STUCK IN THE MIDLIFE WITH YOU

FREYA KENNEDY

Boldwood

First published in Great Britain in 2025 by Boldwood Books Ltd.

Copyright © Freya Kennedy, 2025

Cover Design by Alice Moore Design

Cover Images: Shutterstock

Every effort has been made to obtain the necessary permissions with reference to copyright material, both illustrative and quoted. We apologise for any omissions in this respect and will be pleased to make the appropriate acknowledgements in any future edition.

A CIP catalogue record for this book is available from the British Library.

Paperback ISBN 978-1-83533-843-8

Large Print ISBN 978-1-83533-844-5

Hardback ISBN 978-1-83533-842-1

Ebook ISBN 978-1-83533-845-2

Kindle ISBN 978-1-83533-846-9

Audio CD ISBN 978-1-83533-837-7

MP3 CD ISBN 978-1-83533-838-4

Digital audio download ISBN 978-1-83533-841-4

This book is printed on certified sustainable paper. Boldwood Books is dedicated to putting sustainability at the heart of our business. For more information please visit https://www.boldwoodbooks.com/about-us/sustainability/

Boldwood Books Ltd, 23 Bowerdean Street, London, SW6 3TN

www.boldwoodbooks.com

For
Lesley Price
The best bookseller in Dromore for her age.

1

THE WINDS OF CHANGE

Becca

'Is this supposed to be stress relieving?' I whisper to Niamh as we transition from Plank Pose to Child's Pose. Sweat is dripping from my forehead, my stomach muscles are begging for an early death and I am fighting for my life when it comes to holding in the gaseous emission that desperately wants to escape.

I'm not sure why I'm fighting so hard to hold it in – it seems that a significant number of people in this room have no qualms at all about letting their wind blow free. This room – this hotbox of sweaty, super-bendy people – smells like a twisted combination of old socks, farts and patchouli oil.

'It *is* stress relieving,' Niamh – my ride-or-die best friend of more than forty years – hisses at me with a ferocity that would make Medusa look and sound positively fluffy in comparison. 'Can't you see the stress leaving my body?' she snarls as she folds her body in two with such flexibility I wonder if she removed a couple of ribs before coming to class.

As I try the same move, stretching my arms across the floor in front of me while my bum rests on the back of my legs, I know there is no neat folding going on. My stomach is acting as a sort of oversized bolster cushion between my spine and thighs. The closest I can get to folding in half is hitting a thirty-to-forty-degree angle betwixt leg and belly. Briefly, I wonder if wearing Spanx next time would help me improve on this, but then I think of the inevitable sweaty gusset situation that would ensue and nix the notion. This is hellish enough. We do not need to add a bad case of thrush to the horror.

Niamh is a natural – able to move her body as if she lacks a skeleton. She manages to make each twist and extension of limb look effortless. Only the grunts and moans coming from her mouth give away the fact she's feeling the burn.

I grimace as I realise those grunts and moans are probably not a million miles away from her sex noises. Then I grimace again because I absolutely don't want to think about my best friend's sex noises. This must be what people mean when they talk about intrusive thoughts.

I should not have let Niamh talk me into joining her at one of her twice-weekly ~~torture sessions~~ yoga classes. At forty-six (and a half) I should know my limits by now and yoga should be near the top of the no-can-do list. It's something I've tried multiple times, convinced things will be different with each attempt. They never are.

'You just need to give yourself a chance to get used to it. Your body won't want to move that way at first,' Niamh had said. She certainly wasn't lying about that second part. As I now try to 'deepen the stretch' as directed by the instructor, my body screams in protest. This is not relaxing. This is not giving me a sense of peace.

However, it is, I suppose, at least distracting me momentarily from my ongoing troubles which are three-fold:

(1) I am going to be a grandmother. I can't quite wrap my head around being old enough to be anyone's grandmother. That and the fact that my child, Adam, who is the baby's father, is only nineteen and in the middle of his university studies in Manchester. I am focused on appearing non-stressed by all of that when I am in Adam's company. The last thing his quite sensitive soul needs is judgement and blame. But inwardly? Inwardly I am fighting the urge to grill him about how on earth he thinks they will cope with or provide for a baby.

(2) The baby's mother, Jodie, is the daughter of the very bendy Niamh. I suppose this isn't the worst-case scenario. If I'm going to rock a co-granny dynamic, I can think of no one better to do it with than my long-term BFF – but I'm still worried. What if the stress of it all leads to a major bust-up between Adam and Jodie, and a follow-on major bust-up between us? Niamh and I have only just reunited our triumvirate of long-term besties by making peace with our number three, Laura, after a decade-long falling-out. I never want to go through that again.

(3) Along with the ongoing crises surrounding the news of the unexpected baby in the uterus area – as Niamh described it – has come a whole new list of responsibilities, as Niamh and I support our young people through this life-changing development. If they decide to carry on with the pregnancy, this is only likely to increase ten-fold. Even now, I've found Adam needing almost constant reassurance that everything will be fine and I will fully support them whatever. Where that has created a problem in my own life is that my emotional energy is being entirely swallowed up by navigating these stormy parental waters, and I have little to nothing of me left to offer to what had looked like the beginning of a very lovely relationship.

Conal – brother of Laura – and I had been getting along very

nicely indeed and heading to the point of no return, and hopefully many orgasms, when the shit had hit the fan.

There is nothing in this world that puts the brakes on a fledg-
ling relationship quicker than a surprise pregnancy. Even if that
pregnancy is not your own.

So that romance, and the associated prospect of my decade-
long drought being declared well and truly over, is now on the
proverbial back-burner.

The best I can hope for is that it keeps simmering until I have
the time and energy to turn the heat back up on it again. My fear,
however, is that the proverbial pot will have boiled dry before I
get the chance to give it the attention it deserves.

Our instructor tells us to lie on our backs and get comfortable. I do exactly what I'm told and close my eyes, concentrating
on my breathing and the soft cadence of a whispered meditation.
This is the part of a yoga class I like. The slipping into just being
at one with my body and breath in a space where I can convince
myself that everything will indeed be okay. I even get to enjoy the
momentary smugness of having completed a full-on exercise
class and not being dead. This won't last long. As soon as I try to
walk on shaking legs or lift anything heavier than my car keys, I
will realise I haven't escaped as unscathed as I'd hoped.

Inhaling, I imagine soft warm sand beneath me, and the
gentle rush of clear blue waters to shore. I can almost feel the
warmth of the sun on my face and smell the coconut-scented
aroma of sun cream when a loud voice clip of Stewie from *Family
Guy* calling repeatedly for his 'Mum' starts to echo through the
room.

I know instantaneously that it is my phone that is ringing.
Because of course it is. This is my life now, I think. A series of
unfortunate incidents and embarrassments. I mentally wring the
neck of my older son, Saul, who has clearly messed with my

phone settings while he was home for the Christmas holidays. He's quite fond of playing on my increasingly poor grasp of ever-changing technology. At least, I think, as I scramble to my hands and knees and crawl to the back of the room making an apologetic facial expression, it's not as bad as the time he set my phone to play a loud fart sound when he called me. Then again, I might just have gotten away with that one in this room.

With my phone out of my bag and clamped to my chest – in the hope my matronly boobs will muffle the noise – I get to my feet and make for the exit as quickly as possible.

As soon as the door is closed behind me, I answer. 'Saul? What is it? I was in the middle of a yoga class.'

'Oh, shit, sorry, Mum,' he says, and even though he has only been studying in Manchester for four months I can already hear a northwest of England twang in his voice. He's not quite gone the full Liam and Noel Gallagher yet, but there's a definite deviation from the broad Derry accent I've known and loved.

Saul being Saul – the eldest of my twin sons and heretofore the more problematic of the pair – he needs to be led through a conversation even when he has initiated it himself.

'So, you were calling?' I say, as I open the door of the community centre and revel in a cool blast of icy January air. Somewhere along the way I have gone from being a lover of all things warm and sun-soaked to a woman desperate for icy goodness and Arctic breezes – and this one feels so glorious I step out into the cold, bare-footed. The perimenopause has a lot to answer for.

'Yeah. The thing is, Mum, the extractor fan is broken and I don't know how to fix it.'

He says it with a tone in his voice that leads me to believe he thinks I have some sort of magic electric appliance superpower and can will the fan back into life from the icy car park of a community centre. It would be a handy power to have, I suppose, but I don't think Marvel will be battering down the door to offer me a franchise deal on the back of it.

'Okay, love. What do you mean by broken, exactly?'

'It won't come on. Not even the wee light thing. I was going to make a bacon sarnie, but I can't do that if the fan isn't working. It'll set off the alarms.' He sounds quite distressed at the thought.

'Is everything else working? Lights? Other outlets?' I ask.

'I think so,' he says.

'It might be the fuse,' I tell him, and realise I have come to the end of my useful knowledge. 'Probably best to report it to the accommodation manager and get them to send someone in to look at it.'

'But what about my bacon sandwich?' he says. 'I'm starving, Mum, and I haven't done a shop yet because my student loan hasn't landed in and...'

As he chats, I do what I promised myself I would not do this term and send him over some cash so that he can order a pizza and settle himself for the evening. Saul has two modes – so laid back he's almost horizontal, or able to catastrophise the smallest of inconveniences to the nth level in seconds. There is no in between. So even the absence of his ability to fry up some bacon without setting off the smoke alarms will be enough to have him convinced the world as he knows it is coming to an end.

If I was in good, fully present mother mode and not freezing outside of a yoga class, I would talk him through this crisis until he has made his peace with it. But it's late, I'm tired and I don't have the mental or physical energy to play the part of a counsellor just now. Money for a pizza is a good compromise. That, and the promise that I will call him back in the morning.

Money sent and child soothed, I turn to head back into class, knowing I'm unlikely to be able to get myself into a place of zen again in whatever time is left of the meditation, but willing none-theless to give it a go anyway.

Only the door has closed behind me as I exited and has locked automatically.

Of course it has. Because, as we've discovered, this is my life now. A series of disasters and challenges. I am outside, in the cold; my shoes, coat, hat and car keys are all inside.

As the cool night sky starts to pelt thick, icy globules of sleet onto the bare skin of my arms and my feet start to go numb from the cold, I offer a not-too-silent prayer of frustration to the gods of menopausal women everywhere. One my phone would've auto-corrected to 'Duck my life'.

2

'YE WOULDN'T BE LONG GETTIN' FROSTBIT'

It may only have been three or four minutes since I discovered the door closed behind me, but it feels a lot longer. I have tried battering on the door to attract the attention of my classmates, but I know it's likely pointless. They are down a hall and behind a fire door. They won't hear my pathetic thuds. Especially not as they lie on their backs listening to their guided meditation over the soft sounds of some plinky-plonky music – the kind you only hear in spas or classes which require you to move as if you're playing a one-woman game of Twister with yourself.

I could try phoning Niamh but I know I'd likely be on a hiding to nothing with that. Niamh does not believe in ever having her phone on anything but silent. Especially not when she is having time out from her work or her family.

'There is nothing so important it can't wait a bit,' she often says. 'I mean even if someone is dead, my answering the phone isn't going to undead them, is it?'

She has a point.

As my toes start to turn blue and my poor frozen hands start to turn purple, I console myself with the knowledge that this cannot go on much longer.

The relaxing meditation bit comes just before the 'Namaste' bit, which preludes the drinking from water bottles and smiling smugly at all your fellow classmates, proud that you have survived the ordeal. Not long after that, they will all start to leave and all being well they will find me still alive and not frozen to death, my nipples standing proudly to attention in the bitter night air.

Crossing my arms in front of my chest and plunging my hands into my armpits in a bid to preserve body heat, I contemplate ordering myself a pizza as soon as I get home and undoing what little good I have just done for my body during the last hour.

At least, I think, I could share it with Adam, who has yet to return to his beloved Manchester after the Christmas holidays, while he tries to wrap his head around the news that his girlfriend is pregnant.

It's fair to say that he is very much on an emotional rollercoaster right now and I never quite know what version of Adam I'm going to come home to. When I'd left to come to yoga, he had been sitting on his bed, strumming tunelessly on his guitar and talking to our beloved pet, Daniel the Spaniel.

He has learned, just as I did over the past few years, that Daniel is a trusty confidante. He never spreads gossip, will listen for hours as long as you scratch his belly or behind his ears, and almost never looks at you with judgement in his eyes. If you can handle the noxious aroma of his gassy emissions, he is actually a pretty great companion to have around.

I'm lost in a little jig trying to stave off the impending frostbite when I hear the door open behind me and turn to see a few of the young, more lithe, members of the group stare at me as if I've lost the run of my senses.

'If you're done gawping, any chance I could get past you?' I say, as cheerily as my chattering teeth will allow. They nod a yes in unison, and step backwards. Then, just like Moses parting the Red Sea, my frozen form seems to prompt a parting of the fit and healthy as I walk down the hall, arms crossed to protect the modesty of my still-erect nipples, so I can retrieve my belongings and warm up before hypothermia kicks in.

'Where on earth did you go?' Niamh asks as I walk back into the room. She is standing – her shoes, oversized hoodie and jacket already on – next to my discarded trainers. 'You were there before I closed my eyes and then when we sat up you were gone. I hadn't a clue what you were at!' She sounds cross, but I know my friend well enough to know that in Niamh-land cross is often her way of hiding her worry.

'My phone,' I say. 'You must've heard it. That "Mum, Mummy, Mum" thing?'

'That was you?' she asks.

'Saul has been at my settings again,' I say, and she nods her head in a 'that explains it' gesture.

'Is everything okay with him? Has he lost his left shoe again? Or remembered the time he hid a fiver of his communion money all those years ago and wants you to go and look if it's still there?' she asks. These are, for the record, both things Saul has actually phoned me about in recent times.

'The extractor fan in his kitchen is kaput,' I say. 'And he is in desperate need of a bacon sandwich.'

'Have you scrambled the private jet yet?' she asks with a cheeky smile. 'This seems like a category-one emergency.'

Niamh is perhaps the only person in the world who can make jokes about my children or call out their occasional fecklessness without causing me great offence. Niamh gets it – not just because she is a mother to four herself – but because she has been by my side through every step of my parenting journey (boke at the word 'journey' – overused as it is). She has witnessed every high point, low point and all in between over the years, and I know that when she criticises the boys she does it ultimately from a place of great affection and from a place of great support for me and my occasionally frazzled nerves.

I smile back. 'I sent him money to order a pizza and left instructions for him to contact the landlord in the morning. It was enough to settle him a bit. Only back in England a few days and the crises are already flowing.'

'Thank God for pizza,' she says as I tie the laces on my trainers, glad to be able to feel my toes again. 'I suppose it must be strange for him, Adam not being there.'

And she's right. Even though they are like chalk and cheese when it comes to their personalities, my boys tend to rub along in a nice little codependent manner when they are away from home. Adam is the sensible-headed one who probably knows how to fix a wonky fuse in an extractor fan but can take life a little too seriously and have trouble letting himself go. Saul is the antithesis to this – and the one who will drag his brother down to the Student Union, or up on stage for a karaoke performance of 'Wonderwall' and make sure life has its fun elements. They are the yin to each other's yang in that regard, and neither of them functions quite as well without the other.

'I think it is. And I think it's strange for Adam too.'

'Yeah,' Niamh says. 'Things are a bit arseways at the moment.'

She doesn't need to explain. I know what she means already. It's a strange time for her eldest, Jodie, too. Although both of our children (now adults) have impressed us with their mature approach to things, there's no escaping the, frankly, shite timing of it all. Their relationship has only moved from the friend zone to the romance zone over the past few months. This should still be the super-fun-can't-keep-their-hands-off-each-other stage – which presumably it was for a time, given this unexpected pregnancy.

The memory of Niamh arriving at my door, Laura by her side for moral support, and a pregnancy test in her hand is still embedded firmly in my memory. She regrets telling me in that way now. Wishes she had given Jodie and Adam a chance to work out their feelings before coming to us with the news themselves. But, as I always say, we can only do the best we can with the information we have at the time. At that time, Niamh was in possession of just enough information to freak herself the fuck out and so, of course, it was understandable she would turn to her best friends for support.

Now it is up to us to support our adult children in whatever way they need. For Niamh, that has meant holding Jodie's hair back while she pukes several times a day, and often with little warning.

For me, it has meant assuring Adam that whatever decision he and Jodie make, he will have my full and unequivocal support and that my newfound incontrovertible knowledge that he has had sex has not lessened my opinion of him in any fashion whatsoever. After all, I have always known it was going to happen some day, even if I could've happily lived out my years not knowing it for certain.

'They'll be okay though,' I say, and I'm not sure if it's a statement or a question. Maybe it's a bit of both.

'They will,' says Niamh. 'And it's not the worst news that could come to our doors.'

We have been reminding ourselves of this a lot. It's not an illness, or an addiction. It's not the revelation that they are part of some gangland criminal cartel. It's a baby. Chances are if we had gotten this news ten years, or even five years, from now it would be a cause for celebration. But it is what it is and it's our job to guide our nineteen- and twenty-year-old offspring through the coming months.

It's also our job to try and remain sane while doing so and, as Laura reminded me via WhatsApp earlier, it's my job not to slide into old habits of focusing on supporting everyone else and not pushing forward with my own plans to build a life for myself that sixteen-year-old me would be proud of.

In fact, Laura has been adamant that even with this unfurling domestic drama I power on with my mission to make good on the promises I made my younger self, which I rediscovered when I uncovered the time capsule we made as teenagers.

Laura will not allow me to forsake my plans to overhaul my career, see more of the world and learn to love the life I lead and the body I lead it in. The only area she has kept clear of getting involved in is with my budding – now stalled – relationship with Conal. Her brother. It's not, she says, that she doesn't care – more that she can't bring herself to openly encourage me to have sexual relations with someone who made an art form of directing his farts in her direction when he was a child.

As Niamh and I leave the community centre and reach our cars, we give each other a hug. 'We'll be okay too,' I tell her. 'I mean, I'm not sure I'll be able to move tomorrow without considerable effort and a few choice swear words but overall, we'll be okay.'

'You just need to get used to the moves and then, honest, you'll find it a great stress reliever. I feel much better able to go back and deal with Paul after this.' I hug her tightly, because while Niamh and I are doing our best to support our children, Paul is very much struggling with the news, and as a result there have been some shockwaves in their usually quite wonderful relationship.

'He still being...' I trail off, trying to think of a suitable way to describe how Paul is behaving without being truly offensive.

'A dick?' Niamh says. 'Yeah. But you know the craic. He's my dick, etc. We'll get through it.' She shrugs as she gets into her car, leaving me wondering how bad things might actually be between them.

3

HERE I GO AGAIN

There's a fair chance that I am going to hell. My sin is that I have yet to tell my mother about the pregnancy. To her credit, my mother has always been relatively cool with life's curveballs, and no matter what either of my boys could ever do, she would still think the sun shines brightly from their arses.

But this is a tricky one. I don't want to tell her the news until I know exactly what the news is and, if I'm being completely honest, if Adam and Jodie decide not to proceed with the pregnancy then I am considering not telling her at all. Not because I think she'll be angry about it, but because I know she would find it unsettling – upsetting even. She's of a generation that believes in mortal sin and eternal damnation, and while she's not overly religious herself, the impact of years of Catholic indoctrination still looms large in her conscience.

I feel awful keeping something so colossal from her, and it's made harder that I'm having to add lie on top of lie to cover the tracks of what is really going on.

'So when is Adam going back to university?' she asks, as we sit at her kitchen table drinking tea and seeing which of us will break first and reach for a second bun from the paper bag of treats I've brought with me.

'I'm not sure,' I tell her as the cream-filled, sugar-dusted pastry in front of me tempts me further. 'But classes are starting soon, so I imagine it will be sooner rather than later.'

'But he's okay though?' she asks. 'He's happy over there and happy in his studies?'

I nod. 'Yes. But you know how it is, with first love and all that. He just wanted some extra time with Jodie before the new semester.'

Technically, it's not a lie. He does want extra time with Jodie, and he has been enjoying his studies.

'Ah, love's young dream,' my mother says. 'I'd say I remember it well, but it was quite some time ago for me.' She looks wistful as she thinks of my now departed daddy. How I wish he was still around to offer his usual reassurance and a big hug. There's nothing that ever made me feel as safe and as loved as a hug from my dad.

My mother cuts through my thoughts. 'But speaking of love's young dream – how are things with young Conal?'

That she calls fifty-year-old Conal O'Hagan 'young Conal' amuses me. He finds it funny too. 'Endearing' I think is the word he used, just before he asked if I wanted him to book an appointment at Specsavers for her.

But when I think of how things are with 'young Conal', I can't quite manage to hide the look of disappointment from my face. I do try. I do my best to plaster on a smile but I'm not fast enough and my mother's left eyebrow shoots up in record time. Mammy detection mode is well and truly in operation. Her head tilts just a little to the side. 'What is it?' she asks, as she reaches across the table not, as I think, to grab the tastier of the two remaining buns, but instead to put her hand on mine. 'What has he done?'

The expression on her face tells me this woman is ready to go into battle for me if I need her to.

'He's not done anything,' I reassure her quickly, and it's true. Any cooling off has been on my part as I've had to shift my focus elsewhere. There are only a limited number of 'out of my comfort zone' experiences I can deal with at a time, and the last thing I want is to expose my full melting-down self to the only man I've been remotely interested in in the last decade.

'Oh, love. What is it then? You can tell me.'

The thing is, though, that I can't. I simply can't explain the complexity of what is going on to her without getting her worried sick about everything. And it is my life's mission to make sure my mother does not get worried sick, or any kind of sick, any time in the near, or distant, future. She is much too precious to me.

'We're just taking things slowly,' I say, and again, it's not entirely a lie. We haven't broken up as such. Although we never quite got round to the boyfriend and girlfriend conversation either. It seemed a little icky to talk in such terms given our advanced years. I've tried to reassure myself that as we're still technically together, there is still a sort of glacial pace forward momentum to our relationship. I'm starting to worry, however, our final destination isn't going to be in happy-ever-after land.

I haven't seen Conal since two days after the pregnancy bombshell was dropped, and even then it was hardly a romantic date by any definition. We'd met for a quick coffee in a Caffè Nero, where I had cried a little bit, said the word 'shitshow' four times and he had sympathetically patted my hand, listened intently and told me he will be here for me and if there is anything I need I should just shout.

It was very kind of him to say that, but we all know, don't we, that people don't always mean it when they say such things. It's just what you're expected to say. It's not considered polite to reply with 'Sucks to be you' or sing a chorus of 'On your own, on your own, on your own!' back at them. Conal and I had only been together a matter of weeks before the shit hit the festive fan, so it's unfair to expect him to be 'all in' for any ongoing family drama.

Yes, we'd had a fun few weeks. He's a wonderful man and he'd made Christmas feel extra magical – but we hadn't been together long enough for me to expect him to hang around during a major family upheaval.

It's not like we have even slept together yet. My boys had come home for Christmas two days after our first date, and there was no way I was breaking a ten-year drought with my two nineteen-year-olds in the house. It was embarrassing enough telling them I was dating someone. I'd blushed to my very roots when I told them. I might as well have been fourteen again and asking my parents if I could go to the Creggan disco with the girls – knowing full well there would be boys there and one of them just might be my first-ever kiss. A late bloomer, I was the last of our gang not to have had the 'pleasure' of a skill-lacking snog and boob grope by one of the many teenage boys who frequented the youth club. I'd felt like a marked woman until the deed was done.

To my surprise, the twins had reacted well to the news that I was back in the dating game. Saul had grinned and said, 'Nice one, Mum.' Adam had given me a big hug and said he was happy for me. I could tell by the expression on his face that he meant it.

When I introduced them both to Conal, they had declared him 'pure sound' – which is as high an accolade as you can hope for in our home city of Derry in Northern Ireland.

I'd been so optimistic. Here was a man who actually liked me. As in *really* liked me. He'd told me as much. And I liked him too – probably more than I dared to let on. I knew I wanted to do everything in my power to give us the best chance possible of turning this into something meaningful. Which meant, I soon realised, not inflicting Crisis-Management-Mode Becca on him.

He has enough to deal with without having to take my life crises into consideration. He is, after all, still mourning the loss of his mother, Kitty, who passed away last November. He's also dealing with the practical side to bereavement, including undertaking the emotionally draining task of packing up her belongings and putting her house on the market.

We have said we'll get together to walk the dogs some day this week – Daniel having taken a fondness for Conal's dog, Lazlo – but as yet we haven't managed to make it happen.

I'm trying not to let it get me down. But I'm sad that my dreams of frosty walks in the park, both of us in cute hats and scarves, me wearing mittens because I've suddenly morphed into the star of a Hallmark romance movie, have failed to materialise.

There has been no stopping at a cute little coffee cart to get hot chocolate from a wizened old man who is secretly some sort of angel or cupid figure. There has been no mingling of the steam from our breath as we move closer and kiss beneath branches sparkling with frost.

With every day that passes, it feels as if it's slipping out of my reach more and more.

'You've waited a long time to even think about love again,' my mother says, slicing through my thoughts once again. 'You don't have to rush it. Better to take your time and get it right. And for God's sake, enjoy it!'

I smile and nod and watch as my mother nudges the nicer of the two remaining buns in my direction. 'You have that one,' she says. 'I have a feeling you need it more than I do today.'

I feel my resolve to stay composed and not cry waver. 'Thank you, Mum,' I say. 'You're very good to me.'

'And you're very good to me,' she says with a smile. 'Things will work out,' she says, even though I've made no mention of things not working out.

Derry mammies know everything, I think. I was foolish to think I could keep my troubles from her.

4

YEAR 11 AND THE TEMPLE OF DOOM

Niamh

There's a special place in hell for the person who scheduled a double lesson with Year 11 first thing on a Monday morning, Niamh thinks.

She wonders if it's some sort of cosmic karma biting her in the arse. Maybe, she thinks, she's like the Captain in *The Sound of Music* and has done something in her youth, or in her childhood, to deserve this. Although, now that she thinks about it, Captain Von Trapp's karma came in the form of a lovely new romance with Julie Andrews. Niamh's has come in the form of Ella Devine asking her if she has TikTok.

'No,' Niamh replies. 'I do not have TikTok.'

This is a lie. She, of course, has an account, but she doesn't post anything on it. She can think of nothing worse than her pupils finding videos of her doing comedy skits or viral dances online – except, perhaps, her own children finding her online. They'd never forgive her. Her pupils, however, would just make her life even more of a living hell than it currently is.

'Miss, Miss... but you could talk about science and stuff and teach people all about it,' Ella says. 'We could help you.'

Before Niamh has the chance to reply that she is already talking about science and, allegedly, 'teaching people stuff', Jayden Murray chimes in with some sort of gobbledegook language that everyone else in the room seems to understand and find absolutely bloody hilarious. She's not sure what 'no cap' and 'Ohio' have to do with anything, but this seems to make sense to his classmates. Maybe, she thinks, she's having a stroke. That's why these words don't make sense. Perhaps it wouldn't be the worst thing ever – at least she'd get a lie down and a few sick days off school.

'Miss, Miss. Could we make up a dance? We could go viral!' Ella shouts, already out of her seat and scrolling through her (forbidden) phone.

'Ella! Phone in your bag now, or I'll confiscate it,' Niamh, disappointed that it looks less likely that she has in fact had a stroke, says, just to earn a roll of eyes from Ella and a chorus of groans from her classmates.

'Miss, I was just looking for a song for you,' the dejected teen says, slumping back into her seat and dropping her phone, performatively, back into her bag.

'And I'm just trying to teach you lot,' Niamh replies. 'You have exams coming up, if you haven't forgotten. So maybe we could stop debating the merits of TikTok and instead return our attention to cell division?'

A mumble of disappointment travels around the room like a Mexican wave. Niamh just waits for it to pass. If she had her way, she'd tell them all, very clearly, that she would rather be doing just about anything right now instead of going over the basics of cell division, once again, to a class who really should know this inside and out by now. If she had her way, she'd tell them that, ideally, she'd like to be a on beach somewhere drinking a Margarita for breakfast (yes, for breakfast) and bitching with her friends. She'd like to be as far away from this cold and rainy January day in Derry as she could get, and away from the troubles in her life.

Namely:

(1) Year 11 – the bane of her life and the one year group she would describe as feral, knowing that was putting it mildly.

(2) Her teenage sons, Ethan and Cal, who have taken to communicating in grunts and mumbles and whose shared bedroom has become a biohazard that she just can't find the strength to deal with but knows she has to. A pungent aroma of body odour mixed with God knows what else has started to seep out into the landing and it's enough to make her gag.

(3) Her youngest child, sweet, beautiful, surprise-baby Fiadh, who is almost eight, seems to be fast-forwarding into the tween years with hints of the trouble to come.

(4) Her husband, Paul – heretofore the love of her life and stalwart in every single crisis they have faced together – who is not handling their latest crisis all that well.

Which brings her to:

(5) Her eldest child, twenty-year-old Jodie, is pregnant. This is not what she had hoped for for her precious firstborn who should be enjoying her university years and the freedom to 'act the hallion' that only comes in your younger years.

And last but not least:

(6) Perimenopause is kicking her square in the vagina and nothing seems to be helping. In fact, she is currently experiencing the worst hot flush of her entire life and is afraid she might actually combust – which Year 11 would find totally hilarious and which they would create a TikTok about before her charred remains had the chance to cool off. No one warned her

the hot flushes would come with an unhealthy dose of extreme sadness and rage which she is desperately trying to keep under wraps.

She takes a deep breath and instructs her pupils to read page sixty-eight of their textbooks while she walks to the window and opens it wide, desperate for a blast of cold January air. She is aware that external temperature has no impact whatsoever on the ferocity or length of her hot flushes, but still she feels as if she should be doing something to help her poor, overheated body. She also knows that the quicker she cools down, the less likely she will be to burst into tears in front of her class, which would be akin to a fate worse than death.

After all, the first rule of teaching in a secondary school is 'Show no weakness'. Teenagers will take a rogue fart, mispronounced word, swear or show of emotion and use it to forever change your future for the worse. Niamh knows this. She has seen it time and time again as colleagues have succumbed to unfortunate nicknames that have stuck. You just need to ask Toot Toot McGuigan, the French teacher who, to this day, bitterly regrets the five-bean chilli they ate for dinner one Tuesday night in 2003, how that feels.

'Miss! Miss! It's freezing! Can you close the windy?' Jayden Murray shouts, following it with an exaggerated shudder.

'It's window, Jayden. Not "windy". I'll close it in a moment,' she says.

'But Miss, we'll all catch colds or Covid or the flu and it might start a new pandemic,' Ella shouts.

'You'll all be fine,' Niamh says, a rictus smile on her face.

'Miss, are you like Elsa from *Frozen*? Does the cold not bother you?' Jayden says, clearly enjoying the attention he's receiving. He and Ella make for quite the double act. If they ever combine their powers, Niamh fears for her ability to be able to control her classroom.

Maybe she is like Elsa, she thinks as she glares at Jayden – hoping that her best intimidating teacher look will be enough to silence him. Maybe the cold doesn't bother her. In fact, she actively welcomes it. If only she had the power to control it, and the ability to look amazing in a pale blue slinky frock bedazzled with sequins and sparkles. Instead she's wearing a pair of checked, elasticated-waist trousers and a burgundy jersey top. She hopes she's looking like a professional but fears she might be looking more like Rupert the Bear, or Rupert the Bear's granny.

Even the word 'granny' makes her feel as if she is shrivelling and shrinking into an old-age version of the person she used to be. She has always hoped to be a granny – one day. Maybe when she is sixty or thereabouts. Sixty feels like a proper 'granny' age. Not forty-six. And God, Jodie is only twenty. Lord knows, Niamh felt overwhelmed when she became a mother at twenty-six, but at least she had enjoyed a few years of freedom and adventure between finishing uni and giving birth.

To her relief, the hot flush starts to subside and she finally feels able to close the window and resume her teaching duties. She just has to try and stop her mind from running constantly with Jodie and her 'predicament'. She hates that she even thinks of it that way.

She thought she'd raised Jodie to be careful. She's never put limits on her but has always encouraged her to make sure to be sensible and think about what she wants out of life. That meant being sensible when it came to sex and contraception. But nonetheless, here her daughter is 'with child' halfway through her second year at university. A part of Niamh wants to scream at her. But at the same time she knows that would achieve absolutely nothing except to alienate Jodie, and give herself a sore throat into the bargain.

She sighs as she pulls the window closed, and hauls her brain into the here and now to deal with her teaching responsibilities. How, she wonders, is it possible to feel this hacked off with it at all so early on a Monday morning at the start of a new term? This is the next-level fatigue that normally makes itself known at the end of term – not after a break. She's supposed to be re-energised now, not so tired she wants to cry. It would help if she could sleep, but she seems unable to manage more than a couple of unbroken hours each night. The rest of the time is spent tossing and turning, waking in a pool of her now cold sweat, and wondering if Paul has always snored so loudly and if it would really be that bad to put a pillow over his head.

No doubt, she thinks, as she walks to the front of the class, all this is yet another thing that can be attributed to the menopause. She thinks of the small rectangular patch of plastic currently stuck to her stomach, allegedly infusing her with oestrogen. She's not quite sure it's having any real effect – except for leaving her tummy covered in little grey patches of adhesive that have to be scrubbed with a Brillo pad to have any chance of removing them. They breed down there now, on her lower tummy. One day she will be entirely covered in little grey patches of adhesive, decorated with whatever lint and fluff they have managed to grab.

No one warned her about that. Or that the adhesive would sometimes irritate her skin. No one warned her that if she wanted to stop her vagina from 'atrophying' (she swears she feels it atrophy in fear every time she even thinks of that word), she would have to lie, legs akimbo, as she pops a little pill inside her vagina.

On more than one occasion she has, absentmindedly, swallowed the pill before remembering it is not *that* kind of tablet.

Still, at least her mouth and throat will be safe from the worry of atrophying.

'Miss! Miss! Are you okay?' It's not Ella or Jayden this time, but Hannah – the class swot – who is speaking. 'You face has gone very red.'

Hannah's face is filled with concern. Niamh wishes she had twenty-eight Hannahs in her class. Twenty-eight young people who always remember their books and their homework. Who ask sensible, intelligent questions about topics they are actually studying. Hannah never asks her if she watches *Love Island* (which she did until she started to feel irrationally jealous of the side-boob and under-boob on display. It has been a long time since Niamh would trust her D-cups in a bikini top clearly two sizes too small).

No, Hannah always asks the right questions. And right now, Hannah is clearly astute enough to observe that her most beloved of teachers is well on her way to a full-blown meltdown. It's enough to snap Niamh back into professional teacher mode. She cannot show weakness. She must keep control. She does not want to be known as Cry-Baby Cassidy or something much worse for the remainder of her teaching career. She will push all her worries to the very back of her mind until home time.

'Thank you, Hannah, but I'm fine. Now, let's talk about mitosis and meiosis.'

5

FIRST-CLASS TICKET TO PONTYPANDY, PLEASE!

Becca

I'm quite relieved when Adam slumps onto the sofa beside me and rests his head on my shoulder. It's reassuring to see him come out of his room, where he has been moping, overthinking and carrying on hours of FaceTime calls with Jodie, before disappearing to see her without so much as a 'Bye, Mum!' on his way out the door.

'Jodie is going to come over later. With her mum,' he says, as Daniel rouses himself from in front of the fire and pads over towards us.

I can't pretend I don't feel a little put out that the dog I do 90 per cent of walks for rests his head on Adam's knee to beg for pets rather than on mine. Then again, when I see my lanky six-foot son reach over and scratch behind Daniel's ears, both of them immediately perking up, I get a warm fuzzy feeling.

It's good to see Adam acting silly. He has been too sombre and sensible these last few days – and it's not like he was ever really not sensible to begin with. It has worried me at times just how much of an old head on young shoulders he has always been, so to see him double down on being serious-minded is concerning. Not that there isn't a good reason for his seriousness. The prospect of impending fatherhood is a heavy burden. Especially when you're only nineteen.

I can't help but see a little boy in front of me when I look at him, even now. Yes, he's a tall boy. He has a manly physique – a strong jawline, the darkening of stubble across his face. His hands are much bigger than mine – and a world away from the small chubby hands I used to hold on to for dear life as we crossed the road. His voice is deep and he smells of Tom Ford cologne, which cost more than my first week's wages in my first full-time job.

But he's still a boy. My boy.

Nineteen is no age. And yet he is facing the biggest responsibility of a person's life. Selfishly perhaps, I can't help but worry about the impact it will have on my life too.

'Is everything okay?' I ask him, which seems like a stupid question.

He looks at me with a small, stoic smile and nods his head. He looks so like his father in this moment that it takes my breath away. His is a face I love but I don't love the big reminder of a marriage that failed and of a man who, looking back, I don't quite understand why I married.

We've not told his father – Simon – the big news yet. Adam pleaded with me to hold off until he got his head around it and I agreed. I'm in no rush to pull that particular plaster off. There's no way Simon won't have a considerable amount to say about it. He'll have no qualms about voicing his opinion. Empathy is not his strong point.

'Yeah,' Adam says. 'We've talked and talked and talked and I think we know what we're going to do.'

I raise an eyebrow, waiting for him to tell me.

'But Jodie and I want to tell you and Niamh together,' he says, and while I have to respect their decision I want to plead with him to just give me a clue. Even a little one.

Instead I ask him if Paul is coming too.

'Jodie's going to talk to him herself,' he says. 'You know he's not exactly happy about it, and you know how much of a daddy's girl she is.'

He has also always been his daughter's fiercest protector and her biggest fan. He is not taking the news of her pregnancy particularly well and is failing miserably at keeping his feelings to himself.

'I do, yes,' I say, reaching out to take my son's hand in mine. 'Whatever you and Jodie have decided – whatever comes next – none of it will change how I feel about you, and I will do everything I can to support you both. I'm sure Paul will come round.'

'Thanks, Mum,' he says, and lays his head back on my shoulder, prompting Daniel to spring up to try and nuzzle in between us. How can a dog be ten years old and have no clue about respecting people's personal space? Then again, at least he doesn't try and sniff our bums in the way he does with every single dog he encounters in the park.

'What are you working on, anyway?' Adam asks, clocking the laptop folded shut on my knee and the notebook filled with my messy handwriting on the sofa. 'More listicles? Ten Ways to Beat the January Blues by Being More Productive in Work?' He smirks. He and his brother have a long and illustrious history of teasing me about my work writing copy for business-to-business publications – and most notably writing lists which always nod towards staff working harder for less.

'Actually, no. I'm not. Well, I am... but not like before.'

'Do you care to elaborate, Mother, or am I supposed to guess?' he says.

For some strange reason, I feel myself start to blush. This is ridiculous. I'm not doing anything dodgy. I'm not doing anything wrong. I'm simply writing a different kind of a list in a bid to score a new opportunity. One that means a whole lot to me, as it happens.

'I'm diversifying,' I tell him. 'I've a meeting with an old school friend to talk about maybe writing some stuff for the magazine she edits. You know that *Northern People*? I pitched her some ideas about being a woman of a certain age and she liked them.' My face is blazing as I speak and I know it's ridiculous. I'm a forty-six-year-old woman and have been writing for B2B publications for years. It's not been glamorous but it has paid the bills and kept the boys in shoes. For a while it had been the perfect way to combine earning a living with raising the boys – allowing me to work from home long before it was fashionable. That became an absolute lifesaver when my marriage broke down and the boys needed me even more. It had been enough – or so I had convinced myself – until I uncovered a letter written by sixteen-year-old me to the me who exists now outlining her hopes and dreams for where we might be at this stage of life.

Sixteen-year-old me dreamed of writing for *Cosmo*, or *Marie Claire*. *Northern People* might not be in those big leagues but it's a whole lot closer than any number of interchangeable business-focused titles.

'Mum!' Adam says with such enthusiasm that Daniel launches into a volley of enthusiastic barking, which unfortunately starts right in my ear, temporarily deafening me.

I can see that Adam is still talking but I'm buggered if I can make out what it is he is saying, while Daniel is going full Spaniel with excitement.

'Daniel!' I scold, but only half-heartedly because it's nice still to have someone be excited for me. With his tail still wagging furiously, he nuzzles into my neck and once I've firmly discouraged him from licking my face, he settles contentedly again. This allows Adam to finally be heard.

'I'm really proud of you, Mum,' he says. 'That's really exciting. You'll smash it. So what kind of things will you be writing?'

I think about just how honest I should be with him. I'm aware, of course, that if I'm published there will be no hiding what I've written from him, but I'm not sure he's really ready enough to hear my full pitch right now. I have a long list of ideas about the good, bad and ugly of menopause. How to find your sexual groove in your forties – although given the direction my relationship with Conal has taken, I might have to scrap that particular one. I'll replace it with how to handle online dating as a woman old enough to know better.

I'm also pitching a column on how to survive your children abandoning you to go to uni, and breaking your heart. That kind of thing. Not the kind of thing you want to discuss with your nineteen-year-old and certainly not the kind of thing your nineteen-year-old wants to discuss with you.

'Ach, well, life, the universe and everything,' I tell him. 'I hope to keep it relatively light. But honest, you know. About what it's really like to be in your forties, and going through menopause and maybe dating and...'

I watch as the colour starts to drain from his face, which of course causes the colour to drain from my face. Does he not want me taking such an honest approach? Would he be embarrassed by his mother writing about her menopause, or even S-E-X in a publication? Is he already regretting his bout of enthusiasm and excitement, just moments earlier? Should I be taking his feelings into consideration or steaming ahead with my life? Sixteen-year-old Becki (with an i) hadn't thought this particular scenario through. She'd wanted her older self to have children, of course, but she never factored in any potential embarrassment they might feel if she one day started writing about her saggy boobs, or occasional need for a little help from Mrs Tena. Or if, God forbid, she even considered writing about her desire to reignite her waning libido with a new man.

My momentary euphoria disappears as quickly as it arrived. 'You think I'll make a complete eejit of myself, don't you?'

'No!' he protests. 'Not at all. I don't think you'll make an eejit of yourself. I suppose I'm a bit nervous about just how honest you'll be. There are things a son doesn't need to know...' He trails off and I'm pretty sure we're both sharing the same thought. That there are things a mother doesn't really want to think about either. Like her son impregnating his girlfriend – but here we are.

I see a small twitch at the corner of his mouth, which thankfully heralds the arrival of a smile. 'Okay. I get that I've the ownership of some pretty special double standards here, but still...'

My heart swells with affection for my boy.

'Don't worry,' I tell him. 'I'll be honest. But not too honest. That's, of course, if I get the gig. There's no guarantees. I have to impress Grace... that's the editor. It's years since I've seen her and yeah, we sort of knew each other at school, but we weren't close. It's not like she owes me a favour or anything. But even if she did, I wouldn't want the gig because she feels she owes me. I want it because I'm good.'

God love Adam for having the patience to listen to me. Saul's mind would've wandered somewhere completely different by now and he'd reply to my concerns with a random observation about a TV programme or football team. Adam, on the other hand, understands. He gets me because we have the same personality – the same need to be sensible and the same fear of never being good enough. The mammy-guilt rushes in – my mind immediately thinking of the Philip Larkin poem 'This Be the

Verse' and its premise that parents will always pass their shitty baggage on to their children. Whether they want to or not. Larkin puts it much more eloquently, of course.

'You *are* good, Mum,' Adam says and I feel fuzzy inside. When Adam says it, I know he means it. If it was Saul, I'd be waiting for the inevitable sneaky request for twenty quid to follow.

'And you're good too, son,' I tell him – aware that I always thought it was just old women who use 'son' instead of their actual son's name. At least, I console myself, I have not reached the stage where I use 'son' when speaking to all young men below the age of thirty. That really will mark the beginning of the end.

'I hope so,' he replies and squeezes my hand a little tighter, his head resting a little heavier on my shoulder. I drop a kiss onto his wavy brown locks, thankful there is still a trace of the curls there that I so loved when he was little.

I wish things were still as simple as they were then and all it would take would be a *Fireman Sam* magazine and a Milky Way to make him feel better.

6

MY LITTLE PONY

Niamh

Niamh is fighting a headache that is absolutely not being helped by the Taylor Swift songs blaring from Fiadh's room. Or the exceptionally loud running commentary Ethan and Cal seem to be providing at the top of their lungs as they game together in the swamp of despair that is their bedroom.

Paul isn't home. He says he is working late. Which Niamh suspects is a fib, and he has most likely gone round to his mother's house for his tea. He tends to do that when he's feeling particularly stressed, and she knows that he is definitely feeling on edge at the moment. Just like she is.

Perhaps she should've gone to *her* mother's for her tea? But of course, she couldn't do that because at least one responsible parent has to come home and make sure their brood are fed, watered and kept from murdering each other.

She wants to call him out on it. She wants to lift her phone and send him a sarky message asking him if they have now reached the stage in their relationship where blatantly lying to each other is acceptable.

Instead she is focused on helping Jodie, who is hunched over the toilet – morning sickness having now stretched into the evening.

'I tried to put the dinner on,' Jodie says, her eyes red-rimmed and still watering, her face pale and sweating. 'But I couldn't manage it.'

Niamh feels heart sorry for her daughter as she remembers her own run-ins with morning sickness. She helps her get to her feet and to her room, while shouting at Cal to bring his sister a glass of water.

'What's wrong with her?' Cal grunts as he hands over the glass and eyes his sister with suspicion.

'She's just not feeling well,' Niamh says, tersely. Cal, Ethan and Fiadh are still in the dark about the drama playing out in their home.

'Too many vodkas, Jodie!' Cal teases as he mimes bringing a glass to his lips and knocking it back.

Jodie just grimaces and for a few seconds Niamh is sure her daughter is going to throw up once more, all over the bedroom floor.

'Cal, go back to murdering things in your room!' Niamh snaps, and watches as her son throws his hands in the air in mock offence.

'Chill out, bruh,' he replies, making a stupid hand gesture and turning to swagger out of the room like the member of some super-cool street gang and not just a really annoying teenager who still has to be reminded to change into clean pants each day.

'Should've stayed on the cider, sis,' he offers as a parting shot before disappearing back into his room and resuming the shouting match with Ethan and their online friends.

'Love, you're getting it tough.' Niamh does her best to soothe Jodie as she gently sweeps her hair back from her face. 'We'll have to get some Ginger Nuts or something to see if they help.'

'I don't even want to think about biscuits,' Jodie groans. 'Or any type of food. Or anything with a strong smell.'

'I know. I remember it well. It's a rotten feeling.'

Jodie nods, and closes her eyes. In this moment Niamh can see just how very young she still is. She still looks like her little girl – how on earth is she going to cope with all the demands a baby will put on her?

Jodie lies still for a moment before opening her eyes again and tentatively pulling herself up to sitting, so she can take a sip of water from the glass.

'Mum,' she says. 'Adam and I have come to a decision about what we want to do.'

Niamh feels her stomach tighten. She isn't sure exactly what she wants to hear her daughter say next. She isn't sure she is able to admit to herself her true feelings on the matter. That no option is a perfect option and that whatever they decide is likely to have a long-lasting impact on them both, no matter what. That she wishes her daughter wasn't pregnant at all – even though acknowledging that swamps her with new feelings of guilt and shame at wishing away what would become her grandchild.

That she fears that even though she knows Adam to be a lovely young man – he's the son of her best friend, after all – she knows it is Jodie whose life will be most impacted by their joint decision. It's always different for the woman.

'You know you have choices,' Niamh tells her daughter. 'You know you don't have to rush them.'

'I know, Mum. And believe me, we've talked through every angle.'

With all the naivety of young people barely out of secondary school, Niamh thinks, but she keeps her mouth shut.

'Well, what is it then?' Niamh asks, as tenderly as she can muster.

'Can we go see Becca and Adam? We want to tell you both together.'

'Can you not just tell me now?' Niamh asks, wanting to weep at the thought of putting her coat back on and leaving the house again. She desperately just wants to put on her pyjamas, chuck a frozen pizza in the oven for the children and sprawl on the sofa watching reruns of *Say Yes to the Dress* until the world seems less horrible.

'We really do want to do it together,' Jodie says, her eyes filling with tears, which immediately makes Niamh feel like the worst mother in the entire universe. Here she is making her pregnant daughter cry, all because she feels too lazy to go to her best friend's house.

'Okay,' she says, with a sigh. 'Okay. But I need to feed the others first, and make sure Fiadh has done her homework. And I really need to change out of these clothes into something more comfortable.' What she means by more comfortable is to change into something where she does not feel like she is mouldering with her own sweat, and which doesn't make her look like a menopausal cartoon bear.

Jodie smiles and says she'll just get a little nap while she waits, which Niamh totally understands because pregnancy brings on an exhaustion like no other. *Except maybe perimenopause*, a little voice whispers from inside her. Oh, but how she would love a little nap herself. Or maybe a good coma. Just a few months. Nothing drastic.

Instead, she sets about her tasks and then, having changed into her comfiest loungewear – otherwise known as whatever pyjama set looks least like pyjamas – she's on her way to Becca's and Jodie remains tight-lipped about her decision.

Maybe that's part of what hurts so much. That she is no longer a key part of her eldest child's decision-making process. Jodie has grown up and is well able to make life choices for herself. Someone else – a boy she has only been seeing a matter of months – is now front and centre of the biggest decision her daughter has ever had to make. Someone who has no idea of the impact having a baby will have on them both – but especially on Jodie.

Adam is a good boy – or more accurately a good young man. Niamh knows this. But it doesn't matter that she has loved Adam like one of her own since he was born and that she has watched him grow, and thrive. Or that Adam and Jodie have known each other their whole lives and had been the best of friends before they fell in love late last summer. It still feels wrong to Niamh that he suddenly is the person her daughter is turning to when making big life decisions.

Maybe because the pair of them had kept their romance a secret for months. Both Niamh and Becca had only discovered their children were together by chance shortly before Christmas. Just weeks before this surprise pregnancy had been revealed.

Is it any wonder Niamh's head is spinning?

She glances at her girl, who is absentmindedly singing along to Chappell Roan on the radio declaring she's a 'pink pony girl'. Beautiful Jodie. The first person to call her mama. Not a girl of the pink pony type or any other. Tears prick at her eyes and for the first time she wishes for a good hot flush to distract her from her desire to cry. She has to keep a neutral outward appearance.

'I just want to say, I know you've come to a decision, but whatever it is, you can always change your mind. You have time,' she says.

Jodie turns to her and stops singing. 'I know,' she says.

'And you also know that this is your body, not Adam's, and I'm not for one second saying he would pressure you one way or the other, but ultimately you are the one who has to carry the baby. You have to put your wants first.'

'I know, Mum. Trust me. Adam hasn't put pressure on me. We've made a decision we're both happy with.'

Jodie turns her face back to look out at the window and starts singing again – as if she doesn't have a worry in the world. Meanwhile Niamh is wondering if the palpitations she is now feeling are because she's about to have a cardiac event, a panic attack or just another bloody gift from Mammy Menopause.

7

'HAVE YOU REACHED A VERDICT ON WHICH YOU ARE ALL AGREED?'

Becca

'Why do I feel like I'm on trial and waiting for the jury to deliver their verdict?' I ask Niamh as we sit in my living room. Jodie and Adam have disappeared into the kitchen and to my great disappointment are not talking loudly enough for us to hear them here in the living room.

She looks tense. Her expression stiff and stoic as if she has been Botoxed to within an inch of her life. I know she has not, because we have made a solemn promise that if one of us breaks and gets it done, the other must go with them. If one of us falls, both of us fall. Like modern-day Musketeers.

She doesn't speak. Doesn't utter a single word but keeps her focus on the fire. This is very much not like Niamh.

'I don't suppose Jodie told you what they've decided on the way over?' I ask.

'Nope,' Niamh says, her voice terse. 'Not a word.'

'Are you okay?' I ask her, knowing that it takes an awful, awful lot for my ever-cheerful friend to be anything other than... well... ever cheerful.

She turns her head to look in my direction. There's something in the slow way she does it that makes me fear her head might just keep on spinning and do a full 360 before she projectiles pea soup at me, à la *The Exorcist*. Shit. Something is very off here.

'The thing is, Becs—'

'Sorry for keeping you,' Adam says, walking into the room and cutting Niamh off before she's had the chance to finish her sentence.

She quickly turns her head towards our two children and plasters on her very best understanding-teacher face. The woman is an expert at looking supportive when really she wants to burn the place down using a Bunsen burner doctored to go full flame-thrower instead.

I note that Adam and Jodie are holding hands. This augurs well, I think. They are united in their decision and neither of them looks as if they have been crying.

It dawns on me that this conversation will be one of the more defining ones of my life. That I am about to witness my son make the biggest decision of his. Everything is about to change. If Niamh is nursing the same thoughts, it's no wonder she looks as if she might just boke.

They sit down and I bite the urge to shout at them to just spit it out. I mean, I love a bit of drama as much as the next person, but this is a *lot*. It has *been* a lot to have constantly running through my mind this last week or so. It has been a lot to realise this is a decision that only my son and Jodie can make and that my usual maternal urge to swoop in and make everything okay is extremely limited in its grasp in these circumstances.

I wait for either Adam or Jodie to speak. I can feel the tension coming off Niamh in waves and it's more unsettling than anything our children could say in the next few minutes.

'We've talked this through a lot,' Jodie says, her voice surprisingly assured. 'We've asked ourselves a million questions. It hasn't been easy. And we know this isn't going to *be* easy.'

'This isn't something we planned,' Adam says. 'But I think that's pretty obvious.' His face colours a little. 'But sometimes things happen that just change everything, don't they?'

I nod, but truth be told I'm starting to feel like we're at the final vows stage of *Married at First Sight* and they're dragging the arse out of this to up the drama. I want to remind them that this is not a TV show. And remind them that Niamh and I are both heading towards fifty and have a limited number of years left on this earth, so we appreciate it when people get to the point.

'I know it's not ideal,' Jodie says. 'But I've thought about taking a different route and it just feels wrong for me.'

'And I agree with Jodie,' Adam adds, looking at her. They share a soppy look that screams of young love and the endless possibilities that come with it.

'That's good,' I say, while Niamh stays silent on the other side of me.

'We know it won't be easy, but we also know it will be worth it,' Jodie says. 'We have things to work out, of course. But there's nothing we can't overcome.'

'Jesus Christ, Jodie, would you just spit it out for the love of God?' Niamh blurts. 'It's bad enough you've made me wait so you could tell us together. This isn't the bloody *X Factor*. There's no need for a big reveal!'

Jodie and Adam sit, wide-eyed and their mouths gaping as they look at a now very ruffled Niamh. I'm struggling to take this version of my best friend in too, to be honest.

'Woah there, Mum!' Jodie says. 'I thought I was supposed to be the hormonal basket case in this scenario!'

Niamh glares at her. She's using the best scary mother/scary teacher-demanding-the-coursework-you-promised-would-be-completed-a-week-earlier face I've ever seen. I'm afraid to speak in case she sends me to detention, so I stay quiet. I'm almost intimidated enough to put my finger on my lips as if I was back in primary school, trying not to annoy my teacher.

'Okay,' Jodie says, throwing her hands in the air. 'We'll get to the point. We're going to keep the baby.'

My eyes dart immediately to Adam, desperate to see if he looks content with the decision. It's not a case that I don't believe Jodie that this is a fully joint decision, more that he is my son and of course he is the person I care about most of all in this scenario.

'Okay.' Niamh's voice is even. 'Well, we said we'd support you in every way we can and we will. But have you worked out how you will manage this? I mean, Adam's at university in Manchester. You're halfway through your degree, Jodie. I'm not for one second suggesting you're making the wrong decision – but this is going to be tough.'

I don't speak, but I nod. Niamh is not wrong. This *is* going to be tough.

'We know it will,' Adam says. 'So the plan is that I look to transfer my studies back here. I need to look at course provision and make that decision. I can finish my first year and be back in the summer in time to support Jodie. Hopefully I'll get a summer job and work those months to put some money behind us.'

I feel a huge bubble of emotion rise in me as I watch my son talk about such a huge decision and bring such a level-headed approach to it. These all feel like very grown-up decisions to have to make given that he's not even twenty yet and this morning I had to remind him to change his bed sheets before they walked themselves to the laundry basket.

'We know it's early days in our relationship, but we'd like to think we'll still be together,' Jodie adds as she squeezes Adam's hand.

Just as I can still see the boy in him, I can still see the little girl in her. She was the first of our communal babies – the sole focus of our friendship group until the boys came around. I have loved her from the very moment she was born.

'But even if we aren't together,' my boy says, 'I want to be as present in the baby's life as possible. I don't want to be an absentee parent.'

He sounds so earnest. When did our young people become so sensible? How can we be at this stage already – talking about babies and parenting? Becoming a granny, for the love of God. When I think of 'granny', I can't help but think of my own – my mother's mother – who always, even when I was little, very much fit the stereotype from the get-go. She always had her greying hair set in curlers at the hairdressers once a week, and by some miracle of science that short and boofy style lasted until her next appointment. It always sat perfectly – as if it were a hat plonked on top of her head. She dressed almost exclusively in lined skirts that stopped just below her knees, and soft woollen jumpers or twinsets. She had a brilliant line in brooches which I loved to search through, pretending they were pirate's treasure.

I could always see the trails of spider and varicose veins in her legs through the American Tan tights she wore every day with her slippers. She only put shoes on her feet when she left the house and my abiding memory of them was that they were low-heeled, laced up and definitely prized functionality over fashion.

Granny never wore make-up. She didn't ever fall into the trap I myself have tumbled into many, many times and spent a clean fortune on skincare products in the hope of miracle transformations. She was very much a soap and water type of woman, dabbing on some Nivea creme after. I can still conjure the smell of it, along with the comforting scent of her talcum powder, in my memory, just as I can the softness of her skin. She must've been doing something right.

But I'm a million miles from where she was. My hair has a mind of its own – managing to be neither straight nor curly, instead opting for some sort of frizzy combination of the two. It can be calmed with straighteners when I can be bothered to get them out. Otherwise, given that the majority of my days are spent at home writing copy, or venturing no further than the park with the dog, or my mother's house, I run a brush through it and hope for the best.

My daily uniform is more likely to be leggings, or skinny jeans with a T-shirt and a hoodie, than anything as refined as a twinset.

Last year I bought my first pair of Crocs, much to my twins' disgust, but let me tell you those bad boys are like a hug for your feet and Niamh had to threaten an intervention to stop me from wearing them everywhere. It was only when I bought her a pair for her birthday that she finally understood my obsession. Still, she says they are very much 'inside shoes'. Give it time though. She'll be nipping out to the shop in them soon enough. It will only grow from there. If I'm not mistaken, that 'loungewear' she is wearing is actually her best pyjama set from M&S. Crocs would've finished the look off nicely.

Anyway, I digress, I am not granny-like but yet here I am, listening to my boy telling me that I am most definitely going to be a granny. I want to hug him – and Jodie – and at the same time I want to give them both a good shake.

I want to hug Niamh – then spirit her away somewhere with

wine and ask her how she really feels about it all. I know that, like me, she will support our kids, but I also know that, just like me, she is dealing with a tsunami of emotions. Excitement will be in the mix somewhere, I realise. Deep inside me, my poor, decrepit ovaries have given a splutter of dusty enthusiasm at the thought of there being a baby in my life that I'm able to access for cuddles, head-sniffs and that incredible newborn-scrunched-on-your-shoulder feeling.

But the bigger feeling is worry. How will the kids cope? They have their plans – but how do I really feel about Adam dropping out of his course? Even if he will be picking back up closer to home. He had wanted to go to Manchester to study that particular computer programming course since he was fourteen. It is ridiculously competitive to get a place, but he had done and now he is going to walk away.

Will their relationship – or more importantly, perhaps, their friendship – survive the pressures of being young parents? God knows my own marriage didn't survive being not-so-young parents. It was tough. And if their friendship doesn't survive, what will that mean for Niamh and me? At the very best it will be awkward and uncomfortable. I don't want to think about the very worst.

And God, I think, if Adam comes home to continue his studies that means that Saul will be in Manchester without the support of his younger (by ten minutes) but infinitely more sensible brother. Of course, Adam is not his brother's keeper, but knowing that there has been a guiding hand on side has made me feel a lot easier about Saul studying across the sea.

Now is not the time for worrying about this though. Certainly not this very minute. I'm suddenly aware that Adam is looking directly at me, the same look I remember from his childhood on his face. It's the look he had when he would hand me a painting he did at school, or when he would show me what a good job he'd done of tidying his bedroom. It was a face that was calling out for approval and acknowledgement.

I have to hug him. I need it as much as he does, so I stand up and gesture to him to the do the same before pulling him into a 'giant squish', as we used to call it when he was little. 'I'm proud of you, Adam,' I tell him. 'We'll all get through this together and take it one day at a time. We'll work it all out.'

I'm aware that Niamh has stood up too and is hugging Jodie and it's one of the loveliest, but also most surreal and most terrifying, moments of my life.

8

SORRY, MRS MARTIN

'I shouldn't have brought the car,' Niamh says as I hand her a cup of tea. 'I could do with a glass of wine – a large one – about now. Or maybe some vodka. Turps even, might be good. Do you have any in the shed?'

'It's a lot, isn't it?' I say, staring into my own cup of milky tea and wondering if there is any turpentine in the shed. Adam and Jodie have disappeared up to Adam's room because they wanted to talk through their plans more. In private. Leaving Niamh and me to look at each like two war-weary baby veterans reliving the tough early years of parenting and trying to imagine Adam and Jodie taking on those roles.

It's a good thing my house is currently alcohol – and turps – free. If I started drinking I might not know when to stop.

'It's a school night,' I remind Niamh. 'You'll feel better for not going on a bender when the little darlings are trying to get you to make a TikTok with them in the morning.'

'The fact that it's a school night and that the little darlings will be trying to get me to make a TikTok is part of the reason I want a large glass of wine,' she says, pulling a face and eyeing her tea as if its lack of alcoholic content has personally offended her.

'It must be bad. It's only the first full week of term!'

She shakes her head slowly. 'Feels like the Christmas break didn't happen at all. Probably because of this *situation*.'

The *situation* is how we have taken to talking about the pregnancy over the course of this last week. Niamh had to be very careful of how she spoke in case her boys, Ethan and Cal, got wind of it or, worse still, Fiadh found out before decisions were made. It had been easier for me to fall in line with that, but I suppose now we can think about using the actual words. At least, once we've told those who need to know. I already feel a bit sick at the thought of how Simon – not known for his tact and diplomacy – will react. I know Niamh will be having similar worries about Paul.

'I know the kids can wind me up, but today I swear my patience was through the floor with them. I'm not a grumpy teacher – most of the time – but I swear I nearly summoned my inner Mrs Martin on Year 11 today.'

I grimace. Mrs Martin was our science teacher from first through until third year. The kind-hearted might refer to her as a 'real character', but to those of us who actually endured hours in her lab, she was a full-blown demon. The queen of the passive-aggressive putdown, she seemed to get a sense of pleasure out of reducing schoolgirls to tears or ordering us out of her classroom – where we would wait in fear of the vice principal walking by and starting an interrogation.

She was prone to hysterical shouting fits, and God love anyone sitting at the front of the lab because they would be sprayed with her spit as she roared.

I have never in my life been as scared of a teacher as I was of Mrs Martin, so to hear that Niamh – my lovely, funny, witty

Niamh – felt as if she was coasting dangerously close to that level of full crazy was worrying.

'Shit,' I say, reaching for a chocolate biscuit.

'Shit indeed.' Niamh lifts a chocolate biscuit and examines it before putting it back down again. 'Maybe I need to go to some extra yoga classes or something. So I've somewhere to channel this big, fat feeling of... fuck... I don't even know what it is. Rage? Anxiety? Fear? Hunger?' She lifts the biscuit again and eats it in one bite.

I'm not going to lie, she's scaring me a bit now too. What if she goes all Mrs Martin on me? My PTSD in that regard might be well buried but I'm not sure it would stay so if Niamh started spit-shouting at me in my own living room.

'Becs, will you hate me if I tell you I don't know how I feel about all of this?' She gestures around the room, looking up to the ceiling – a nod to where Jodie and Adam are currently in their blissful baby bubble.

'Of course I won't hate you. I could never hate you. And as I've said, it's a lot. There's so much to consider. They're both great kids, with sensible heads on them, but...'

'Kids,' Niamh says. 'They're kids. I know that technically they're adults but nineteen and twenty these days is nothing like it was in our day and even then I would have had a conniption at the thought of having a baby. They can't have thought about it properly.'

'No,' I say, shaking my head.

'And I'm not saying that I want Jodie to have an abortion... I mean if that was her choice... but...'

'I get it,' I tell her. 'It's scary. It's a lot of responsibility on their shoulders. And Adam giving up his place at university? He loves that course. And Saul relies on him so much. God only knows how Simon will react. As I said, it's a lot.'

Niamh, quiet for a moment, takes a sip from her tea before putting the mug back on the coffee table and rubbing her temples.

'Jodie has her final year at uni to complete, and was hoping to go on and do her PGCE,' Niamh says. 'I suppose that will go on hold. She'll not want to be committing to that level of study when the baby will be so young. I was going to get her a placement in the school. And Paul? He won't be able to hide his disappointment. You know what he's like – his voice mightn't say it, but his face will. Him and Jodie have always been so close... he's wanted everything for her. Was so proud she was following in my footsteps into teaching. But now this? All because of a boy!'

I bristle. Not because I don't agree with her, but because the 'boy' happens to my boy. Who will be making sacrifices in his life plans too. When I think of the scary teacher version of Niamh, who shouted at Jodie to get on with it not half an hour ago, I decide to keep my feelings on this to myself. Emotions are running high. It won't do me, or any of us, any good to lose the head right now.

'And Becs... grannies! You know that big wobble we had last year about ageing – when we found those letters we wrote when we were sixteen? I think that was just the precursor to this even bigger wobble. Is this it? Is my life going to be Year 11, and all future Year 11s, making me more and more ratty until I retire on the grounds of insanity in ten years' time? I mean... what age was Mrs Martin when she taught us?'

'God knows,' I say. 'Every teacher seemed to look the same kind of old-lady old to me back then.'

'But maybe she wasn't old at all? Maybe she was just our age, and menopausal? I'm tempted to try and find out if she's still alive and call round to apologise personally to her.' Niamh punctuates the end of her sentence by stuffing another chocolate biscuit – in one bite – into her mouth.

I let her eat her biscuit before I answer, not wanting to try and speak over the din of crunchy digestive topped with chocolate.

'If it helps, I'm freaking out a bit too. This was not on my bingo list for the latter half of my forties. I'm grateful I don't have Year II, or any year group for that matter, to stand in front of because I can tell you now that I *would* go full Mrs Martin. All you teachers have the patience of saints.'

Niamh gives a small smile, but it doesn't last long and I know she is well and truly down in the dumps.

I proffer her the plate of biscuits but she shakes her head. 'If I eat any more biscuits, I'll barf. I swear I'm 90 per cent biscuit at the moment. I've no stomach for anything else and I'm so tired all the time that I just want as many sugar hits as I can get. We went and got the patches, Becs. Should they not be tackling all this hormonal depression-laden nonsense by now? I don't feel any different, except that my boobs hurt like a motherfucker. It reminds me of when I was pregnant, which I'm absolutely not. I'm not going down that rabbit hole of madness again.'

The 'madness' being the not too distant past where she was convinced she was indeed pregnant, until a negative test and a subsequent visit to the doctor assured her she was not. She was, instead, in perimenopause. As am I. We were both prescribed HRT patches to wear, and while I have found them to be a great boost to both my mind and body, Niamh is still accursed with menopausal woes – including the aforementioned sore breasts.

'Maybe HRT just doesn't work for me?' she says. 'I had such high hopes that I'd get the Davina McCall effect and get all snatched and super healthy, but instead I'm suffering through yoga, sweating buckets all the time and my mood – God, my mood, Becca! I've become a complete shite-craic cry-baby. How am I going to find the patience to help Jodie through her pregnancy when I just feel so pissed off all the damn time?'

I let her speak because, to be quite honest, I'm now quite scared to interrupt her but I know she needs my help.

'Maybe your HRT just needs a wee tweak? The doctor told me it's not one size fits all, and it's a matter of playing around with it until you hit that sweet spot.'

'You make it sound like a sex toy,' she says with a bit of a smirk. There's a flash of the old, happy, not-afraid-to-make-inappropriate-jokes Niamh still there after all.

'Well, maybe it is a bit like that,' I say, a blush creeping over my face. That's the problem with being a born-again virgin who hasn't actually had any sex in the ten years since her marriage broke down – I get ridiculously embarrassed talking about anything remotely sex adjacent. It's something I'll need to get over if I'm to write the column I'm pitching to Grace Adams. Or, more importantly, if I'm to get things back on track with Conal. 'Look, make an appointment to see the doctor again. I'll go with you. We're not giving up and giving in just because we're going to be grandmothers. Didn't we say when we found those letters that we were going to grab life by the balls and do the things we've always wanted? That means getting ourselves in the right place, physically and emotionally, to do that. Make the appointment. We'll make this work.'

'If we're not babysitting instead,' she says, glumly. 'Ach, listen to me, I've become such a long streak of misery. I can't even stand listening to myself.'

'You're grand,' I reassure her, secretly worrying that yes, we might just be babysitting all the time and not able to do all the things we promised our younger selves we would. Younger me wanted to travel more. She wanted to write because she loved it. She wanted to fall in love and dance under the stars and do all the things that would be difficult if there was a baby on her hip.

Niamh brushes the crumbs from her biscuit off her trousers and into her hand, where Daniel dutifully licks them up. 'So, forgetting about the babysitting and going back to grabbing life by the balls... what's the sitch with Conal? Any... you know... ball-grabbing action going on in that regard?'

'Sadly, no. We still seem to be stuck on pause. I haven't wanted to not be there for Adam, and then I've been working on this pitch for Grace – which is happening tomorrow, by the way. I don't want to spend time with him when I'm distracted by everything else and then he has been busy at work too...'

She shakes her head. 'The course of true love doesn't run smooth.'

'Except for you and Paul,' I say. 'As the young ones would say, hashtag couple goals.'

'I'm not sure the young ones would say that right now,' she says, slouching back in her seat, defeated. 'If I'm grumpy, he's grumpier. We're like Statler and Waldorf from *The Muppets*. Only more crabbit. Jodie's news has knocked him for six.'

'It has knocked us all for six,' I say.

'Yeah, but Paul, I don't know, he seems only able to see the negative. He's wallowing in it and I'm bearing the brunt of his frustration and sadness and I have enough of my own frustration and sadness to be coping with. I don't have the mental or physical energy to lift him up too. He looks at me as if it's my fault, somehow. Or something. I don't know. But I don't like this side of him. I've never seen him this way.'

It's certainly not the case that Niamh thinks the sun rises and sets in Paul Cassidy's eyes. She is not blindly in love with the man, and they have had their share of ups and downs over the years, but for the most part they have been on the same side when it comes to the big issues. Their clashes have been minor and infrequent. So I can totally understand why this is worrying to her.

'He'll come round though,' I say, hoping that I'm right. 'He's not an arsehole. There's no way he would've been able to hide his arseholey ways from us all these years. He just needs to process it all.'

Niamh shrugs. 'I just wish he would process it faster, or in a less grumpy fashion. God knows how he's going to react to this decision of theirs. Jodie is insisting on talking to him herself, but what if he says something he can't take back?'

I nod and listen as she continues venting.

'I'll be stuck in the middle between them. And it's not like this is easy for me either. I feel awful saying that. That's my grand-child in there, after all. Ah, fuck, Becs. It's all a mess. Maybe Paul is handling it the right way and being honest about his feelings. Maybe it's me that's the problem.'

Shaking my head, I grasp her hand. 'Darling, you could never be the problem. Even at your worst, you're still not a problem. You might have an unhealthy yoga addiction—'

'It's the only thing that stops me losing my shit!'

'I know that. And I know it's good for you, and me. It's just really, really hard.'

'It will get easier,' she tells me. 'I promise.'

'Hopefully that's true for all our worries. Things have a way of working out, and if I have to give Paul a stern talking-to, then I will. Just tell me when.'

Niamh gives a small laugh. 'I think I'd pay good money to see that.'

9

WE'RE GONNA NEED A LONGER YOGA CLASS

Niamh

Niamh feels a little calmer when she leaves Becca to make her way home. Her best friend is right, things do have a way of working themselves out. It might take a while, but that doesn't mean it won't happen. Hadn't she given up on ever reconnecting with Laura – the third member of their friendship triumvirate – only to be brought back together towards the end of last year?

Driving home, she thinks of Laura now, and the challenges she has faced over the last while. She watched her mother battle with cancer before the cruel disease finally took the inspirational Kitty O'Hagan much too young. Laura has been remarkably stoic in front of others, but Becca and Niamh know just how hard it has been for her. They've seen her when she has let her guard down and fallen apart – her pain just too overwhelming. Of course, thinking of Laura leads to a tsunami of guilt washing over Niamh. Here she is getting her comfortable Marks and Spencer knickers in a twist over the menopause and the prospect of a grandchild while Laura is living under the weight of grief.

She can almost hear her mother's voice in her ear – 'Sure, there's folk a million times worse off than you. You need to haul yourself out of it, love.' It was one of her mother's most frequent refrains.

While she knows her mother doesn't mean to make her feel worse when she doles out that particular nugget of maternal love and care, that is in fact the outcome of this gentle 'encouragement' all the same. And it's something so ingrained in Niamh these days that she doesn't even need her mother to say it any more. It's ever present in her own mind. It's why she so rarely allows herself to slip into a maudlin mood or ruminate on her worries – instead always feeling compelled to pull herself together and 'count her blessings' instead.

There may be some sense in it, but God damn it those feelings have to come out sometime. Deep down she's starting to worry that all the messy feelings she has pushed down over the years have just been biding their time, waiting for the perfect moment to burst forth into the world.

Best case, they arrive in spectacular 'fuck it' style wearing a feather boa and high heels, singing 'Get the Party Started' by P!nk while quaffing Tattinger. Worst case – and the one she thinks might be looming imminently – is that they stumble out of her, hungover, in grubby dressing gowns and mismatched socks, mascara streaked all over their faces as they sob about their past, and it won't matter how hard she tries, she will never be able to make them sit down and behave.

Maybe, she thinks, she'd have less cause for worry if she hadn't spent all these years suppressing the urge to occasionally feel sorry for herself.

Starting to feel uncomfortable with just how dangerously close she is to having a full-on ugly cry in her car, she practises her emergency slow breathing to find her centre. Yoga has its benefits and this is certainly one of them. To her surprise, even though she finds each yoga class to be a form of torture, she has started to look forward to her classes – even booking a few extra sessions. It's impossible to focus your energy on your problems when you're contorting your body into some unholy shape while trying not to fall over or pass wind. Maybe she should book one every day.

Maybe she should ask Laura, again, if she'd like to come along too. It might do her good to get out of the house and do something that will distract her from her grief, even if it is only for an hour or two. A guilty thought hits. Should they have invited Laura over this evening? No. It would have been weird for everyone to have her in the middle of their conversation with the kids about their baby. Both Adam and Jodie are only really getting to know her again after the 'great falling-out' which happened when Becca's marriage disintegrated and Laura chose to stay friends with her ex, Simon.

As her husband Aidan's best friend, Laura didn't feel she could leave him out in the cold, but when Simon moved into their house for a while post break-up, their friendship had imploded spectacularly. Niamh had got caught up in the crossfire when she chose to take Becca's side.

The ten-year gap in their friendship hasn't stopped Niamh and Becca from picking up from where they left off with Laura and very quickly building on the sisterly bond they had shared from their first days at secondary school. But with the kids, it was different. Yes, Laura had been ever present in their childhoods – until the point where she simply wasn't any more. Jodie had been just ten, and Adam just nine, when the great falling-out happened. A lot has changed in their lives in the intervening decade. They have grown into young adults, who need to get to know Laura all over again.

But still, Niamh feels guilty that Laura was excluded from proceedings – worrying that her friend might still feel like a bit of an outsider to the incredibly close bond she and Becca share.

To assuage her growing guilt, she instructs Siri to call Laura so she can fill her in on what has happened.

Laura doesn't answer with hello, but instead with, 'Well? What's the craic? I've been sitting here on my nerves waiting to hear from either of you.'

'I'm sorry,' Niamh replies. 'We were talking for a while and then Becca and I had a chat about it. They've decided to keep the baby.'

There's a pause for a second or two before Laura speaks again. 'And how do you feel about that?'

'Mixed feelings, if I'm honest. But they're taking a very sensible approach to it all and they seem to have given it a lot of thought.'

'And Paul? How has he reacted?'

'Jodie went home earlier to talk to him. I've been driving around trying to avoid going home, but I suppose I have to find out sometime, so I'm on my way back now.' Niamh flicks the indicator on and pulls into the forecourt of the garage closest to her home. She's going to buy some chocolate. Possibly a lot of chocolate. Her raging hormones have her wishing she could get melted Cadbury's infused directly into her veins. Not hot chocolate, mind. That's not pure enough. She would have them melt down at least three family-size Dairy Milks and run its thick, gloopy goodness in on a fast infusion.

They chat for a while before making plans to meet at the weekend to catch up. Wine, Laura tells her, is not optional.

'It will probably be Becca's house. I'll message her when I'm done talking to you. Oh and Laura, don't forget tomorrow is her big pitch with Grace at *Northern People*. Let's be on standby in case she needs some emergency support measures before or after.'

'I'll consider myself on call until I hear different from you,' Laura says, and Niamh can't help but smile. At least, she tells herself, she has her girls. She might feel completely at sea in regards to just about everything else in her life, but she knows her friends will keep her right. That, and her yoga and her chocolate – which she will keep in a secret stash in the glovebox so that none of her children will get a hold of it. Becca had warned her that teenage boys can eat you out of house and home but she'd never quite believed it until her own offspring had begun to land like a plague of locusts every time she brought food into the house – devouring everything and leaving nothing but empty boxes in the cupboards and empty milk cartons in the fridge.

Once she has stocked up, Niamh heads for home, unsure of what atmosphere will greet her when she gets in the door. She's not sure how she will cope if it's anything less than peaceful. A rush of anxiety starts to claw at her and she does not like this feeling. Niamh Cassidy does not get anxious. She is renowned for her ability to keep her cool in every situation. She was the first person Becca turned to when her marriage broke up. She's the first person the head turns to when the printer breaks, or the heating breaks down, or Year II start a fire in the home economics classroom. Niamh doesn't get flustered. She does what needs to be done. She is practical and logical. Her scientific brain helping her keep a hold of her senses.

Or at least she used to be like that. Increasingly, she seems to be swamped with bouts of anxiety so severe she feels as if someone is compressing her chest, making it hard for her to breathe. Her skin crawls as if anxiety is a poison spreading through her veins.

Rationally, she knows that it isn't. Everything is okay, she reminds herself. She knows her husband. She knows he will get his head around things. She knows her daughter and knows that, even though she is young, she will cope.

The thing she doesn't seem to know, or trust in any more, is her own ability to cope. Could Becca be right? Could this be down to the menopause? Is that why her ability to cope with life's many shit-hitting-the-fan scenarios seems to have disappeared? Because if it is, she is *not* a fan. The menopause, and the hot, sweaty, anxious horse it rode in on, can fuck right off.

Unable to face whatever is waiting for her inside her own front door just yet, she pulls her car over to the side of the road at the top of her street and inhales a full family-size Whole Nut bar, and immediately hates herself after. She'll have to work extra hard at yoga to try and undo the damage. She shovelled it into her mouth so fast she doesn't even think she tasted it.

Tears prick at her eyes. 'Oh, pull yourself together, Niamh!' she scolds herself. Tomorrow she'll phone the doctor and make that appointment and that will be when she starts putting herself back together.

10

ZIP-ITTY DOO DAH

Becca

Daniel is looking at me with his full-on sad face as I try on my third outfit of the day, trying to find something that screams 'funny, fresh and talented writer' instead of 'I haven't bought any clothes other than leggings, hoodies and fluffy socks in the last few years'.

I was sure I'd have something suitable for my meeting with Grace Adams in my wardrobe. I was sure I had something work appropriate which also managed to make me feel relaxed and fabulous, but of course I didn't check, which was absolutely a fatal mistake.

I am now in my bedroom, red-faced and sweaty as I struggle into a Hell Bunny pencil dress, wondering if it might just scream a bit too much 'gangster's moll' than 'brave new journalistic voice'. I'd bought it in the sale three years ago, promising myself I would start to reclaim my social life. The plan was to drag Niamh out for drinks in a nice bar so that we could dress up and remind ourselves we weren't just overworked and underpaid mothers of teenagers. I'd bought a nice pair of patent Mary Janes to wear with it. I'm sure they must be in the back of my wardrobe somewhere.

I pull the zip up on the dress, thinking that whoever invented side zips in dresses is assured a place in hell. I can't imagine the thought process behind that particular joy.

The side zip – that most wretched of creatures – and specifically the side zip on this lovely dress goes a step beyond that particularly hellish task. It requires a balancing act to get the tension just right so I can pull up the zip without hauling the entire dress northwards and exposing my knickers to an already sad and depressed-looking dog.

The implied sorrow in Daniel's pleading eyes is reminding me that I have not walked him this morning. In fact, I've shown him a startling lack of attention today, and he is not happy. My 'scritches and scratches' count is far below what he normally expects in a day and this wounds him deeply. A day cannot be considered a success in Daniel Land unless he has had his fur ruffled and that sweet spot behind his ears scratched at least three times every hour.

If there was a TripAdvisor equivalent where dogs could review their owners, I'd be scored a disappointing two out of five – 'Must try harder. Standard used to be higher but has dropped significantly in recent days. Could do with revamp.'

Thankfully, however, no such site or app exists, and so far his unhappiness is only at the emotional blackmail stage and not at the teach-himself-how-to-write-so-he-can-leave-a-scathing-review-online stage. With Daniel, I can't help but feel the latter is only a matter of time.

When I sit down on the bed, he doubles up on the sad-eyes look, and scooches across the covers before laying his head on my lap and exhaling loudly into a 'boof' of sorrow.

'I'll take you out when I get back from my meeting,' I assure him, which only makes him 'boof' again, and louder, turning his head away from me as if he can barely bring himself to look at my hateful face. He really can be quite the drama queen.

Trying to ignore him, I instead allow myself a moment of celebration at managing to win my battle with the zip in my dress. Sadly, however, when I look in the mirror I do not see the put-together professional I'd been hoping would stare back at me. It's giving less Peggy from *Mad Men* and more Peggy from *Hi-de-Hi*. My hair is extra frizzy and hanging damp around my overheated face, the pale skin of arms and décolletage is blotchy. It's not a great look.

Pushing down the panic that is threatening to overwhelm me, I try to work out if anything from this particular look is salvageable.

The dress, I can accept, looks quite well. It hugs but doesn't suffocate my figure, managing to look chic rather than slutty. The skirt skims my knee in a way that flatters, and the neckline doesn't dip outrageously low. This isn't bad.

But perhaps it's too sculpted office professional? What do journalists at *Northern People* wear to work anyway? Is it the latest fashion? Will my three-year-old sale rack Hell Bunny frock mark me out as being totally out of touch with current trends? Are they all in some modern designer? Maybe dressing in 'fashion forward' creations – shapeless billowing dresses made out of parachute fabric cut in asymmetric patterns, with cut-outs to show off some part of their bodies that I'd only ever show to a doctor or lover. Or perhaps those ridiculous extra-super-wide-leg trousers which make young trendy folk look like Borrowers, but which would make me look five times the size I am and as if I'm trying too hard. It might even be the case that they all are the complete opposite of fashion-obsessed media darlings and spend their days dressed in jeans and tees and can get away with it because they are young and lithe and have flat stomachs and a flawless tan. What if I show up in my body-con but business-friendly dress and heels and they all just gawp at me from the comfort of their band T-shirts and Converse?

I feel like lying down on the bed and 'boofing' along with Daniel.

If only I had someone to come along and offer me some scritches and scratches of encouragement around now? My mind immediately goes to Conal. We'd spoken on the phone for a full hour last night when I'd called to fill him in on the big decision. He'd listened with just the right amount of understanding, and then he had made me laugh by sharing some of Lazlo's recent antics. I realised I had been listening to him while smiling so broadly that my jaw now hurt.

'I miss you,' I'd blurted, without really thinking.

There was a pause. Not a long one, but one long enough for my bruised heart to convince me he was horrified at my declaration and was currently booking himself a one-way ticket to Australia.

There was a sigh. 'Becs,' he said, and the low timbre of his voice, heavy with longing, actually vibrated through me. 'I miss you too. I know we were only getting going, but I was enjoying the ride.'

Chance would be a fine thing, I thought, and immediately blushed. It has been a long time since I've had 'the ride' and nervous as I am about it, I can't help but let it creep into my thoughts every now and again. Especially when I'm with Conal.

No. I cannot allow myself to get distracted, or hot and bothered, thinking about Conal O'Hagan. It will bring out a hot flush to end all hot flushes, then I'd look even more of a mess arriving at my meeting with Grace. Overdressed and overheated. It's not the first impression I want to make.

I'm scared I'm getting ready to make a holy show of myself. Maybe this indecision and self-doubt is the universe's way of signalling this isn't the right time for me. Maybe I'm mad to think I have (a) the talent and (b) the energy to chase a gig like this.

Maybe I should be putting all my efforts towards my impending granny-hood. Perhaps there's a class I could be taking? It could teach me all the basics, such as how to slip a fiver into the hand of a grandchild without their parent noticing, or the best place to store a secret supply of nice biscuits and sweets that only come out when the children visit? What else could it teach, I wonder, thinking of my own granny. How to knit? How to bake an apple tart? How to have a prayer for every occasion? None of these sound particularly like me.

I wish I could phone Niamh or Laura for a last-minute pep talk, but they are both at work. Instead I read over the messages they sent me just this morning telling me I'm brilliant and how I've got this, etc., etc., but it seems my doubt is too loud to allow me to believe them.

I sit on the bed again and allow Daniel to scooch his way back onto my lap, not caring about the dog hairs he is currently covering me in. He'd certainly be happier if I stayed doing what I'm doing and being at home every day, free to walk him between writing uninspiring nonsense for ungrateful clients who rarely even bother to say thank you.

He's not a fan of being left alone, but then again Grace might be happy for me to write from home. I'm only pitching some columns. I'm not expecting to be offered a corner office and a parking space. There's no reason to believe I won't be able to continue in my role as Daniel's servant and almost constant companion.

I take a deep breath to settle myself, and I try to think what my beloved daddy would say to me if he was still living. I'm sure he'd very gently, while also managing to be firm in that way only a father can be, tell me to stop self-sabotaging and to hold my head high and go for it. 'You're as good as anyone else,' he'd say. 'If not better. So stop telling yourself that you're not, or that you don't deserve it. You're a fierce one for sabotaging your own happiness, Rebecca. My dearest wish is that you find a way to break that habit, because I know you are capable of anything you set your mind to. If you don't believe in you just yet, then know that I believe in you enough for the both of us.'

With a shaky exhalation, I wonder if that belief of his still exists in whatever form of the afterlife he has found himself in.

Or maybe it's my turn to believe in me enough for both of us.

'Daniel,' I say, standing up and brushing the dog hairs off my dress. 'It's time I get myself ready. And there's no need for you to look so sad. Adam is home. He'll mind you. And I promise I'll bring you back a sausage from the deli counter.'

His ears pick up at the mention of the word sausage. He's so easily bought. A total sausage slut.

Forty-five minutes later I have transformed myself into a reasonable representation of a woman who knows what she is doing. I've put on some opaque tights which have the added benefit of sucking my stomach pouch in a little. It's not flat. It never has been flat. Not even before I had the twins. Needless to say, after I'd had the twins I had to make my peace with the fact it will never, ever be flat. But at least it's less wobbly. With the addition of the now uncovered Mary Janes, and a cropped leopard-print cardigan I bought in the sale in Asda, I look presentable. I've opted for a natural yet groomed make-up look, with the help of some concealer, blush and a hint of mascara. The straighteners have been dragged through my hair and, while I'm certainly not giving any stylist anything to have a sleepless night over, I have managed to calm the frizz. As long as it doesn't rain on my way to *Northern People*, it should remain so.

Now I just have to grab my folder with my pitch ideas – which I have also emailed to Grace so she can read in advance – and get across town without bottling out.

'I'm doing this for you, Daddy,' I whisper to his picture, wishing I could just get a sign from him that he's proud of me for stepping out of my comfort zone.

That my phone chooses this exact moment to ping to life makes me swear, loudly, earning yet another disappointed 'boof' from Daniel. I know, of course, the text is really bloody unlikely to be the aforementioned sign from beyond the grave that my father is proud of me. I'm not completely delusional.

But as it turns out, it's still something very lovely. A message from Conal.

> Good luck today. You're class. You'll walk it. Chat soon. I still miss you. C xxx

I might be a forty-six-year-old woman but the 'I still miss you' and the three kisses at the end of his text make my heart flutter just a little. Three kisses is intentional. It's not a force of habit single 'x'. It requires a level of forethought. It shows he is still interested. And he misses me. There is still time to salvage this.

I'll message him after and let him know how it has gone. See if we can't work out a mutually agreeable time to get together. As long as it goes well, that is. I might need to lie down and have a cry in a darkened room if it doesn't.

Before I fall into another doubt spiral, I swear I hear my father's voice in my ear once again. 'What's for you won't pass you, Rebecca. If it's meant to happen, it will happen.'

11

AMAZING GRACE

Grace is surprisingly approachable and enthusiastic. I'm sitting in her office, looking around me as I wait for her to finish on a phone call. She's speaking to a photographer about a shoot she has organised, and it all sounds impossibly glamorous and exciting – and a million miles away from 'Ten Ways to Increase Productivity and Wow Your Boss'.

Her office is relatively small, but it's tidy save for a pile of *Northern People* magazines in the corner that I'm pretty sure poses a significant fire hazard. It's not my place to point such things out, so I stay quiet and instead look at the selection of framed magazine covers on the walls. There's the first edition, published in the eighties, featuring a woman with permed hair, shoulder pads and bright blue mascara.

There's also a cover featuring a smouldering shot of Jamie Dornan. He's giving his best sexy serial killer expression, which makes me think this edition must have coincided with the success of the Northern Irish-based drama series *The Fall*.

I remember thinking, at the time, that I wouldn't mind the likes of him climbing in my window one evening. I wasn't so keen on the notion of being murdered, mind... but still, Jamie Dornan was very good at setting my heart (and other parts) all a flutter.

The other covers on display mark different landmarks in the magazine's decades-long history. I spy their one hundredth edition, and one celebrating their ten-year anniversary. It's an impressive sight and I can hardly believe that I am in with a chance to actually become a part of this magazine's story.

My stomach fizzes with what I hope is excitement, but which could also be an incoming bout of gastroenteritis. Please God, it's the former.

Grace looks very comfortable behind her desk – as if she was made for the role. I'd been low-keyed worried she'd turn out to be a Miranda Priestly clone and immediately see right through my pathetic attempts to be relevant and fashionable.

But she hadn't been like that at all. She'd come to greet me in reception, smiling broadly, instead of sending one of her minions. She's dressed in a neat pair of black trousers, with a stylish white shirt, open just low enough to be classy and to show off the simple gold necklace around her neck. Her entire look could probably be described as effortless, but I'm sure it wasn't. I am not blind to the extra flourishes.

She is a well-polished and more confident version of the girl she used to be at school. If she had been in the same year group as Niamh, Laura and me, we would probably have been friends. We were cut from the same slightly nerdy cloth – neither part of the popular set nor cool enough to hang out with the emo crowd who, for some reason I've never understood, were known as the Fraggles. They were certainly nothing like the brightly coloured puppets of one of my favourite childhood shows.

Grace was always, always passionate about what she wanted to get out of life. She was determined, even then, that she would become a journalist and she would climb that career ladder.

Unlike me, she never found herself a comfortable spot on the bottom rung and took up permanent residence there.

There's a lot to admire in the version of Grace I see in front of me now.

Her nails are manicured and painted a subtle taupe, while mine are bare and could probably do with a good massage with hand cream and cuticle oil. Her highlighted hair is pulled back in a neat chignon, but a few stray hairs have managed to escape, which puts me at ease. I think I might have cried if I'd been faced with perfection personified. Women who don't look just a little harassed make me suspicious – even more so if their make-up and cosmetic touch-ups mean they could be any age between twenty-five and fifty-five.

Grace Adams looks her age – in a good way. Her eyes crinkle when she smiles, and her lips are not unnaturally plumped and filled. I can see the hint of grey roots in her hair. She looks as if she is very comfortable in her late-forties style which I find deeply reassuring. It's always a bonus when I don't want to slide under a table with embarrassment at how out of place I feel. There's a kinship here. I can feel it.

She says goodbye to the person on the other end of the line and puts the phone down. 'Sorry about that,' she says. 'I should be able to leave the photographer to get on with things but sometimes he can need a little more guidance. We've a big edition coming up and it's all hands on deck to make it really special. No one wants to fuck it up.'

'That sounds exciting,' I say with a smile.

She shrugs. 'Between the two of us, it is and it isn't. There's a lot of pressure to get it just right. Print editions are fighting for their lives out there at the moment. Who wants to pick up a magazine when they can get the latest fashion, features and gossip online in minutes? We're pushing hard to keep selling and keep relevant.'

'That must be a lot of pressure for you?'

'It is and isn't,' she repeats with a smile. 'I love it, which is why I keep doing it. I think I've learned to thrive under pressure, but at the same time I'm responsible for keeping the show on the road, keeping my staff in a job and growing our digital content too. It's certainly busy.'

Her phone rings again and she lifts it before hanging it straight back up, then lifts the handset and lays it on her desk off the hook. 'But listen, you didn't come here to listen to me talking about how busy I am! Thanks for sending over the sample columns. I had a good read of them last night and Becca, I'm in.'

I hardly dare to believe what I think I'm hearing. She's in? In what? In for having me on board? 'I'm in!' is usually a positive statement, isn't it?

But what if I'm wrong? What if she means she's in a state of disgust that I would insult her with such nonsense? Or in shock at my audacity at thinking I had a voice her readers would want to entertain?

I don't know how I should react – whether to smile or cry – so I just stare at her while trying to remember how normal human beings use their own faces. It's possible that I look as if I'm mid stroke. *Speak, Becca!* I think, *For feck sake! Open your damn mouth and say something sensible!*

'You're i-in?' I stutter.

'Yes. I loved them!' she says enthusiastically. 'You have such a relatable voice – and not just because I'm a similar age and my children are leaving me behind while they forge ahead into their futures like yours are. You just get that mix of humour and heart that our readers love so right. I laughed when I read them, and I had a little cry too because, seriously, when you wrote that motherhood inevitably breaks all our hearts, I felt that in my bones. I mean, we put all the work in and then they just clear off! When I showed them to my deputy and features editors they agreed with me. We think you'd be a great asset to the magazine.'

'You d-do?' I stutter again, watching for signs on her face that maybe she had but now that she's met this stuttering eejit who doesn't even know how to react like a normal person she might just be reconsidering that decision.

'I do. Look, I don't have unlimited means. I'd like to tell you that I do, but truth be told, every month I get through without having to go full Hunger Games with my staff to appease the powers that be is a bonus. What I do have, though, is a modest budget for contributors. We'd love it if you were able to provide us with five to seven hundred words on surviving your forties each month. I'll have to brainstorm with the team, and you of course, but we'll come up with a name for the column and branding. You'll have editorial freedom, within limits. Write what you want – but try and stay clear of ripping into the industries most likely to advertise on our pages. I like your warts-and-all approach. What it's like trying to figure out who you are, while caring for older relatives, your children and your friends, while working and trying to maintain a relationship – or build a new one,' she says with a wink. 'Give us menopause chat. A forties-is-the-new-thirties attitude. I want that "there's life in the old gal yet" approach – but without using that phrase. It makes me feel queasy. Something about "old gal" feels like we should all be wearing tweed skirts and twinsets and supping gin out of hip flasks down at the stables.'

I'm listening as she chats excitedly about the words I've written, and the style I've adopted. I beam with pride when she tells me she almost peed laughing at my menopausal take on 'Position of the Fortnight', which had been the closest thing to porn many a teenage girl in the nineties saw in each edition of the now sadly defunct *More* magazine. But my version wouldn't be about sex, but instead about getting a good sleep while dealing with night sweats, aches and pains and a back that goes out more than I do.

'I'm so glad you liked it,' I say, delighted with myself for being able to speak a coherent sentence with the appropriate facial expression in place.

'Seriously! I loved it. And when I say I almost peed, I'm not lying. I've had two vaginal births, and a hysterectomy. I'm always just one belly laugh away from needing Tena Lady.'

Her honesty and willingness to talk about the things we have often been urged to keep under wraps warms my heart. It's exactly how I want to write. I don't want every word women read to be aspirational. I want what I write to be relatable. Life is bloody hard enough without thinking you're getting it wrong all the time and everyone else is sailing along in a state of near perpetual bliss.

I don't want my words to amount to a how-to guide of how to look younger and fight off the natural ageing process. Women in their forties and fifties are not solely fixated on their looks.

There's an incredible warm glow inside me as I listen to Grace, and for once it's not a hot flush. It's just sheer pride.

'So,' she says, cutting through my little internal celebration, 'here's the catch.'

Catch? I freeze. I don't like catches. I don't like little surprises on the end of nice news. I am always immediately suspicious of them. They scream of 'if something looks too good to be true...'

My concern must be written large all over my face as Grace immediately moves to reassure me. 'Oh, God. Don't look so stressed. Don't worry. It's not bad. It's... well... let me put it this way: how good are you at working under pressure?'

I snort. Everything in my existence seems to be under pressure at the moment; what difference would throwing one more log into the bin-fire of my life make?

'I may require a large glass of wine at the end of the day, but as it happens, I'm quite good at pressure. Most of the time,' I reply, wondering if it's appropriate to start regaling her with stories of my sons, the unexpected pregnancy *situation*, the new romance or making sure my mother doesn't kill herself by climbing into her attic or breaking a hip trying to shovel snow on her own. But then I remember this isn't actually a friendly natter over coffee. This is a work situation and I am supposed to be professional – even if we were only discussing incontinence a few moments ago.

'Look,' I tell her, 'I'm used to working to frequent and shifting deadlines. The majority of the business-to-business clients I have worked with over the years have very exacting standards and are never afraid to shift the goalposts at the last minute and expect everyone to fall into line behind them. This creates pressure all of its own.'

She nods.

'I juggle creating content with hitting their deadlines, targeting specific issues within their industries and making even the driest of copy sound entertaining. This gig... well, this is me doing something for me. Something that feeds my soul. Truth be told, this is something I should've pursued years ago but, you know, life got in the way in the way it tends to do. Parenting. Lone parenting. That kind of thing. And then I got too settled in my comfort zone. But this? This is what I want to do and I'll do anything to make it work. Pile the pressure on. I'll make it happen.'

I'm hoping my speech has come across more Jerry Maguire– esque than just the desperate ramblings of a woman who knows this might be her last chance to take control of her career.

I'm also hoping that even though I've told her to pile on the pressure, she doesn't pile too much on. I can't help but feel a little like a human version of Buckaroo right now. One cowboy hat too many and I'll be kicking my emotional baggage all around me.

'Great,' she says, grinning. 'Because here's the thing. April is our fortieth anniversary edition and I really think that will be the perfect time to launch you as our latest voice.'

April? Well, this is January, and February and March are still to pass. I'm pretty sure I can write a seven-hundred-word article by then without giving myself carpal tunnel syndrome or RSI.

'I know what you're thinking,' she continues as if she's reading my mind. 'April is ages away. Except in magazine land, it's not. We bring our April edition out mid-to-late March. And yes, I know you think that mid-to-late March is, what, nine weeks away?'

I nod.

'You'd be right on one level, but the thing is, we like to get the magazine planned and the freelance features all to bed around six weeks before publication. We keep certain pages for closer to deadline, obviously, but your copy? We'd need that sooner rather than later.'

'That won't be a problem,' I tell her, knowing that I have several sample columns already drafted beyond those I've sent to her already. There's bound to be something among that which will be suitable.

'Great!' Grace claps her hands together. 'That's what I was hoping you'd say. Now, before we get down to talking money and the like, I want to run one more thing past you. I think it could be right up your street, but it is a bit out there.'

12

GIRLS' TRIP

BECCA

Girls, would you both be free to pop round to mine tonight? Or even on your way home from work? Or we could meet at Caffè Nero for a quick coffee and chat? I have news! And a favour to ask.

NIAMH

An excuse to stay away from home for an extra hour and possibly avoid having to make three different dinners to appease my ungrateful brood? Sounds like heaven to me!

LAURA

What time? I'm at the dentist with Robyn and then I've to meet Conal at Mum's to sign yet more paperwork. *sad face*

BECCA

What time works for you, L?

LAURA

Six gives me time to drop Robyn home first. Does that work?

NIAMH

It's good for me. But I'm going to tell Paul that we're meeting at five. I'll treat myself to a hot chocolate and an hour reading my book in peace before you get there.

BECCA

Perfect! I'll see you all at six.

LAURA

Is everything okay? The meeting with Grace?

BECCA

Well, that's exactly what I wanted to talk to you about.

Parking close to Caffè Nero, I really hope I can get the girls on board with what Grace and I discussed. I think it could really be good for them. I know it could be good for me. Or at least I think it would be. And if not, then at least we'll be able to tell ourselves that at least we stepped – nay, jumped – outside of our collective comfort zone.

It's not often an opportunity like this comes along and I can't help but feel that this is fate in some way. Perhaps Kitty O'Hagan weaving her magical spell from the afterlife and looking after us in the way she always had. Maybe I can pitch it to them that way?

Pushing open the door, I'm greeted with a rush of coffee-scented warm air and the chatter of customers catching up with friends. It's surprisingly busy for six o'clock on a Tuesday night in January and it takes me a moment to spot Niamh, curled onto a soft armchair, looking down at her book. She looks completely at ease – amid the hissing of the coffee machine, clatter of cups on saucers and hubbub of conversation. Then again, I suppose she is used to the non-stop noise of a school environment. Silence might be a bit overwhelming. I'm just about to start walking across the café to her when the door opens behind me, bringing with it a rush of cold and a semi-frozen Laura.

'That is not a nice evening,' she says, shivering before pulling me into a quick hug. Niamh has spotted us and is waving for us to join her. I mime bringing a cup to my mouth and raise an eyebrow in the universal sign language for 'Do you want another drink?' and she mouths 'Hot chocolate' in an exaggerated fashion. It's probably a good thing. My increasingly shoddy eyesight means I need everything to be large and in my face. How I wish for the days I could take my glasses off long enough to lose them – and not have to panic about it.

'What would you like?' I ask Laura. 'I'm getting these.'

'You're not,' she replies. 'I'll get them. You'd a big day.'

'Wise up! Just tell me what you want! You got them the last time.'

'Becs, just go and sit down and I'll bring them over...'

There is only one way to end this coffee-related stand-off. I need to act. Fast. I give her a gentle shove out of the way and barrel my way through to the counter, from where I grin at her triumphantly. I get a filthy look in return before she rolls her eyes and informs me she'll have a cappuccino.

Neither Niamh nor Laura have to tell me they also want a slice of cake. You can't be friends with women for close to four decades without knowing that they always, always have cake – and none of that extra fibre, low sugar, wholemeal flour, bird-seed-topped healthy option stuff either. It's go big-and-covered-in-chocolate or go home.

Once we are all seated with our tasty treats, Niamh urges me to 'get to the bloody point'.

'As if Paul's reaction to *the situation* isn't enough to try my patience, it's a Tuesday in January and the heating was on the blink in the school today so my nice-girl persona has already been tested enough for one day,' she says as she scoops a partially melted marshmallow out of her hot chocolate and swallows it. 'And yes,' she adds, 'this is my second hot chocolate. It's also my second slice of cake but I dare either one of you to say anything.'

We both raise our hands in a 'surrender' pose. 'I'm not that brave,' I say, and I mean it. Niamh had texted me earlier to ask me to recommend a good divorce lawyer. I'm only about 90 per cent sure she was joking.

'Me neither,' Laura says. 'Have as much cake and chocolate as you want. This is a judgement-free zone. I raided Robyn's leftover selection boxes over the weekend when the PMS hit hard, and had to replace the bars before she noticed.'

'It's medicinal. Anyway,' Niamh says before turning her attention back to me and glaring pointedly.

I put my cup down. 'Okay! First of all, yay! I got the gig! It's only a column once a month and it doesn't pay much. So now we have cast-iron proof that Carrie Bradshaw was a lying baggage with her fancy shoes and New York apartment all funded by her column-writing career. But still, I'm going to be paid to write about something I really want to write about.' I can't help but smile.

Niamh grins. 'That's brilliant. I am absolutely delighted for you. But if I hear you saying it's only a column again I'll not be responsible for my actions. It's a bloody column in a well-known, well-read magazine. And as for payment – as long as they're not taking the piss and being ridiculously stingy then it doesn't matter that it's not enough to live the Carrie Bradshaw life. She's a train wreck anyway. Never should've let poor Aidan go and chosen that Mr. Big gobshite instead, if you ask me.'

I should've remembered that Carrie Bradshaw is on Niamh's List. Niamh's List is a thing of legend and once you find yourself on it, nothing you do can or will ever do can get you removed from it. To earn a place on it, all a person has to do is annoy Niamh in one of countless ever-changing ways. This can include being mean to her in her dreams, not saying thank you after she holds a door open for them, ever having appeared on *Love Island* and, of course, being Carrie Bradshaw.

'I'm so happy for you,' Laura adds, reaching across and giving my hand a squeeze. 'And fair play to you for making it happen! I'm proud of you and my mum would be proud of you too!'

A lump forms in my throat. I really hope Kitty would be proud.

'Thank you,' I say, my voice breaking like a thirteen-year-old boy's.

'There's no better reason for cake!' Niamh brings a fork-full of chocolate fudge cake to her mouth before devouring it as if she hasn't eaten in a week. I wait until her semi-orgasmic noises have died down before I drop my next bombshell.

'There's more,' I tell them. 'As well as the column, Grace asked me if I would write a feature on a new retreat that's going to be run in Donegal.'

'Ooooh! Is it going to be all luxury spa treatments and delicious organic food, and only the best non-hangover-inducing wine?' Laura asks, her eyes wide.

'Not quite.'

'Tell me it's not some sort of wacky survivalist shite where they make you plunge into ice water and drink some sort of hallucinogen which makes you boke your anatomy and go on some sort of spiritual journey?' Niamh might be a fan of yoga, but you'd be wrong to assume she is in anyway a hippy chick. And as for 'survivalist shite' – she is very, very clearly not a fan.

'Well,' I say. 'It's not that either. At least I don't think so. The details are a bit sketchy, but *Northern People* wouldn't be interested if it was a complete shite-hole. I'd say it's probably somewhere in between the two? It's a retreat for women of our age who are looking to empower themselves and embrace the next stage of their life.'

'I like the sound of that,' Laura says. 'So kind of a Crones Are Us type of thing?'

'Who are you calling a crone?'

'Crone isn't a bad word, Niamh. We've talked about this before. The three stages of womanhood? Maiden, Mother and Crone? All centred in Celtic mythology and the belief that older women are wise and powerful. Like the Bean Feasa.'

Laura seems to have an increasingly unlimited knowledge when it comes to the folklore of ageing women. It seems to have become her special interest since her mother's death. I imagine it's because she saw that strength in Kitty, and she's determined that we'll hang on to it too.

'Bean Feasa?' Niamh asks.

'That's the Irish for wise woman – an older lady imbued with knowledge and healing powers.'

'That's it exactly,' I add. 'It's a weekend retreat. There will be some meditation, but as far as I know no hallucinogens.'

'More's the pity,' Niamh replies. 'I would pay good money to read about you getting yourself off your tits on mushrooms.'

'Let me stop you there!' I raise my hand. 'First of all, once again, there will be no mushrooms and even if there were, I would not be partaking. The last thing I need or want is to lose control of my senses. No. I want to be fully present. Second of all,' and this is where I finally get to the point, '*Northern People* have offered me three places on the retreat – as long as you two don't mind bunking in with me.'

The expressions on their faces are a mirror image of each other. Eyes wide. Eyebrows raised. Not quite sure if this is a good thing, or a bad thing.

'Sorry, what?' Niamh asks.

'Look, when I submitted the columns I wrote a little about, you know, the importance of female friendship groups and about how much you girls mean to me.'

'Awww! That's so sweet,' Laura says.

'So,' I continue, 'when I saw Grace and she agreed to the column she also said this opportunity had come in but really she didn't have any suitable staff for it and she's too busy to take the weekend away herself. She thinks it will make for great copy and sure, it means the three of us can get away for a weekend together and when was the last time we did that? It's not going to cost us anything except for whatever snacks we want to bring and it will be an experience. Something different. Something the sixteen-year-old versions of us would want us to do?'

'And where is it? I need more details than just Donegal,' Niamh says. 'Is it a nice hotel at least? Will the food be decent? It won't be superfoods and sawdust, will it?'

I shift awkwardly in my seat. This might just be where I lose them. 'I don't know about the food. And, well... about the accommodation... the thing is...'

'I'm not sure I like the sound of this,' Niamh says.

'Shush! Just let her speak.' I knew I could count on Laura to be the voice of reason. Lovely hippy-centric Laura.

'The thing is, it's not a hotel.'

'Self-catering cottage?' Laura asks, hopefully.

I may be losing her too.

'Yurt,' I say, in little more than a whisper. 'Near Clonmany. Not far from the beach. Apparently you can hear the sea from your bed.'

There's a pause that lasts longer than is strictly comfortable for any of us before Niamh speaks.

'A weekend, in a tent, near a beach, on the Atlantic coast... when? In the summer? Spring at least?'

'This weekend.' If there is a volume level that is one step lower than a whisper, I am speaking at it.

'Sorry, did she just say this weekend?' Niamh is incredulous.

Laura just stares at me for a moment, eyes blinking.

'I know it's a big ask, but very last minute and—'

'Fuck it, I'm in!' Niamh says. 'A weekend away from the bosom of my family who I simultaneously love but want to kill? In a tent? At the will of the wind and waves rolling in off the Atlantic? What could possibly go wrong? But here... fortune favours the brave.'

We both look at Laura. 'You don't even need to ask,' she says. 'My mum would kick my arse if I didn't, and to be honest, it would be nice to get away from all the grief and the house-selling stuff. Even if only for a weekend.'

I am absolutely thrilled silly. The thought of the three of us going away together is so exciting. I don't even care that it's to a yurt. Or that there will be workshops and self-improvement sessions we will have to attend. I've survived yoga. I can survive this. I might even enjoy it.

13

PACK UP YOUR TROUBLES

Niamh

Niamh is simultaneously both looking forward to and dreading telling Paul she is going away for the weekend. Things have reached a new level of frosty between them and for the first time in her life she has felt intense dislike for him.

Yes, he has ragged her happiness on many an occasion during their long time together, but she always remained secure in her belief that he was her person. She loved him and he loved her and she could cope with the fact that no one is perfect all of the time.

Today though? Today she has fantasised about packing a bag and walking out the door to leave him to manage the shitshow that her home life has become. There will be no sneaking round to his mother's house for his tea when it is his sole responsibility to feed the children and keep them in clean clothes.

He can pick his own dirty boxers up from the bathroom floor and wash them. He's big enough and ugly enough to use a washing machine.

He can sleep all night in their bed in whatever position he wants and snore his head off for all she cares because she will have run off somewhere. Preferably to rent a little cottage by the sea, where she will keep her garden wild and her hair wilder.

Forget teaching, she will become a witchy herbalist and give not a single solitary fuck about anyone other than herself. And especially not Paul, whose very existence seems to irritate her these days.

When Jodie told him about her plans to keep the baby, he played the role of dutiful father admirably, telling her that he loved her and would have her back. He gave her a huge hug and they both had a bit of a cry and then he had made her some tea and toast and they'd watched an episode of *Ted Lasso* together.

It was only when he came up to bed later that night that he had started to vent his concerns to Niamh, telling her over and over again how Jodie had no idea how much she was going to limit her life. 'I can't believe she's been so stupid,' he raged while Niamh sat and listened – every protective mama-bear fibre in her body fizzing.

First she'd listened to Becca telling her how tough it would be for Adam to have to change his university course, as if it was anywhere near what Jodie would go through. And now she was listening to Paul's tirade. It didn't matter that she had her own concerns. Or maybe it was precisely *because* she had her own concerns that his ranting got under her skin so much.

She didn't have the energy to start into any kind of heavy discussion with him at ten o'clock on a Monday night. She was tired, cold and hormonal.

Being honest, what she'd really wanted was for Paul to hug her and tell her he loved her and would have her back too. She'd have loved it if he had made her tea and toast and invited her to snuggle on the sofa beside him and watch an episode of *Ted Lasso*.

Instead she'd put a wash in the machine before going up to their bedroom to do some marking. Having finished her work, she'd climbed into bed, desperate to get some sleep, and had just been reaching over to switch off the bedside light when the bedroom door opened, flooding the room with light.

Paul's silhouette had been framed perfectly in the doorway and as he'd stepped further into the room she could see he had an expression on his face that would curdle milk.

'Do you think she's really thought it through?' he'd started as he sat down on the edge of the bed and kicked his trainers off. Niamh had cursed her lousy timing. If only she hadn't fallen down that TikTok rabbit hole of investigating the beef between two American influencers she neither knew nor cared about, she could've been asleep by now. Or at least she could've done a good job of faking it.

It wouldn't be the only thing she'd have been faking in their bedroom these days. Whatever fresh hell had taken control of her body, it seemed to have taken her ability to have an orgasm with it. Her one reliable stress buster had been cruelly snatched from her, leaving her worried it would never return.

'Niamh?' Paul said, his back to her as he pulled his sweatshirt over his head. 'Well? Do you really think she has thought it through?'

Before she even had time to take a breath, let alone answer, he had started to talk again. 'Like, do you think she knows how hard it's going to be? This isn't playing dolls. You can't leave a baby in a crib for a week or two at time while you get distracted with something else.'

Niamh opened her mouth to tell him that Jodie was smart enough to have an idea of what the expectations would be for both her and Adam. Both of them are smart young people – and determined young people, at that. She wanted to tell him she understands he is worried – she's worried too – but truth be told he was coming across as a bit of a patronising dick.

But again Paul spoke before she could.

'God, the responsibility she's putting on her shoulders at this age. She can't possibly realise that once she's made that choice, there's no going back. And there's no way to reclaim her early twenties. She should be having the craic, not worrying about finding babysitters, or up all night with a colicky baby! How's she going to cope at university? I'd be surprised if her housemates would be happy to have a newborn sharing with them. It's hardly conducive to the student lifestyle, is it?'

Niamh sighed – the kind of deep sigh that comes from your very soul. Did he really think that Jodie hadn't thought things through? He was giving her no credit at all for her intelligence or how much of a sensible young woman she was. Yes, she'd found herself unexpectedly pregnant, but that didn't mean she was incapable of making rational decisions. Dear Lord, but hadn't they found themselves unexpectedly pregnant on two occasions in the past? Cal had been a bit of a surprise, and as for Fiadh? She'd been a plot twist of epic proportions. Niamh had been thirty-nine and perfectly happy that her childbearing days were behind her. Instead she'd had to get used to being the oldest mammy attending parent-teacher meetings or class assemblies. More than once she had been mistaken for her daughter's granny. Which was ironic really, given that she is now actually going to be a granny and can't help but think she feels and looks too young.

She'd wanted to say all this to Paul. She'd wanted him to listen while she spoke of her own concerns and worries. She'd wanted him to do what he used to do best and reassure her that everything was going to be fine and there was nothing that they, as a team, couldn't tackle together. But she couldn't, because that fierce mama-bear sized protective urge to support Jodie was overpowering her. If Jodie has decided that she will have this baby then they have to honour that. It's not for anyone to tell a woman what she should do with her body. No man could ever understand how everything changes the moment a woman knows there is a potential life growing inside her. She had to dampen down her worries, not give a voice to them. Not to Paul anyway – who had so many of his own.

So she had let him say everything he'd wanted to say and she had nodded and acknowledged him until, eventually, he had sighed and rolled over in bed, pulling her in for a cuddle. Normally Niamh welcomed each and every hug from her husband. Even after all this time together. But lately she was feeling the need for personal space more and more. That had been especially true as they lay together last night, him feeling better for having voiced his worries and Niamh unable to escape a niggling feeling that something was very, very wrong. She didn't know if it was in her marriage or something within herself, but it had unsettled her and she hasn't been able to shake the feeling since.

It's almost as if she doesn't know him any more – or maybe it's more that she doesn't know herself any more? She thinks of the letter she wrote when she was just sixteen – the one Becca had uncovered in the time capsule last year – and how she was so full of life and *joie de vivre*. While it's not exactly the case that she isn't now... it's just that everything feels a little duller. And this growing disconnect with Paul is troubling her more than she dares admit to anyone. She isn't exactly sure what the hell she will do if things fall apart with him. He's her soulmate. Her other half. She's not a really schmalzy person, but when it comes to

Paul Cassidy, he is undoubtedly the person she was destined to be with, and never before in all their many years together has she felt such an urge to give him a good shake. There's no way he doesn't sense it too. He can't have failed to notice how her body tenses when he wraps his arms around her, or how often she tells him she doesn't want a hug because she's in the middle of a hot flush. Niamh being a person who wears her thoughts on her face means there is no way he hasn't noticed her increasing eye rolls, or weary stare back.

So with things far from how they usually are Chez Cassidy, raising the subject of a last-minute weekend away with the girls isn't something she particularly relishes – but deep in her soul she knows she needs this weekend away more than she is willing to let on.

In fact, she could do with a full week away, or maybe a fortnight? She wouldn't be opposed to a month or two on a deserted island, if she's being entirely honest – but only as long as there was running water, electricity and a steady supply of food and drink. Niamh is not built for the rugged lifestyle, which of course makes her wonder why on earth she has agreed to a weekend in a yurt of all things – and that's not to mention the fact she forgot to ask Becca what the toilet/showering situation is. Visions of dashing through icy pellets of rain in the pitch-black night to a freezing outhouse or having to shower under the tumbling streams of an Irish waterfall while actively trying to ensure she doesn't freeze her tits off cross her mind and she shudders in anticipation. And it's not the good kind of shuddering in anticipation either.

Weighing it up though, the fear of sub-par ablution stations is not greater than her need to get some much-needed headspace. She'll rough it. It's not exactly *I'm a Celebrity...* She's pretty sure there will be no animal testicles to eat or tunnels of rats to crawl through. She can handle it.

Paul is scrolling through his phone in the living room, looking perfectly relaxed on his favourite armchair with his feet up on the footstool in front of him. His face, one she can recognise is ageing now and far removed from the young man she fell in love with, is set in a sour expression.

He doesn't even look up as she comes into the room, but that doesn't stop him from talking. 'The Kerrigans at the top of the street have put their house up for sale. You'll never guess what they're asking for it...'

'Paul,' Niamh says, sitting on the sofa opposite him.

'Our house is definitely nicer than theirs and they're asking—'

'Paul,' Niamh says again, more firmly this time, and he looks up.

'£260,000.' He turns the phone screen towards Niamh, who wants to scream that she doesn't give a damn what the Kerrigans are selling their house for.

She bites her tongue. This is the kind of thing they talk about often. They've been debating upsizing a bit now that the children are all getting bigger. Of course, there might even be a new baby coming into the house... but still she feels irritated by him waving his phone in her face. Worse than that, she feels irritated that she feels irritated by him. Mustering all the essential relaxation skills she learned in yoga, she takes a deep breath and centres herself before she dares open her mouth. She feels it in her very bones that one of these days when she speaks it will not be the support-ive, loving wife coming out of her mouth but the vicious, snap-ping beast that menopause is turning her into. When she visualises it she can't help but think of the Gmork from *The NeverEnding Story* – the scary, growling black dog/monster that gave every child watching that movie in the eighties the biggest jumpscare of their young lives.

'Very good,' she says as he shakes his head in disbelief at the asking price of his neighbour's house.

'They're chancing their arm, looking for that,' he mumbles and goes back to scrolling across his phone screen.

'But I need to talk to you about something else,' Niamh says.

He looks up from his phone and grimaces. 'Oh, God, what now? Don't tell me there's another bombshell coming our way? What is it now? Cal been expelled? Fiadh getting an ASBO?'

'No. It's nothing like that.'

'Thank feck,' he says. 'So what is it? God. Don't tell me it's worse?'

She tenses and wonders when did he ever become such a drama queen? 'It's not something worse. It's just, well, Becca got the gig at *Northern People*.'

'That's brilliant news!' For the first time in two weeks he looks genuinely happy.

'It is. And they've already offered her a great opportunity to go to a women's retreat – a kind of menopause boot camp.'

He grimaces again and she wants to throw a cushion at his face. 'Don't pull that face! You wouldn't be doing that if you actually had to go through menopause.'

'Yeah, but I have to live with you going through menopause. Maybe I'm the one who needs a retreat? Could you ask Becca?'

He's joking, of course, in the sarky gentle ribbing way they always joke, but Niamh doesn't find it funny and it's more than a cushion she wants to throw at his face this time. But along with the anger, another emotion bubbles up, taking her by surprise. Tears prick at her eyes. Dear God, she thinks, I'm going to cry. As a lump forms in her throat, and embarrassment causes her face to flush a fierce red, she gets up and leaves the room because she does not trust herself to speak.

Even though this is Paul. Her Paul. Her soulmate and life partner – who she has cried in front of too many times to mention over the years but who she doesn't seem to recognise any more.

Has he changed that much, she wonders. Or is it her?

14

PAPA DON'T PREACH

Becca

I'm excited about our trip. Ridiculously excited. Even if it will involve a yurt and meeting new people and probably some weird workshops. Three things that would usually send me into a tailspin of anxiety.

That I'm so excited probably says a lot about how little I've managed to get away from normality over the last few years. It's been so infrequent that I'm at the stage that even a night in a haunted hotel being forced to watch *Mrs Brown's Boys* reruns on a loop while someone scrapes their fingernails down a blackboard beside me would sound a little appealing.

Between raising the boys and simply trying to get the bills paid and the dog looked after, nights away from home have not been on my list of priorities. Admittedly the boys and I did get a night in a hotel when we went to my cousin's wedding – but I'm not sure sharing a hotel room with two twelve-year-olds, as they were then, off their tits on Fanta counts as a relaxing break.

I'd stayed in a Travelodge when I'd dropped the boys at

university but I was too emotionally fragile to fully appreciate the luxuries of a budget hotel buffet breakfast.

But apart from that, I am embarrassingly not well-travelled. My boys have seen more of the world than I have thanks to Simon taking them on holidays. I am, at least, grateful for that.

Last year, when we uncovered the time capsule, I made myself a promise that I would finally make plans and start to travel to far-flung places. It's what sixteen-year-old me dreamt of. While I'm pretty sure Inishowen doesn't count as 'far-flung' by anyone's standards – being just an hour's drive from home – I quiet her with the reassurance it's just a start.

Having the girls with me will make it extra nice. It will make it feel special – a little like those girls' holidays we dreamt of all those years ago. That's enough to make me look forward to it. It's even enough to make me feel less guilty about using the weekend to go to a 'Female Empowerment' retreat instead of blocking out some much-needed time with Conal. Thankfully he has been more than understanding, if disappointed. 'It's work,' he reminded me when I felt that disappointment wash over me too. 'You have to go. It's too good an opportunity.'

He's right, of course. It's exciting, or it will be after I get through some of the less appealing conversations I have to have with both my mother and Simon.

Adam offered to talk to them both himself, but I've known him long enough and well enough to recognise the flicker of panic in his eyes as he told me that. Telling his granny, and his father, that he is going to be a dad is a lot for a nineteen-year-old to deal with. Even one as sensible and reliable as Adam. In fact, maybe even more so given his reputation as the sensible and reli-able one. I know my son is cut from the same cloth as me. A cloth that is permanently terrified of disappointing people.

Surprisingly perhaps, the person he is most worried about

disappointing is not his father but rather his granny. He revels in her pride at his achievements and can't bear the thought of upsetting her.

It doesn't matter that I've told him a hundred times over there is nothing he could ever do that could change how she feels about him. My mother loves him and his brother more than she loves the children she actually birthed herself. I knew this within seconds of the first time she and my father met these tiny, pink-faced little babies who had just arrived in the world kicking and screaming. My mother had held Adam, and my father had cradled Saul, and I had witnessed their transformation into doting grandparents in all its immediate and overwhelming glory.

As for telling Simon, well, there's a different kind of trepidation tied up with that one. Adam fears his dad will lecture him and tell him he's ruining his life – choosing to focus only on the negative aspects of parenthood and not the blessings. If we'd describe Niamh's Paul as being a 'bit of a dick' about the *situation*, then it's likely Simon will react in way that makes us see him as a 'whole dick, and balls' about things.

Simon's not a bad person, per se. Yes, he did up and leave me with two shellshocked nine-year-olds when our marriage crumbled around us, but apart from *that*, I can see that he tries. I'll give him that. A solid B for effort.

He tries to be a hands-on father with the twins but he always seems to shoot himself in the foot by saying or doing the wrong things just as everything has reached a peaceful impasse.

He will unleash the side of himself that is prone to overreacting instead of taking the time to listen, and think through his response, before he opens his mouth. And I'm often left to pick up the pieces and try to put everything back together after.

I dread to think what absolute clangers he's likely to drop in the course of this conversation, so Adam needs me to be there, and more than that, he needs me to bring my A game with me. I need to be calm, rational and on his side. I have to realise this is not about me, but instead entirely about my son and his new family.

Adam and I plan Operation Break the News with military precision. We know we have to schedule our metaphorical bombshells to land at times in the day when the recipients are likely to be most receptive to listening and giving us their full attention.

For example, everyone who knows my mother knows that you do not try and conduct a conversation with her – no matter how important – when *Coronation Street* is on. There is nothing, she insists, in this world so important that it can't wait half an hour so she can catch up with the latest events on the cobbles. We often joke that if Jesus Christ himself decided to descend from the heavens to bestow onto her all the mysteries of this world and the next, she would make him take a seat and keep his mouth shut until the Rovers Return was closed for the evening.

As for Simon, it's always wise to make sure he has been fed and watered and has changed out of his work suit into his joggers and T-shirt. Even more advisable to wait until his two younger children – Saskia and Theo – are in bed. This is especially important today because they love the very bones of their big brother and the last thing he needs is to have them clinging to him demanding he play when he's trying to have a serious conversation.

In what is either an act of self-preservation, or absolute masochism, we decide to get both of our visits over and done with on the same night.

We debate which order to carry them out in, and not just because of the timing of *Coronation Street* and the bedtimes of Adam's half-siblings.

We wonder if we should face the potential shitshow with Simon first, and then uplift proceedings by visiting my mother afterwards. Or do we gird our loins with the love and acceptance of Granny Burnside before we walk into Mordor (aka Simon's house)?

In the end, we opt for pulling the stickiest plaster off first and going to see Simon. After a pep talk to end all pep talks, we get in the car and set off, but very soon I can tell that even my most encouraging words aren't hitting quite where I hoped they would.

As we park, I turn to face my son and even though it's dark in the car, it's not dark enough to hide the fact he is a sickly shade of grey.

'Darling,' I tell him, taking his hand, 'you've not hurt anyone. You've not done anything wrong. You're having a baby. You and Jodie are approaching this with so much maturity – more maturity than I'd have had, or your dad would've had, at your age. You keep that very firmly in your thoughts as we talk to him.'

Adam nods and gives my hand a squeeze. 'I will, Mum. I just hope he doesn't start talking about it like it's the worst thing in the world that could ever happen. We didn't plan it, and in an ideal world' – he pauses and takes a deep breath – 'well, ideally we'd be older and settled, but it is what it is and this baby is my son or daughter. I don't want to listen to Dad or anyone else talk about it like it's a disaster in the making.'

My throat tightens. I'm momentarily overwhelmed by the emotion – and more specifically the love – in my boy's words. He's right, of course. This is his baby in the making, and my grandchild for that matter. Whether we chose for this little life to come into ours now or not is largely irrelevant – they are already on their way and now we just have to celebrate that and make the most of it instead of treating it as a tragic event.

'You're absolutely right,' I tell him, and I'm struck by a wave of maternal love and a protective instinct so strong I'm tempted to turn the key in the ignition and just drive home. I want to take him away from the possibility of anyone saying the wrong thing.

At the same time, I know I'd not be doing him any favours by putting this off any further. And who knows... Simon might just surprise us.

* * *

Simon does not surprise us.

It initially looks like he might. He nods and sits back in his chair, his face emotionless, and he says nothing. I'm happy with that. I'm perfectly okay with Simon Cooke saying nothing and continuing to say nothing for as long as possible. But of course, he has to speak eventually.

'Oh, son,' he says, his voice laden with woe. 'What a colossal fuck-up.'

I immediately feel Adam bristle beside me, and that sense of irritation quickly moves, like a Mexican wave, right into my bones.

'Simon!' I chastise. 'It's not the end of the world!'

'The boy is nineteen! He's just gone to university. He has his whole life ahead of him and now what? He's going to be saddled with a baby for the rest of his days. How's he going to provide for it and get his education? Dear God, Adam, do you not know how to use protection? You've no idea what responsibility is about to be landed on your shoulders. You can't just hand a baby back when it gets too much!'

'Really?' Adam says, and there's a steely determination to his tone. 'Because isn't that exactly what you did? Walked away from us when it all got a bit much? I know we weren't babies. Maybe it would have been easier if we were. Maybe we wouldn't have felt so rejected. So I don't think you've any right to be lecturing me on how to deal with responsibility.'

My stomach clenches. A mixture of pride in Adam and anger at Simon. And a healthy dose of guilt that our failed marriage has clearly left its mark on our son.

'It wasn't like that,' Simon sputters while I sit frozen to the spot, not sure what to say or if I should even speak at all. 'I didn't hand you back or walk away because it got too much. Things weren't working between your mother and me and it was better that we went our own ways.'

'Better or easier?' Adam asks, and I feel my face burn.

'It wasn't easy,' I mutter, almost afraid to say the words out loud.

Both men stop and turn their heads to look at me, as if I'm the oracle of this situation and know exactly what pearls of wisdom to share.

'It wasn't easy,' I repeat with more confidence. 'But it was better for us all.' I smile apologetically at Adam. I don't want him to think I'm taking Simon's side, so before my ex-husband has the chance to plant a smug expression on his face I speak up again. 'But that doesn't mean it was easy. Especially not on our boys. Nor does it mean, Simon, that this situation is a colossal fuck-up. Or that Adam isn't aware of the responsibility he and Jodie are taking on. They are smart young adults. Smarter in a lot of ways than we were when we started our family. And they have support around them. Me. Niamh. Saul. Whatever they need. Obviously, we'd like to include you – and Jessica and the kids, for that matter – in the equation, but if you can't be a helpful part of it then we will manage well enough on our own. Still, we thought you had a right to know and we've fulfilled that responsibility. The next move is entirely up to you.'

Dear God, but I'm proud of myself, I think, as I finish my

second Jerry Maguire–esque speech of the week. My voice has not even wavered and while I can't say Simon looks wowed, he does at least look chastened.

'Come on,' I say to Adam. 'Let's go and leave your father to mull it over.'

The two of us leave Simon's house in silence and it's only when we reach the car that I dare breathe out.

'Mum, that was so bloody cool!' Adam says, grinning.

'Mind your language, Adam,' I find myself saying, and it's as if I'm hearing my mother's voice leave my own mouth. So I very quickly throw in a 'but it was bloody cool, wasn't it?'

15

ENOUGH IS ENOUGH

Niamh

The following night, Niamh tries again to tell Paul of the weekend away with the girls. It feels easier this time – mostly because she had once again gone head to head with Jayden and Ella in their quest to be TikTok famous.

'Miss! Miss! It's a trend. If you do it with us, it will have a better chance of landing on people's FYPs and going viral,' Ella had said as she tried to thrust her phone under Niamh's nose in much the same way Paul had done the night before.

Never in her entire life had Niamh felt the urge to tell a pupil to 'fuck off' as strongly as she did in that moment. Ella had invaded her personal space so much that the fumes from the half-bottle of Sol de Janeiro the teen had clearly doused herself in were making Niamh's eyes water.

Jayden chimed in with, 'C'mon, Miss! We'll show you how to do it. You just lip sync and—'

'*Enough*!' Niamh had shouted, hoping it would be enough to put the fear of God into her most unruly class.

As she was greeted with a chorus of 'Oooooooooh!' and giggles, along with some ham acting from Jayden as if he was shaking with fear, she had felt something in her snap. This could be it. This could be the day she gets her embarrassing nickname. This could be the day she cries in front of these children. It would be the day that everyone would talk about, never mind her almost twenty-five years in the classroom before it.

She took a deep breath to try and steady herself, knowing that if she backed down she would be done for.

'I. Said. *Enough!*' she repeated, and her voice had reached a new, higher volume. 'This is a classroom. Not a playground. Ella – I'm confiscating your phone.'

Ella had opened her mouth to protest but one look at the fire in Niamh's eyes shut her up. She handed her phone over and slunk back to her seat.

'Sorry, Miss,' she muttered.

Niamh eyeballed Jayden Murray, who had already sat back down. The boy raised his hands in a mock surrender gesture. 'Sorry, Miss,' he'd said.

'Right!' she had told them, glad to have the room back in her control. 'Let me be very clear here. You lot have exams coming up. Important exams which will count towards your final GCSE grades. It's my job to teach you so you get through the exam and do well in life. Maybe you don't have the gumption to realise yet that it's a bloody hard world out there and you are privileged to have access to a free education. Let me be very clear: it is *not* my job to learn dance routines, or lip sync, or watch videos all day. Some of us have higher ambitions than becoming TikTok famous. If you had half a brain in your head, you'd feel that way too. If you're not prepared to learn, then you can get your lazy, disruptive arses out of my classroom now. You can go straight to the principal's office where you can explain your decision. Otherwise, you sit down, you shut up and bloody well behave yourself!'

Silence fell across the classroom, but it had felt like a hollow victory. She had lost her cool. She had called her pupils lazy. She had used phrases she remembered only too well from Mrs Martin's classroom back in the day. Threats and slights. It was not who she was as a teacher.

Yes, Year 11 had listened for the remaining fifteen minutes of the lesson. They had even filed out in silence after the bell rang – not even Hannah the class lick-arse stopping to say thank you – and Niamh had gone into her prep room and cried.

By the time she got home, she had come to realise that she needed the break away from it all. She needed it in the same way a person might need medicine, or food, or air even.

This has all put her in the right frame of mind to tell Paul, and not be distracted by any other conversation or end up as a sounding board for his woes. She reminds herself she is not asking for permission. She is telling him. Out of respect. And maybe out of a need to let him just how close to the edge she finds herself skating these days.

When they've had their dinner and their children have gone back to their rooms, save for Ethan, who is currently grumbling about it 'not being fair' that he has to load the dishwasher and wipe down the surfaces, she follows Paul into their living room and sits down close to him.

As he moves to lift the TV remote, she stills his hand with her own. 'I need to tell you something,' she says.

Immediately she sees the colour drain from his face and he gives an exaggerated sigh. 'What now? Any more unexpected pregnancies? The boys have been arrested for arson? Fiadh has started smoking?' This act is getting both tired and repetitive.

'No. No. Nothing like that,' she says. 'I'm going away this weekend. With the girls. Becca got offered the chance to take us on a—'

'Hang on. You're going away? Just like that? This weekend? With everything that's going on?'

Niamh bristles. 'It's precisely because of everything that's going on,' she says, tersely, trying not to slip into the same Incredible Hulk mode she did with Year 11 earlier. 'I need a break, Paul. In case you haven't noticed, I'm struggling at the moment. Between work and the menopause and Jodie...'

'You don't think I'm struggling too?' he asks, sitting forward.

'I didn't say that,' she says, willing herself to stay calm. 'I just said I need a break. And Becca was offered the chance to bring Laura and me to a retreat this weekend. For free. I'm taking that chance.'

He gives his head a little shake and she imagines giving his entire body a little shake. A sick, heavy feeling of dread nestles in her stomach. This is Paul. Her Paul. And right now – this very second – she could gladly tell him to go and eff himself.

'Sounds like it's a done deal then,' he says, in a tone so defeated Niamh would almost swear she'd dropped a major bomb on him – such as telling him she wanted a divorce, or was having an affair, or was moving to her dream Hag Cottage by the Sea with her wild garden and wilder hair.

'It is,' she says, realising she doesn't even have the energy to tell him what happened today in school. That she had cried in the prep room. That she feels she is losing her mind. That menopause is kicking her square in the vagina, even though she is wearing those blasted patches. That she is angry at just about everyone in her life right now – not least him.

'Well, I suppose there's nothing else to say,' he replies, petulance dripping from every word. 'Now, if you don't mind, I want to catch up with my programmes.'

He lifts the remote again and points it towards the TV, while Niamh tries to summon the energy to get up, go upstairs, ignore the stench from the swamp of despair and climb under the covers.

16

A VERY PARTICULAR SET OF SKILLS

Becca

'Well, sure, won't it be nice to have a wee baby in the family again after all these years? If God is good to me, I'll live long enough to see it.'

My mother is the antithesis of Simon. She didn't so much as blink as we told her the news. No, she said it would be 'nice' and I saw the tension leave my son's body in an instant.

Of course, being my mother, she couldn't get through her response without alluding to her own demise ('It's coming, Rebecca. One of these days. You may enjoy me now because this time next year I could be pushing up the daisies!' is a frequent retort).

'Of course you'll live long enough to see it,' I scold. 'You're going nowhere, Mum. Remember, I've told you that. You're here for the duration.'

'Aye, well. Maybe. We'll see, won't we?' She winks at me and I know she is well aware how her teasing sets me on edge. Still, she can't stop her cheeky side from escaping every now and again and today she must be feeling extra cheeky.

'If you're not careful, I'll make sure you're gone myself!' I tease back.

She smiles. 'Sure, you know I'm only joking, Rebecca. I've no plans on shuffling off this mortal coil any time soon. And sure, hasn't this just given me the motivation I need to make sure to stick around. Hang on one moment!' she says, getting up out of her chair and leaving the room.

'Well, I wasn't expecting that,' Adam says.

'Why? Did you think she'd cast you out? I told you that she loves the bones of you and there is nothing in the world that could change that. You need to start believing me, pet.'

I take his hand and give it a squeeze. 'Besides, your granny has overseen enough crises in her life to be able to tell what's a worry and what's not. She practically carried me through my divorce with your dad. And then losing Grandad...' Those last words still have the power to stop me in my tracks. Even if only for a moment. Even now, it doesn't feel real that my father is gone. Adam squeezes my hand and it's enough to bring me back into the here and now. 'Anyway, as I was saying. It's not a tragedy and nor is it a scandal like it would've been back in your granny's day. Have faith in her!'

At that, my mother bustles her way back into her living room with two large shopping bags. I immediately recognise them and can't help but smile. Sitting back down in her chair, she reaches into the first bag and pulls out a stack of patterns – glossy pages with images of cardigans, jumpers, hats and scarves on the front.

'Rebecca, you go through those and pull out any of the baby ones for me. I'll have to get started.'

I do as I'm told and as I'm thumbing my way through the pile, she reaches into the second bag and pulls out a selection of tiny woollen hats, mittens and a couple of blankets. 'What is it they used to say on the TV? Here's one I made earlier? Well, here's a few. I know the colours might not be to your choosing, but sure you let me know what colours you'd like, son, and I'll get to work.'

She hands over the items, in a variety of colours from baby pink to dark purple, and smiles broadly like a child handing over their artwork after a day at school. Adam starts looking through them.

'Granny, these are brilliant. Did you knit these yourself?'

My mother's face clouds over. 'Indeed I did not knit them myself, Adam. That's not knitting. It's crochet and it's a whole other set of skills.'

I should probably have warned my son that his granny takes the art of crochet very, very seriously indeed. In fact, there's a touch of the Liam Neeson in *Taken* menace about her when she starts to explain the difference between knitting and crochet to anyone who dares mistake the two.

It had always been this way – but since my father died, her fervour over crochet has ratcheted up several gears. There's not a baby born in the parish who isn't furnished with a full pram set almost as soon as it is ejected from the womb. And yes, I might be exaggerating – but only slightly.

I should have realised that the news she was to have a great-grandchild would only send this habit into turbo-charged orbit. I hope her crochet hooks can hold out to it.

As she explains the difference between crochet and knitting to Adam, I am incredibly grateful for the woman she is. I am grateful that the years have mellowed her enough to know that things happen in this world that can take us by surprise but that doesn't mean they're all bad. I'm glad she has realised that what Adam needs most of her is love and support, not a lecture or criticism. The milk has been spilled. There's no use in crying over it.

To his absolute credit, Adam asks her questions and shows a genuine interest in her patterns. Before we leave, he has picked out a cardigan, hat and bootee set for her to work on in soft cream.

'Sure, we can add pink or blue buttons when we know what flavour the baby is,' my mother says with a smile. 'And maybe a little ribbon! Oh, this has really given me something to look forward to. I'm going to start on a baby blanket straight away.'

From that point on, she is lost to us as she takes a ball of soft lemon yarn from her bag and starts to chain stitches with a speed I can only marvel at.

I've tried crocheting before but I know when I'm sunk. I do not have the dexterity, or the ability to keep count, needed to make anything I'd be happy to show anyone, let alone gift to them.

'Granny's pretty cool, isn't she?' Adam says on the way home.

'She is,' I admit. 'But you might want to warn Jodie about all the cardigans, jumpers and blankets that will be coming her way.'

'Jodie will love them,' he replies with a nod. 'She's pretty cool too, Mum.'

In all our conversations about the pregnancy and what choices the pair were going to make, and in all our questions about the practicality of how things will pan out, we have not actually spoken all that much about what really matters at the end of the day.

And that, of course, is how my son really feels about this woman he will now be tied to, in one way or another, for the rest of his life. Even if their relationship founders, co-parenting is a bond that doesn't go away.

Does it make it easier that I have known Jodie Cassidy from the moment she was born? That I have watched her grow up and find her feet as a confident young woman? That I have watched her friendship with both Adam and Saul flourish all those years? Of course it does. But it's not about what I think about Jodie. How I love her. How I have viewed her as an extension of her mother and therefore automatically worthy of my love. It's about how Adam feels.

'She *is* pretty cool,' I agree, face forward as we drive through the city.

'She means a lot to me, Mum,' he says, and I can hear the softness in his voice. There's affection there, but also vulnerability. That damn lump is back in my throat.

'I know we're young and I know it's going to be hard. We're not stupid, no matter what Dad might think.'

'Your dad doesn't think you're stupid. He's just worried.' Even as I say the words, I know I'm not being honest with Adam or myself. Perhaps Simon doesn't think they're stupid. But he does think they're making a stupid decision. Maybe because parenthood never engulfed him the same way it did me. Yes, I resented at times that he missed so much because it meant that so much fell solely on my shoulders. But I also pitied him – because he missed out on so much that was wonderful, even when it was bloody hard. We'll not even get into my feelings about how he is a much more hands-on, and better, father to the young Saskia and Theo.

'You don't need to defend him,' Adam says, as if he's reading my mind. 'And it's okay. It's Dad. It's how he reacts. He'll come round in his own way, but even if he doesn't, it won't really matter. I have my own wee family unit to look out for now. And I know we are supported by you and Niamh and now Granny too. We're doing all right as things go.'

The lump in my throat springs forth from my mouth as a sort of weird, alien sob of a sound.

'I love you, son,' I say, through my tears. 'And you're right, of course. You have our support and you've got this. Both of you. Just... just be kind to each other. Listen. Share your worries. And remember you are both so very, very loved and this baby will be loved too.'

He doesn't reply. But that's okay. I can see he is wiping his eyes and I hear him sniff. I know he gets it. I know we're all doing all right – as things go.

17

AND PEGGY…

'Now, you be a really good boy while your mum is away,' I say. 'Don't be making a mess or making a nuisance of yourself. I'll be back on Sunday night and I'll make it up to you then. I promise. I love you so much!'

'Mum, he's a dog. He'll be fine. I'll look after him.' Adam is highly amused at my pep talk for Daniel before I leave for my weekend retreat with Laura and Niamh. He doesn't seem to realise how much I've come to value Daniel's company since my boys upped and left for university. Yes, Daniel has always been a much-loved family pet, but since he's become the only person I've spoken to some days, and he's the only creature who has cuddled up beside me at bedtime for a very, very long time, he has become my de facto third child.

Just as I've been lost without my boys, Daniel has been lost without them too. Gone are the boys who have loved him since he was a puppy and who were always on hand to play catch or tug of war with him. Instead he was left with a middle-aged woman with limited upper-body strength who can't throw a ball for toffee. Still, he has come to rely on me and I like to think we've come to a special understanding as we take our daily walk together. To give him his dues, he's a great listener – and he's intuitive too. He always seems to know when I need an extra cuddle, or when I need to be nudged off the sofa and forced out into the cold.

I'm not ashamed to admit that, as I get ready to leave him for two whole nights, I am experiencing the kind of guilt I used to when the boys were small and work took me away for a night.

It's a guilt I also have about leaving my mum. Who will she call if she has a fall? Or needs something from the shops? Or if Mrs Bishop, her elderly neighbour, runs out of gas again? I carry this worry with me, knowing that my only brother lives a good ninety minutes away and is about as useful in a Mum-related crisis as a chocolate teapot anyway.

I kiss Daniel on the end of his nose and enjoy the feel of his warm fur against my face. I do love this dog, even if he can drive me to distraction at times.

When I'm finally ready to release my furry child from my embrace, I stand to hug my human child. 'You be careful too. Don't make a mess or get into any trouble.'

He gives me a cheeky soft smile. 'I think that ship has sailed, Mum.'

'Fair point,' I laugh. 'Try not to get into any more trouble, then.'

He hugs me tighter – this six-foot man who I can hardly believe once wriggled and kicked in my stomach. If I thought I was prone to feeling overwhelmed with affection for the dog, it's nothing compared to how I feel about this boy in front of me.

'And don't worry about Granny either,' he says. 'I'll check in on her and run any messages she wants me to. I've promised to go with her to get some more wool for her crochet.' To his credit, he doesn't pull a face, but instead reassures me. 'She'll be fine and you'll get a break from worrying about all of us. Enjoy it!'

'I'm not sure you are understanding how this whole parent-hood vibe works,' I say with a smile. 'We're always worrying about our kids, and our parents too, if we're lucky to have them.'

Adam steps back from me and takes hold of both my arms so that I can't step back towards him. As he starts turning me towards the door he says, 'I'm sure I'll find out soon enough, but that doesn't mean you can't try to relax! Now on you go. Jodie says Niamh was like a woman possessed this morning, getting all her bits together before she went to school. You won't want to keep her waiting at the school gates.'

He's not wrong. On Fridays, Niamh gets to leave school almost as soon as the afternoon bell has rung. Last night she told me she'll be at the school gate waiting for me before the last ding has donged, and I better not be late because she needs to 'get the hell out of dodge'.

We've then plans to go on and pick Laura up at her house before it's all systems go down the road to our yurt for the evening.

There we will meet Peggy McCabe, who is running the retreat. I'm told that despite her name being more common about the older generation, she is only in her early fifties and, according to Grace, 'just the loveliest person you could hope to meet'.

Grace sent me a media pack and itinerary to brief me on what to expect. Peggy is the 'brain behind' the 'Free Your Inner Goddess' retreat, which comes with the sub-heading of 'how to grow and thrive through menopause and beyond'.

Peggy, it tells me, is a certified counsellor, herbalist and practi-tioner of a host of complementary therapies – only some of which I have heard of. When I opened the PDF Grace sent me, I saw this image of a woman with curly grey hair, dressed in loose cotton clothes, smiling serenely at the camera.

This is the first time she has brought the 'transformative' weekend retreat back to her home county of Donegal and says this makes it extra special. 'This is my homecoming. It has long been my dream to bring my work back to the windblown hills of Donegal. Where better to connect with our true selves?'

The blurb promises that this weekend will offer an 'exploration of our inner selves' in a supportive and nurturing environment, harnessing the healing powers of nature.

It was relatively scant on the details though, apart from promising a warm welcome with their 'Fire Starter' session, which it promises will involve a bonfire on the beach, blankets and the chance to informally get to know the retreat staff and our 'sisters in menopause'.

Yes, it does sound a bit cheesy, but as the brochure also recommends going with an open mind, I'm going to embrace the experience. How else can I write about it authentically?

'I better get my arse in gear then,' I tell Adam, giving him one last hug before starting off on a whole new adventure.

* * *

As expected, Niamh is standing at the school gates when I arrive and she waves excitedly before throwing her weekend case in the boot and climbing into the passenger seat.

'Road trip!' she squeals, as she fixes her seatbelt and reaches into the canvas tote bag she'd placed at her feet, pulling out a large bottle of Fanta.

I get a sinking feeling that Niamh circa 1994 is back in business. 'Tell me that's just Fanta,' I say, as I pull off into traffic.

'Okay then. It's just Fanta.'

I don't have to look at her face to know she is smirking. 'Right, so now you can tell me what's really in it.'

'Well, there's Fanta,' she says. 'But there might also be a wee smidge of vodka.' I can hear the giddiness in her voice.

'Admittedly, if I was being really true to our younger years, it would be Malibu or Peach Schnapps but lookit, I'm forty-seven now. I have a limited tolerance for alcohol these days as it is, so it's important to me that every drop that passes these lips is a drop that I enjoy. So not only is it vodka, but it's Grey Goose vodka – the remainder of which is in my case for later. Don't tell me you don't have a sneaky bottle in your case?'

This, I realise, is going to be a little awkward.

'I don't,' I say, eyes straight ahead. 'I don't think this is really a drinking kind of a weekend,' I tell her honestly. 'This is work for me and I want to keep my wits about me. Imagine the first job they send me on is one I get steaming at and make a show of myself.'

I'm trying to keep it light, but somewhere deep inside a little alarm bell has started to ring. Niamh seems to be chugging back the Fanta a little too quickly. She's a grown woman, of course. I can't tell her what to do. But if I'm there representing *Northern People*, does this mean my guests are too? What would Grace think?

Niamh laughs. 'You wouldn't make a show of yourself. But how about I make you a promise. If you even start to do anything remotely likely to make a show of yourself, I'll up my game and distract them all with my silliness.'

I smile. Awkwardly. I love Niamh. She is the sister I never had. But she is making me really nervous. Niamh has always been one who is up for the craic, but this is whole new levels of craic seeking. She's like a woman possessed.

'How are we supposed to find our inner goddesses without

the help of some adult beverages? They won't mind. They're having an event called a Fire Starter, for God's sake. Doesn't that sound like it should absolutely involve something a bit more hardcore than a bottle of Football Special?'

A core memory is unlocked when she utters those two magical words – which mark the name of a legendary soft drink made and sold only into the north-west of Ireland. Memories of warm sunny days on the beach and washing down salty chips from the Four Lanterns takeaway in Buncrana with ice-cold Football Special flood my brain. We are absolutely and definitely stopping on the way down to pick some of that up.

She brings the bottle to her lips again, takes a long swig and grimaces. 'I think I might've been a bit heavy handed with the vodka,' she says. 'But it's been a bit of a week.'

'You okay?' I ask.

'As much as any of us,' she replies, taking another swig followed by another grimace. I'm about to ask her what's going on, but she has lifted my phone and is scrolling my Spotify playlist with the intensity of a detective studying fingerprints.

'Ah, this will do,' she says as the opening bars of Salt-N-Pepa's 'Shoop' start to blast through the car. Niamh is immediately lost in rapping and singing along.

'Come on, Becs!' she says, urging me to join in.

I push my concerns about her to one side, telling myself I'll circle back to them later, and join in – the words flowing effortlessly. It's like I'm back in the nineties and everything is simple and easy again.

'How do I remember all the words to this, but this morning I couldn't remember the word "handcuffs"?' I ask, and Niamh raises an eyebrow and gives me a cheeky smile.

'What on earth were you at this morning that you needed to

be remembering the word for handcuffs? Is there saucy gossip you should be sharing with me?'

'I wish! Sadly no. I was watching the news and they were showing a perp walk. The arrestee was cuffed and had his arms twisted so far up his back that it looked like he was about to dislocate his shoulder. I commented on it to Adam – but I had a complete brain fart when it came to the word for cuffs. The best I could do was "wristy-things".'

Niamh honks with laughter.

'I had myself convinced I was succumbing to early-onset dementia,' I say. 'It wasn't funny.'

'Bloody menopause!' Niamh says. 'Scrambling our brains. Messing up our lives.'

'But not enough that we don't remember that Salt's – or is it Pepa's? – weakness is "men". I suppose that's something. You never know when you're going to be asked some nineties RnB trivia to get you out of a tricky situation.'

I'm grinning and enjoying rapping very badly along with the music, stepping it up a gear when the song ends and is replaced with 'Whatta Man'.

'*Absolute tune!*' Niamh declares and we stutter and rhyme our way through it. There's not much as sad as two forty-something women with strong Derry accents rapping their way through some of their favourite songs of their youth. Given our performance, I'm pretty sure Lin-Manuel Miranda will not be calling us up any time soon to ask us to step in as understudies in *Hamilton*. It's worth noting, however, that Hercules Mulligan was originally from Northern Ireland, so if Mr Miranda wanted an authentic accent for him, I could absolutely do that. The rapping would be rubbish, mind, but the accent would be on point.

It feels so nice to just embrace this little bit of silliness. So nice, in fact, that I can easily keep my creeping concerns about

Niamh towards the back of my mind. She seems happy now, after all. As long as I can stop her getting absolutely shit-faced before we reach the campsite, it should be okay.

So I choose to metaphorically bury my head in the sand a little longer and just keep singing as we head towards Laura's house to pick her up.

18

YURTS SO GOOD

It's dark, and thankfully dry, by the time we reach the glamping site. Niamh is more than a little tipsy, and Laura is a little giddy too, having helped Niamh get through her bottle of Fanta. I have a feeling there will be no fires started by these two tonight and they're likely to crash as soon as we reach our accommodation. It's not ideal and even though it's nice to see them enjoying themselves, I can't help but feel a little annoyed. They know what this gig means to me. They must know I want to put a professional foot forward.

I remind myself that they are not working here. I invited them away to get a break. I can hardly start laying down the law.

The relief that washes over me to see the site itself looks lovely is immense. I'd feared we would be arriving at a boggy field and would need welly boots and torches to find our way to wherever the mysterious Peggy would be waiting for us.

Instead we arrive at a car park a short distance from the sand dunes. Grabbing our bags, we walk through a twisted willow arbour, which has been strewn with fairy lights, to reach our home for the weekend. Six yurts circle around a central meeting space, which is dominated by a large wooden gazebo.

'Oh, this is verr, verr pretty,' Niamh slurs. I'm not sure how much of her 'Fanta' she drank but I haven't seen her this wobbly through drink in a long time.

The sound of voices drifts on the evening air towards us, along with the sound of the waves a short distance away crashing to the shore. There's a smell of woodsmoke in the air and music is playing somewhere. As we get closer, I can just make out that the gazebo seems to be populated by a group of maybe nine or ten people, all dressed in heavy coats and hats and clutching mugs of steaming liquid. Hopefully it's coffee and it's plentiful and I can throw some down Niamh's neck, and possibly Laura's too, and bring them back into the land of the living.

Thankfully, given their unsteady gait, we're not having to traipse through soggy bogland; instead, we're walking on a pathway of mulch and bark chippings. We come to a wooden sign which offers directions to a 'meeting house' – which I can't see from this circle of yurts.

Truth be told, the name 'meeting house' is giving me kind of old-world American puritan vibes. My nerves are definitely starting to kick in. I'm hoping the laughter emanating from the gazebo means I'm wrong and it's not a place where suspected witches are put on trial.

Other signs point to the different yurts, which all seem to be named after Celtic gods and goddesses. It's all quite nice, if basic and, in the absence of being able to see any obvious toilet or shower block, I start to worry about the availability of facilities. Might we have to schlepp to the meeting house for a middle-of-the-night pee? With my menopausal bladder, there's a chance I could get my ten thousand steps in overnight.

'Do you think we could move here permanently?' Laura asks. 'And not tell anyone where we've gone?'

'Don't tempt me!' Niamh laughs, and takes another swig from her now empty bottle. When she takes it away from her mouth, completely disgusted that there is nothing left in it, she looks totally confused. It seems she's the level of drunk who can't make the connection between her current state and the now-missing Fanta. 'Later I'm going to tell you about my Hag Cottage dream, for when I tell the whole world to go and shove itself up its own arse.'

Laura flashes me a look of concern – now realising just how inebriated Niamh is.

'We'll get her coffee and something to eat. She probably hasn't eaten anything since lunch. We'll be able to help her,' I say, looking around for any sight of Peggy, who is supposed to be greeting us. I don't want to bring Niamh into the throng of other attendees if I can help it. Their first impression of her should at least be something akin to her usual self and not this person I can hear whisper-singing 'Push It' beside me.

I'm starting to lose hope in achieving that particular goal though, until stepping into the light and in a fog of woodsmoke there appears an ethereal vision in a dryrobe.

'Tell me one of you is Becca Burnside,' she says in a lilting Donegal accent. As she steps closer I notice she has what I can only describe as a very kind smile. I immediately relax.

'That would be me,' I say, raising one hand. 'And these are my friends, Laura and Niamh.'

'Lovely to meet you,' she says, reaching out to shake my hand. 'I'm Peggy, and you're very welcome here to our Inner Goddess retreat at Wild Water Falls. I'm really hoping you all get something very special out of this experience.'

Seeing her in the flesh, it would be hard to pin an age on

Peggy. Not that it matters. She gives off a quiet air of confidence that is quite enticing. Her age doesn't actually seem to matter. What matters is that she is one of those people who makes you feel almost immediately at ease.

'I hope so too,' I tell her, warmly. 'This sounds like just exactly the kind of thing we were looking for.'

'Great!' Peggy claps her hands. 'That's exactly what I like to hear. And Grace has told me about your new column for *Northern People*. I am absolutely delighted to see that our generation of women are finally being given a voice – and a real voice at that. Women who aren't afraid of ageing and want to embrace life without focusing on trying to pretend they're younger than they are. We've earned our stripes.'

I blush, and hope the dark surroundings make it impossible for her to see. Then again, I don't want to hide my 'real self' – the kind of self she admires.

'Truth be told, we're a little afraid of ageing,' Laura pipes up.

'A *lot* afraid,' Niamh adds. 'I feel too young to be getting old. I'm going to be a granny, you know. And Becca here too. How are we old enough to make that even a possibility?'

Her voice is a little too loud, her words a little too slurred. I hate myself for feeling embarrassed but I do. This is not the first impression I'd wanted to make.

Peggy just smiles and doesn't seem at all fazed. 'Ageing comes to us all,' she says. 'And I think most of us freak out a little at first. Or even a lot. I still have moments when I look in the mirror and expect to see myself at thirty looking back at me. That jumpscare can be real.' She laughs. 'But what I hope this weekend will help you realise is that most of our fears and worries about growing old are because of what we have been fed by society for decades. We've been led to believe that old can't be beautiful. That older women have little to look forward to apart from becoming invisible. There's been a lack of representation of us on TV and in books and movies and it's no wonder we associate ageing with disappearing. What I want this weekend to do is to help reframe the ageing process. Embrace it even. Celebrate our positives and our strengths and show that "women of a certain age" have a lot to offer.' She pulls a face as she says 'women of a certain age' – one that screams of thinking the world who would write us off can go and take a long jump off a short pier.

It's hard not to feel warmed by her positivity. Or at least *I* find it hard not to feel warmed by her positivity. Niamh has other things on her mind.

'Peggy, this is all very lovely,' she says. 'And I'm very excited by everything you're saying but is there any chance you can say it a bit quicker and then direct me to the nearest loo before my pelvic floor is tested beyond its limits?'

It's only then I realise she is standing with her legs crossed. 'I may have had a little drink or two on the way down and, well, I've had four children and...'

'Say no more!' Peggy says with a smile. 'Let me direct you to your accommodation!'

'And there's a toilet there?' Niamh asks. 'Because I don't think I can hold this much longer.'

'Don't worry. All the yurts come with their own bathrooms,' Peggy says with a smile as she starts walking along a pathway away from the gazebo and meeting house and towards the yurt signposted as 'Danu'.

'Danu is the mother of the Irish goddesses, and is associated with wisdom, regeneration and prosperity. So I think this will be perfect for the three of you.' When we reach the entrance to the yurt, she pulls aside the tarpaulin and directs us inside – and Niamh directly to the bathroom which, to my surprise, is through a proper door at the right-hand side of the tent.

I don't have time to think about it too deeply, though, as I take in our accommodation for the weekend. It might be a tent in a field, but it looks relatively cosy. It helps that we've walked in to find lamps lit and a fire already burning in a small pot-bellied stove close to the bathroom door.

'Okay,' Laura laughs. 'I'm already thinking I'm moving here permanently. I'll claim squatter's rights! This is gorgeous!'

And, I think, it's warm and there is a proper bed – iron framed and king-sized at that, strewn with luxury throws and crocheted blankets. At the foot of the bed there is a wooden blanket box on which sit three soft, extremely fluffy cream robes and three pairs of slippers.

'Grace said you were okay with two of you sharing the bed?' Peggy asks. 'And one of you on the sofa, which of course pulls out into a bed. I've slept on it myself and I can vouch for its comfort.'

I don't doubt her. Everything in this room screams comfort. There are cushions, and deep-pile rugs underfoot. A dresser complete with a kettle and selection of teas and coffees is accompanied by a small, buzzing fridge – just big enough to store milk and maybe a bottle of wine.

I didn't expect there to be electricity, or a stove, or what looks like a proper bathroom. This really is impressive.

'Peggy, this is all just wonderful,' I say, surprised to feel a little emotional. This place is absolutely exceeding all my expectations – and then some. Surely Grace must've known how fabulous this place is? That she so willingly offered this opportunity to me suddenly feels a little overwhelming. But, I think, overwhelming in a good way. Still, I don't trust myself to say any more. It's bad enough that our first impression to Peggy has been a drunken Niamh and a mad rush for the toilet. The last thing she needs to see on top of that is me in emotional-meltdown mode.

'I'm happy to take the sofa,' Laura says. 'Or whatever suits. It all just looks amazing.'

'It's more than amazing,' Niamh says, walking back in through the door. 'There's a proper loo in there. Like a proper bathroom. With walls. And a proper shower. I was terrified we'd be piddling into a hole in the ground and wiping our bums with leaves. This is unreal!'

'We found that people like certain home comforts,' Peggy explains. 'That's why we have the fridge, and the kettle, for example. And, of course, the toilets.'

This is all starting to sound a little too good to be true. My inner pessimist starts whispering in my ear that something is bound to go terribly wrong any second now. That's how life is for me. There cannot be good without the bad.

'Right,' Peggy adds. 'I'll leave you to it for now. The Fire Starter ceremony is at eight. We're starting at the meeting house for a quick health and safety briefing before we go down to the beach. I'd definitely recommend wrapping up warm. If the notion takes you to come meet the other attendees before then, some of them have gathered at the gazebo, as you might have seen. There's hot chocolate there, or tea or coffee if you don't have a sweet tooth. We're asking everyone to drop any devices they may have with them in our lock box in the meeting room before we go to the beach tonight, so don't forget to bring any phones, tablets, laptops or whatever with you later. They will be secure until home time on Sunday when they will be returned to you.'

Peggy turns and leaves, and the three of us look to each other, slightly stunned.

'Did she say we had to hand our phones over?' Laura asks.

'I think so,' I say, anxiety settling in my stomach where it will no doubt stay for the weekend.

'Did you know about this?' Niamh asks, her tone blunt and accusatory.

'No!' I tell her. 'I didn't know. It didn't say in the brochure.' I start to mentally scan the pages in my mind. Had it said something? Had I not seen it? Or ignored it? It did say this would be a chance to 'unplug, unwind and escape' but I didn't take that to mean unplugging our phones. There are other things here clearly very much plugged in.

And how can she expect any of us to unwind without our phones? We're mothers, for God's sake. We need to be contactable. My mother is elderly and lives on her own. She needs to be able to reach me. And what about Saul, over there in England without his brother to deal with whatever inevitable crisis he will pull onto his shoulders? No. This can't happen.

But it's work and I agreed to do it. I agreed to give it all I have.

'I'm sorry,' I mutter meekly.

'Well, that's just perfect!' Niamh snaps, and storms back off to the bathroom while I find myself looking at Laura and just hoping she doesn't hate me right now too.

19

WICKED WITCH OF THE (NORTH) WEST

Niamh

Niamh is sitting on the bathroom floor, her back to the door, and her head in her hands. Unsurprisingly, given the amount of both vodka and sugary drink she necked on the way down, sitting in this position does not stop her head from spinning.

But it's not just that she is coming to realise just how much her tolerance for alcohol has changed since her young, free and single days – or even since her thirties – she is vibrating with anger.

Somewhere, deep inside, she can hear the quiet whisper of a rational voice telling her 'it's only a phone' and 'you don't have to have it attached to you all the time', but that voice is being drowned out by a louder, definitely rage-fuelled and irrational voice.

Bloody typical of Becca to leave out this important little detail. She knew we'd not come if we knew it! Release our inner goddesses, my arse! I'm going to release my inner wicked witch of the west! Maybe that will stop Laura harping on about it being a privilege to become a crone! If I hear one more story about some far-flung culture and how they deify their grannies, I will explode. All I bloody wanted was a weekend away. To relax. To do what I wanted for once. To be me. I didn't think we'd be checking into bloody Colditz.

A knock at the door makes her jump – even though it's relatively gentle. She feels like a coiled spring. She dares not answer because she doesn't trust herself not to say something they will all come to regret. It's almost as if she can feel every little knotty muscle in her body contract. There's this fizzing of nervous, angry energy just waiting to burst forth from her and she's afraid it will destroy everything in its wake.

Work is breaking her. She doesn't understand why she struggles with it so much now. She seems to have forgotten how to manage a classroom and engage pupils.

And then there's home. Her family, who she would die for. Her family, who she loves and is proud of more than anything else in this world. Suddenly they just seem to irritate her with their constant demands for her time, attention and endless, thankless tasks. Gone are the days when they would all sit around the table, chatting animatedly about their days. The days when her children were all young enough to hero worship just a little, but also to blow her away each and every day with their unique views on the world, their funny mannerisms and their innocence.

Everything is changing. Everything she thought was solid under her feet is shifting and she just can't cope.

'Niamh.' Laura's voice comes through the door. 'Are you okay? Will you come out and talk to us?'

She doesn't answer. She just thinks of Jodie – how her life is going to change. How Niamh's own life is going to change. She knows how this goes. Grandparents everywhere taking on the responsibility of mopping up the childcare tasks that the parents can't. She can't see Jodie moving out. Not soon. Which means a baby will be moving in. It will be a huge struggle for Jodie to continue her studies with a newborn. And those things are expensive.

Guilt swamps Niamh as she thinks of the extra laundry she'll have to do. The middle-of-the-night help she'll have to provide. How Paul will react to it. How the boys will cope with being told to knock the volume of their chanting down a level or ten so they don't wake the baby.

As the first tear falls, she thinks again that she just wanted to get away from it all and have a break. She thought it would be a laugh, but it's clear Becca is playing things straight. Maybe even judging her for drinking. Oh, God, she wonders, did she behave really badly? Has she humiliated Becca in front of Peggy?

A second knock makes her jump again.

'Niamh, love, let us know you're okay? I'll talk to Peggy. Tell her your circumstances. Maybe it will be okay for you to keep your phone?'

Becca sounds like she is trying to mollify an overtired toddler and Niamh is most definitely not in the mood for it.

'I'm fine,' she says, through gritted teeth. 'I'll be out when I'm ready.'

She knows she sounds vaguely unhinged. She knows she's behaving badly. Slamming doors, hiding in a bathroom, drinking all the way here, but isn't she allowed to get overwhelmed sometimes? Does she always have to be happy, positive, laughs-at-everything Niamh? Why can't she be angry?

One thing she knows for absolute certain is that Becca and Peggy can take their Fire Starter ceremony and stuff it up their arses. She won't be going. She might even use her phone, which she is absolutely keeping by her side, to call a taxi to take her home. That it will cost a small fortune doesn't matter. She's sure Becca and Laura will manage perfectly well without her. If anything, they'll probably enjoy themselves more.

20

KELLY CLARKSON EAT YOUR HEART OUT

Becca

'I don't think Niamh is going to the Fire Starter ceremony,' Laura says, as I sit on the bed pulling on a pair of thick woollen socks.

She has been locked in the bathroom for the better part of forty-five minutes and it's not long until we have to leave to make our way to the meeting house.

I've tried talking to her. I've tried apologising. I didn't know that we were going to have to hand our phones over. It's hardly ideal for me either. I've just called Adam, Saul and my mother to let them know I'll be out of range for the next two days and they are not to worry if they don't hear from me. I've given them all the phone number of the glamping site for use in an emergency, which I've had to stress to Saul does not include any minor electrical appliances going on the blink, or his requirement to be reminded of what he got from Santa in 2011.

I didn't phone Conal. I don't think we're at the stage where I can presume he'd be worried about getting in touch with me and I don't want to come across as super needy. Even though being super needy is a big part of who I am as a person. I popped him a quick text instead, telling him I'll talk to him when I get back on Sunday. I added two kisses to the end. It seemed appropriate.

Laura has informed her nearest and dearest, and while she was initially a bit put out by the notion of handing over her phone, or 'my precious' as she refers to it, she is now embracing it wholeheartedly.

'I think it's actually a really good idea. We've all messed up our ability to concentrate and focus thanks to these mini-computers in our hands. Our foremothers didn't have iPhones and they still made shit happen. It can't be easy to unleash our inner goddesses while we're wondering about the latest trend on TikTok,' she says.

The bathroom door opens.

'Fucking TikTok,' Niamh says, walking back into the room. It's obvious she's been crying.

Immediately I stand up and move to give her a hug.

'Don't,' she says, and it's very much not in a 'don't hug me because I will just cry again' way. It's very much in a 'if you touch me, I will cut you' way. Niamh is in full-on scary Niamh mode. It's not seen often, but when it arrives it is brutal and unforgiving.

I take a step back.

'We're just getting ready to go up to the meeting house,' Laura says. I can hear the fear in her voice.

'I've a headache. I'm not going,' Niamh says as she walks to the bed and climbs in, fully clothed.

I suppose I could offer her a coffee, or some paracetamol, but I have a feeling the reply I get won't be the nicest. So I stay quiet. I don't remind her that this is my work and her actions might reflect badly on me. I know I'm already in the bad books.

'I'm not handing my phone over,' she says, petulantly, and pulls the duvet up over her head.

Laura and I look at each other, aware that things have definitely slipped into the Very Bad Place.

'That's okay,' I say, worried I sound too chipper. Or not chipper enough. 'Rest up. Enjoy the peace and quiet.'

There's a muffled grunt of a response and I'm certainly not brave enough to push it any further, so I just finish getting ready in silence, as does Laura. Occasionally we look at each other, raising our eyebrows in a silent 'do you think she's okay?' gesture. The truth is that neither of us really knows.

* * *

Walking to the meeting house with Laura, I try and pull myself out of the doldrums that now seem to hang over us.

'She'd had quite a bit to drink,' Laura says, trying to reassure me. 'I think she probably just needs to sleep it off. And I can understand her not wanting to hand over her phone – not with Jodie being pregnant. She probably needs her mum more than ever now.'

'Maybe,' I say. 'But she does have Paul and Adam to help her and it's only two days.'

'It's not the same though. No shade to Adam, but he doesn't know what it feels like to be pregnant. With the best will in the world, he can't understand the clusterfuck of hormones running through her body right now.'

'I suppose,' I say, still feeling a little over-protective of Adam. 'But still, the ceremony down on the beach would be the perfect way to clear her head.'

'True, but I think it's very clear she has made her mind up, Becs. So we just have to make the most of it, just us two. Let's get our spirits lifted – this is your big chance! Your magazine feature! We're going to embrace the ever-loving shit out of it!' Laura has injected extra energy and enthusiasm into her voice – so much so that I can't help but smile. She's absolutely right, of course. This is my big chance and I can't let Niamh's sour mood, or anything else, stop me from embracing it fully.

What, I think, would sixteen-year-old Becki (with an i) think of what we are doing just now?

Would she think we are off our rockers or would she be impressed that on a random Friday night in January, we are sitting around a campfire on a beach marvelling at just how clear the night sky is, and how bright the stars?

Chances are she might think we're boring. At her age, I held the belief that really *living* would come in the form of mad nights out – doing the things forbidden to me then. Really living would surely be throwing back drink after drink, dancing on tables and singing until my throat hurt. It would be walking home in my bare feet – my soles burning from hours in painfully high heels. It would be finding someone to snog before the lights came back up in the club and maybe exchanging phone numbers – for land-lines, on scraps of paper.

At her age, I thought really living meant having to live big – to travel, to experience new cultures, to take risks, to experiment, to be a bit wild. I've spent a long time regretting that I never fulfilled that brief. Or certainly not enough of it to count. I bypassed my wild era for my sensible and settled era, and something deep inside me has felt disappointed by that. I didn't so much at the time. At the time I probably felt annoyingly smug that while others were still out getting wrecked each weekend I was falling into a cosy, but ultimately unsatisfying, relationship with Simon. They were sharing houses with their mates and having parties at the weekend. I was sharing with Simon and having dinner parties with him, Laura and her then boyfriend – now husband – Aidan. Aidan and Simon were more joined at the hip than Laura and me, which caused its own share of problems when my marriage went south.

But still, I'd congratulated myself on getting on the property ladder early, avoiding the worst of the early twenties hangovers and having my personal life all sussed.

It was only when my twenties started to roll into my thirties – and I was under the cosh of motherhood and mortgage payments – that I started to wonder if I'd done the right thing after all.

Increasingly, I've been sure that when my time comes, I will look back on my life and, while I'll never regret being there for my parents, and being a mother to my boys, I will wonder where I was in all that. Where was the me who did things *for me* and not for others? Who did things I really wanted rather than things I thought were sensible? Where was the wild child I was still sure existed on some tiny level inside me?

When that day comes, I've wondered if I'll hear the voice of sixteen-year-old me outlining my crazy ambitions and I will realise I failed her. And myself.

Until I found the time capsule and the letter that girl wrote me – the letter that has given me a giant kick up the bum. It's given me the courage to start trying to find that version of myself.

So sitting on this beach right now, surrounded by the noise of the waves rushing to shore, the chatter of female voices and a guitar being strummed as someone with an angelic voice sings a cover of 'Stay (I Missed You)' by Lisa Loeb, I get the tiniest flicker of a feeling that I haven't failed me at all.

Closing my eyes, I breathe in all the sensations around me as they combine with the crackle and hiss of the bonfire.

I do what Peggy suggested at the start of this session and I focus on each of my senses in turn. I marvel at the contrast between the cold of the night air and the warmth of the fire. The taste of the rich, smooth hot chocolate. The gorgeous, heady smells of smoke and salt in the air. The twinkle of the stars against a midnight-blue sky, the red and orange of the flames licking at the darkness around us. All the sounds – the music and the laughter – and the rush of wind whipping around my face, and it all feels so very perfect.

I feel at peace, I realise, with a bit of a start. It's been such a long time since I felt anything close to this that I almost don't recognise it. It has been forever since my mind stopped racing and the conflicting voices in my head stopped talking over each other with their big to-do lists and their loud self-deprecation.

Closing my eyes, I start to sing along, as do many of the other women – each of us lost in a memory of the women we were when we first heard it. When life was so much simpler in many ways, but nowhere near as rich. It's a huge deal that I'm singing. One that most of the women around me couldn't possibly understand. I have not been gifted in that department and always felt too self-conscious to open my mouth to sing in front of others. Alone in my shower or my car is a different story, of course. I'm a one-woman Kelly Clarkson tribute act. But among these women, in this wonderful space, I find myself automatically comfortable enough to sing along too.

I feel Laura rest her head on my shoulder. I remember that Kitty loved this song so very much. She'd join in singing when we played it over and over again in her front room. Dropping a kiss on my friend's head, I know I don't need to say anything. I know we are both thinking of her incredible, strong and resilient mother.

21

BLINDED BY THE LIGHT

Niamh

After waking to a silent yurt, and a silent campsite for that matter, Niamh looks at her now contraband phone and sees that she has been asleep for around an hour and a half. She should probably get up and change out of her work clothes, maybe brush her teeth or, even better, get something to eat. Right now, down on the beach, they'll be enjoying s'mores and hot chocolate and the thought makes her tummy rumble.

She'd absolutely kill for a couple of slices of toast. Surely there will be someone up in the meeting house who can direct her to a toaster. She was sure Becca had told her there was a shared kitchen they could access when they wanted outside of designated mealtimes. There's no way she can face the myriad sweet snacks they had packed into their cases. Not with her stomach now rebelling strongly against the alcohol she's consumed. It has to be something plain. And carb loaded. It wouldn't hurt to walk up to the meeting house and check.

Pulling on her coat, and lifting her phone, she leaves their yurt, listening for any sounds rising from the nearby beach. She wonders if this Fire Starter ceremony has already started the goddess-unleashing process. Maybe her bunking off will mean her inner goddess will forever stay trapped within her, beside her annoying inner child and whatever inner demon voices her self-doubt. Maybe it's better to leave her where she is.

She'd never admit it to Becca or Laura – the truth is she doesn't even believe in all this inner goddess mumbo jumbo. Spirituality is not her thing.

Science is her bag. Science, she finds, has an explanation for almost everything. She doesn't believe that there is anything anyone can do involving dancing around a fire and chanting affirmations that will really make a difference. It's all just hocus pocus and placebo effects.

We all just cling onto our beliefs because the alternative is too grim. Dear God, she thinks, she might just be in danger of releasing her inner depression demon if she carries on thinking and feeling like this.

Using the torch on her phone to help light the way, she tries to think happy thoughts as she walks. Thoughts of hot toast with melted butter. A nice cup of tea. Then back to bed, and hopefully asleep again before the others return. If she's lucky, she can sleep through the worst of the impending hangover.

The sound of her name being called on the wind stops her in her tracks.

'Niamh!' the voice calls again. It's not a voice she recognises. It's neither Becca nor Laura. She knows that for sure. She absolutely does not want to talk to whoever it belongs to. Sadly, whoever it is seems to be more persistent than she gives them credit for and they call again. This time their voice is louder, which means definitely closer.

As she hears the voice a fourth time, louder again, it's clear she can no longer, believably, continue to ignore the caller – so she stops, turns around and is immediately blinded by the flash of a torch.

'Jesus!' she exclaims.

'Sorry! Sorry! Not Jesus. Just me!' the faceless voice sputters, lowering their light. Blinking, Niamh slowly sees their face come into focus. It's Peggy, looking ethereal against the night sky and the soft glow of their torches.

For all Niamh's cynicism, Peggy looks as if she might just have materialised behind her, like some sort of otherworldly creature. She's giving off a distinctly Celtic goddess-y vibe with her soft curls falling around her face. Admittedly, Niamh isn't sure any apparition of a goddess would come wearing a dryrobe and beanie hat but, she supposes, she doesn't really know. She's never experienced an apparition before. For all she knows, every apparition since time began involved dryrobes and beanie hats. The angel Gabriel might have appreciated good insulation.

'Didn't mean to blind you there,' Peggy apologises, stepping forward. 'I just wanted to check in on you and see how you are. We didn't see you at the beach.'

Niamh notices Peggy's eyes darting towards her phone, which is impossible to miss given that she is using it as a torch. She blushes, feeling well and truly caught out and embarrassed by her own bad mood.

Looking as if she can read exactly what's on Niamh's mind, Peggy adds, 'There's nothing wrong with skipping it. This isn't a prison camp. You're not the only one who missed out. This Friday night session can be a bit much for people – especially those with busy jobs who have been at it all week. You're a teacher, aren't you?'

Just how much does Peggy know about her, Niamh wonders.

Has Becca filled in some sort of crib sheet outlining a potted history of Niamh Cassidy?

Niamh Cassidy. Married. Four kids. Stressed teacher. Not quite right in the head these days. Has watched *Schitt's Creek* all the way through four times and sometimes has to stop herself from speaking like Moira Rose.

That kind of thing.

'I am, yeah. Secondary school. Science. It's...' She wants to say it's challenging but she loves it, but something stops her. Probably the fact that she doesn't love it at the moment. In fact, at this twenty-five-years-in-the-classroom mark, she feels really rather fed up with it all. It has changed. The rules have changed. The admin has changed. The kids have changed. God, the whole damn world has changed, especially in the wake of the pandemic. She's just not sure she has the energy for it any more. Not enough energy to be the kind of teacher her pupils deserve. Even her Year 11s.

'I imagine it's not easy,' Peggy interrupts, saving Niamh the trouble of putting her moment of self-discovery into words. Even though she senses that Peggy might be a safe pair of ears to talk to.

'It's not,' Niamh says, feeling her chest tighten. She is not a person who blurts her life story to others. These days she can't even seem to spill her guts to her nearest and dearest.

'Were you just heading up to the meeting house?' Peggy asks, before linking her arm through Niamh's and starting to walk.

'Yeah, I just... well, I was going to get something to eat. Some toast maybe. Becca said it was okay.'

Peggy laughs. 'And it is. Kitchen is always open and snacks are available. I'll even let you have some of my real butter if you want. We only keep it for special people.'

In other circumstances, Niamh might have felt as if she was

being patronised by Peggy's soothing tone, but right now it is exactly what she needs.

'That would be lovely,' she says.

'These types of weekends can seem a little strange to people,' Peggy continues. 'If you want my honest take on it – they feel *particularly* strange to the kind of people, and by people I of course mean women, who spend their lives taking care of everyone else and not so much themselves.'

'I do yoga,' Niamh says, defensively. 'Two classes a week.'

'That's a great start,' Peggy says. 'We've a yoga session tomorrow morning, if you fancy it.' There's a pause before Peggy speaks again. 'I hope you don't think I'm being sarcastic when I say yoga is a great start. It really is. It's better than a lot of people do. But maybe, if you're feeling a little burned out, you might want to look at other things too. Sometimes we need to look at the big picture.'

'I didn't say I was...' Niamh begins before she trails off. No, she did not say she was burned out but it's now increasingly clear to her it must be written all over her face.

'I know,' Peggy says sagely. 'It's just something to think about.'

They come to the turn-off to the meeting house and while Niamh expects Peggy to turn and leave at this point, she feels comforted by the other woman continuing to walk with her. 'I know it can be very, very overwhelming when there is so much going on in your life. It's very easy to want to hide away and sleep it all off. I've been there. I've lived that version of life and it's not all that it's cracked up to be. All I want to suggest to you, Niamh, is that you keep an open mind to what this weekend might bring. Approach it with an open, grateful heart. There's nothing to lose here.' Peggy's smile is soft and warm, as she opens the door to the meeting house and guides Niamh in.

'So I should probably hand over my phone, then?' Niamh asks, red-faced.

'Only if you want to,' Peggy assures her. 'As I've said, it's not a prison camp.'

Peggy's words about people who find it hard to care for themselves and spend all their time worrying about others play again in her mind.

What she knows she will end up doing if she holds on to her phone is that she will no doubt end up piling more worry on her shoulders. Paul is unlikely to have suddenly found peace with their newfound situation in the hours she has been away. She's not sure she wants to listen to him go over his notes about it all. Again. Either that or she will listen to Fiadh crying that she misses her – that child is a dote and a darling but a master of emotional blackmail. The boys will be in touch but only to beg for money for Robux, or FIFA points or... God knows... hard drugs.

If Jodie, and her raging hormones, comes on the line Niamh knows she will likely pack her bags and head back home, the guilt having got the better of her. Even though her own hormones are raging and she wants someone – anyone – to step in and help her instead.

'I think it might be for the best,' she says, handing her phone over.

Peggy takes it with a smile.

22

ICEBERG! RIGHT AHEAD!

Becca

'Do you think we should go back?' Laura asks. 'I know she was sleeping but I don't want to leave her alone all evening.'

Still sore that she didn't join us on the beach, I shrug. She chose to be alone. We might as well let her enjoy it. Of course I immediately feel guilty for being annoyed at her and try to make myself feel better. 'If I know Niamh like I think I know Niamh, she will be appreciating a little time alone. God only knows she gets little enough of it,' I say.

And it's true. She's generally either surrounded by feral teenagers at work, or by feral teenagers at home. (And I'm allowed to call them feral teenagers because I love them with all my heart.) I used to tell myself Niamh had it great – the chatter and constant company must be brilliant. She has a house that is constantly busy and filled with love. I'd think of them all around their dinner table at mealtimes, while I was sitting on my sofa eating my Marks and Spencer ready meal for one, with Daniel giving me the mega sad eyes, hoping I'd take pity on his forlorn fizzog and share my food. After the boys left, there were entire days when Daniel was the only creature I spoke to and it made me sad. At first.

But then I'd come to appreciate my quiet, still life and adapt to a house now largely empty of the clatter and bang of my own feral teenagers. There's a special kind of joy in going to bed only to get up the following morning to find the kitchen hasn't been raided and left like a war zone overnight. There's a comfort in not having to do at least one load of washing each and every day of your existence – knowing full well you're washing clothes that you folded and left on your teenager's bed just hours before. Yes, it's an adjustment but it's not all bad. It's nice to not feel responsible for feeding and clothing multiple people each and every day. Niamh doesn't get that chance. Niamh doesn't get to enjoy and appreciate silence.

'So I think we let her enjoy the peace and quiet for a wee bit,' I tell Laura. 'Let her catch her breath.'

'You've noticed it too?' Laura looks at me.

I raise an eyebrow. Laura has a quick look around. We're still sitting amid the group of around twenty other women, chatting and singing. 'Let's talk over here,' she says, nodding towards a patch of unclaimed sand just outside of the glow of the bonfire. I follow her, already anticipating what she will say. That Niamh is very grumpy? That she's hard work these days?

'She's not quite herself, is she.' Laura says just after we sit down. 'And look, I know I was absent for a long time, but I still know what it looks like when a person is spiralling. She's either much too happy – almost manic and doubling down on being the wacky friend – or she's... well... a bit...'

'A bit get-drunk-on-the-way-to-a-wellness-retreat?' I offer.

'Well, yeah. I obviously had a drink too,' Laura says. 'But I didn't get wasted on Fanta and vodka. It's not really her, is it. I can't help but feel as if we're walking on eggshells around her.'

She's not wrong. Niamh is a tricky customer at the moment. I can't help but feel as if something is just off-kilter with her and between the two of us.

'I know she doesn't think her HRT is particularly effective,' I say. 'She said she'd go and see the doctor again but I don't know if she has.'

'She's probably been too busy with everything that has been going on with Jodie. It's a lot to deal with,' Laura says, as if I don't know it's a lot to deal with. I'm living with the impregnator, after all. I'm coping with a nineteen-year-old who is half excited and half absolutely shitting his pants about it all.

Laura must guess what I'm thinking from the look on my face. 'I'm not saying you aren't dealing with it too, but it must be different when it's your daughter. Don't you think? All those hormones for one thing. The combination of pregnancy hormones and menopause hormones...' She widens her eyes before making a 'BOOM!' gesture with her hands.

'I suppose,' I say. 'Adam's hormones are mostly stable, at least. And at least some of the time Saul is out of sight and out of mind – which is probably the only way I survive without worrying myself to death over him.'

I feel guilty, again. Something I'm becoming increasingly good at. I hadn't really allowed myself to think too much about how Niamh was dealing with all this, or what was going on in her life because my own has been so full of late. Have I been too obsessed with thinking about my big shot with Grace or my budding romance with Conal to really pay attention to how my friends are? I can admit my focus regarding the pregnancy has been on Adam and what he's going to do, and the impact it will have on Saul, to give too much thought to how Niamh is coping.

Because Niamh is just one of life's copers. Or at least she was. I think to how she reacted when she thought she was pregnant herself last year, how she became almost hysterical before she had even taken a pregnancy test, and I wonder how on earth it didn't register with me that something was very much wrong.

'The thing is, you know Niamh,' Laura says. 'She doesn't ask for help. She's always been so stubbornly independent. I think we have to tread very carefully.'

'You're not wrong,' I say as the fire crackles and starts to collapse, stick by stick, just a little in on itself, each time sending sparks into the sky. It's quite beautiful.

But given that the fire is dampening down and no one is adding any more driftwood to it, I don't imagine this 'ceremony' will go on for much longer.

We've mingled, introduced ourselves to our fellow goddesses and listened intently as Peggy introduced her small but mighty band of facilitators and support staff. We've held hands in a circle and welcomed the 'spark which will reignite our fire' into our souls.

Yes, it was low-key, and possibly even high-key, cheesy. I'd had to stifle a laugh for fear I'd descend into the kind of giggles that only come at the most inappropriate of moments. If Niamh had been here she would absolutely have laughed too and we'd have been done for. Thankfully Laura was taking it all incredibly seriously and I didn't humiliate myself.

But now, everyone seems so chilled out, sitting on blankets and rocks and watching the flames lick the sky. The guitar player has moved on to 'With or Without You' by U2 and I'm warmed by memories of before Bono turned into a bit of a gobshite. I notice a few people yawning, stretching as if to make a move and go back to their own little piece of yurt-y heaven.

'This is really lovely, isn't it?' Laura says, breaking through my quiet contemplation. 'I don't even think I realised how much I needed this until just now. Thanks so much for inviting me along, Becca. I know you're not obliged to and we've not reconnected that long...'

'Don't be an eejit,' I say softly, with a smile. 'Of course you were getting invited along. Kitty would've haunted me from beyond the grave if I'd left you at home.'

Laura rests her head on my shoulder. 'I wish she'd haunt me sometimes, you know. I wish I'd see a robin redbreast or a butterfly or even a white feather and think "Aye, there you are, Mammy. Thanks for letting me know you're home safely."'

I nod. I know exactly what she means. 'I was the same after Daddy died,' I tell her. 'I went to sleep every night saying, "You'd better bloody show up in my dreams!" but he didn't. Not for ages. But I feel him near me now. I mean, not all the time because that would be a bit ick. I don't want to feel his ghostly presence when I'm having a wee, for example. But he's been there, just at times when I need a bit of extra reassurance maybe; I swear I can hear his voice.'

'I'd give anything to hear my mum's voice again,' Laura says.

'It'll come, love. For now, I know this sounds stupid, but try not to think about it too much. You'll drive yourself mad.'

'You mean I'm not already a bit mad?' She raises her head, and an eyebrow.

'I think we probably all are. Here's me about to expose my inner thoughts in a national magazine, and there's Niamh getting full drunk on the way to a wellness retreat and acting very out of character. You're in good company.'

'I think I'm in the best company as these things go,' she says and rests her head back on my shoulder. 'So... speaking of company. And given our ongoing policy of not allowing elephants to spend any time in any room with us, what's happening with

Conal? But before you answer, please be aware that if your answer involves sex stuff, then you can keep that to yourself. I'm very happy for you but I don't want to think of my brother in that way.'

I laugh, of course, then tilt my head and rest it on hers. 'I'm not sure there's much to tell. Things were going well. Really well. We'd been out a few times. Chatted a lot. Kissed a bit.'

'No sex talk!' Laura laughs.

'There is no sex to talk about! I'd have let you and Niamh know in unspecific ways if there had been. I mean it's been a long time. If and when it ever happens again it will be an event of note.'

'A great day for the parish!' Laura teases.

'Indeed! But we're not there and I don't know that we will be. When the boys came back for Christmas that obviously made things a little awkward and, being honest, I didn't want to rush it. I want to feel comfortable and confident. But then, of course, the big baby bombshell—'

'—the *situation*,' Laura reminds me.

'Yes, the big baby bombshell situation arose and he's been giving me a bit of space to focus on supporting Adam. Then we were supposed to take the dogs for a walk, but he got caught up in work. So we rearranged, but then my mum needed help with her shopping and apart from occasional WhatsApp chats where we promise to meet up again, we've become a bit like ships that pass in the night.' A wave of sadness washes over me. Unlike the Unexpected Waves of Sadness that have been so characteristic of my menopause, this one is real, and justified. I don't want to be just a ship that sails past Conal O'Hagan. When I was with him – when we could devote time to each other – I remembered the person I used to be. Only he made me feel like a new, improved version of my old self. And my God, I loved it when he took my hand in his.

There's just something about the size and strength of a good man's hands that makes me weak at the knees, you know? He made me feel cared for. Cherished. And I know we're supposed to be strong, independent women who do not need a man and I *do not need* a man but I'd like one. This one. I liked the way he teased me, but never with malice. He made me take life less seriously. I liked the way he listened and asked questions and didn't just turn every conversation back to him. I like how he cares for his family. And his dog.

I liked how he kissed me. I'd forgotten the power that existed in a good kiss. How he brushed my hair behind my ears and cradled my face in those big manly man hands, tilting my head upwards so that I was looking at him as he looked down at me. The soft brush of his lips, the delicious scratch of his stubble, the warmth of his mouth. I close my eyes for just a second and enjoy the tingle of pleasure that always comes with remembering how he kisses.

'Well, you just have to make sure you don't pass in the night,' Laura says, hauling my dirty mind right back to the here and now. 'The thing is, I know my brother and he's a good man, Becca. He really is. I say that with sincerity. But he, like most men, I suppose, can be thick as champ sometimes.'

'In what way?'

'Well, he's not very good at reading signals. If you want to progress with him then you need to be more than a ship that sails past in the night. You need to be there, all lit up like Christmas.'

I can't help but laugh.

'No! Actually. Wait. You need to be a bloody iceberg!'

'You know icebergs aren't traditionally very good for ships, don't you? You've seen *Titanic*?'

She laughs and sits up to look me square in the face. 'I have and here's the thing, in that particular incident, it didn't end well for the ship. But no one ever forgot the iceberg.'

I think there's a point in there somewhere that might just make sense.

Niamh is asleep by the time we get back to the yurt. She's curled on the left side of the bed and bundled up in the blankets like a burrito. She has, very kindly, already folded down the sofa bed and made it up so that all Laura has to do is change into her pyjamas and climb under the covers.

We move about the yurt in the dim light, doing our very best to make as little noise as possible – although part of me wants to accidentally-on-purpose give Niamh a little nudge and wake her up just to ask if she's okay.

Thankfully, I have wit enough about me to know that if I wake her from her sleep now she is very unlikely to feel okay, and in turn she's very likely to ensure I don't either. So I let her sleep as I go to brush my teeth and wash what little make-up I was wearing off my face. This is the first time I wish I hadn't handed my phone over to Peggy. I'd love to be able to send Conal a message. Then again, I'm tired and emotionally wrung out from all our chatting and worrying about Niamh and trying to think about icebergs. Any message I send would probably not do my cause any good.

I take a deep breath. Morning will come soon enough and I have, in a moment of utter madness, agreed that the three of us will do a sunrise dip. I'm already regretting it, and low-key worried this could be what finally pushes Niamh over the edge. But at the same time, we kinda knew what we were signing up for and I do want this article to absolutely knock the socks clean off Grace and let her know she made the right call when she took me on.

Sixteen-year-old us would also totally think we're badasses for doing it. How cold can it really be anyway?

23

THE CASE OF THE FROZEN VAGINA

Sweet baby Jebus and all the saints and angels in heaven.

It's cold. So very, very cold. It was bad enough when the water hit my ankles, and I have had to remind myself to both inhale and exhale with every forward step, but I am now at the point of no return. With the next step this icy-cold Atlantic water will reach my 'area'.

I'm aware that men experience a certain degree of shrinkage in extreme temperatures as their body tries to protect more sensitive areas.

I don't think we women have anything like that to protect our sensitive areas, but I swear my entire vulval region is doing its best to stay as far away from the cold water as possible.

I can almost hear her scream. 'I suffered to birth you your babies and now you want to repay me with *this*?'

At least I'm hoping it's just my internal voice screaming and not my actual voice. Given the trauma of the cold water currently bathing my pubic area, I'm not sure I'm in control of my thoughts and deeds any more.

Never mind waterboarding, the CIA would just have to walk

me into the water on the Atlantic coast and I'd be spilling the tea like a weak-wristed waitress with an over-filled china pot.

'It's invigorating, isn't it?' Peggy is shouting. 'Just remember to breathe.'

Maybe, I think, *maybe* I don't want to breathe. Maybe I just want to stop breathing and cease to be before I can walk any further into this water and definitely before the icy waves hit my nipple area. Dear God – the inhumanity of it.

'Come on, Becs,' Laura says, through chattering teeth. 'All for one and one for all. Or is it the other way round? One for all and all for one? I can't remember. I do remember the cartoon from the eighties though... with the dog. What was his name again? Dogtanian?'

'And the Muskehounds, I think,' I stutter, actually grateful for the distraction to my brain of trying to remember the theme tune.

'That's the one!' Laura says. 'They'd be right in here being heroic little dogs and doing heroic stuff. They'd keep going even though it's absolutely bloody freezing.'

'They're dogs, Laura. They'd drown,' Niamh says tersely as she walks in, arms wrapped around herself and hands clamped firmly into her armpits in a bid to conserve heat.

Needless to say, Niamh is not happy at being dragged to the beach this morning. It was only the pep talk from Laura, assuring her that the cold water and fresh air will clear her hangover, that got through.

'Ladies! I know it's cold, but honestly, by the time you get out you won't even feel it any more. And you'll just get a big rush of endorphins to buoy you up.' Peggy doesn't seem one bit bothered by the cold.

While the rest of the nervous dippers arrived in a variety of rash vests, wet suits, swim leggings, gloves and shoes, all wrapped up in a variety of dryrobes and big coats which were discarded at the very last moment possible, Peggy McCabe had walked down the beach in a simple one-piece. A beanie hat atop her head was the one nod to the bitter cold. She and two of her support staff – who are definitely nowhere near menopausal age – practically skipped into the water.

They are rosy cheeked and smiling broadly. Peggy looks the picture of health and as if she belongs on the front of a healthy-living magazine, while I'm sure that if I could see myself at this very moment I'd look like Leonardo DiCaprio just seconds before Kate Winslet yeets him into the ocean once and for all. 'I'll never let go,' my arse!

I feel Laura link her arm in mine. 'We'll get through it,' she says, bravely, with the stoicism of a soldier about to go over the top and into no man's land.

She tries to link onto Niamh and is met with a shake of the head. 'I am not taking my hands out from under my pits for anyone,' she chatters. 'At the moment they're the only thing stopping me from freezing my actual tits off.'

'It's not as bad as cross-country running in second year through the snow. If we survived that, we can survive anything,' Laura says, determined to keep proceedings as upbeat as possible.

She's right, of course. It feels positively tropical in comparison to the hour-long PE lesson from hell we endured when we were at school. Three times around the school grounds, through the long grass and up the slippery, mud-rich hills, dressed in T-shirts and PE knickers. Not even shorts. But PE knickers. Grey knee-high socks pushed down so they didn't look completely ridiculous over our plimsoles. Plimsoles which had very, very little grip in icy conditions, as it happens. It had been bad enough when we set out, but when the sleet started to fall sideways, blinding us, and feeling as if we were being stung by hundreds of icy bees, it took on a whole new level of endurance challenge.

I still remember the look of horror on our PE teacher's face as we stumbled back into the hall one by one, our faces now as blue as our PE shirts, our skin mottled and our toes frostbitten. My hands had gone a fetching shade of purple and were numb to the touch. Kelly Gallagher had an asthma attack. It was all incredibly dramatic as the teacher whacked on a large heater to maximum and we crowded around it, trying to get some heat into our bones.

The upside was that she felt so guilty she did an emergency run to the hot drinks machine by the canteen while we were getting changed, and returned with twenty-three can't-believe-it's-not-hot-chocolates (a strange warm liquid which tasted like someone had stirred some water with a stick of a Twirl bar).

'We can have hot chocolate after this,' I say. 'If we survive. Proper hot chocolate. With marshmallows and cream!'

Laura snorts, her teeth still chattering. 'That's it! The spirit of adventure!'

'Okay, ladies! It's time to get down into it now! Trust me, it's easier if you submerge yourself up to your neck. Your body adjusts faster. So let's count back from five then everyone hunker down. Swim if you want but it's okay to just let your body float a bit.'

Laura, Niamh and I look at each other with a mixture of fear and mild hysteria. But I suppose, in for a penny, in for a pound. We haven't come this far to only come this far, etc., etc.

'I can't believe this is how I'm spending my Saturday morning,' Niamh hisses, very reluctantly freeing her hands to hold on to ours.

With a courage we don't necessarily believe in, we count down from five and submerge ourselves almost fully into the icy ocean waters.

It's akin to a religious experience. Which at least explains how often I call on our Lord as I wait for the promised numbness to kick in. This high better be worth it.

Laura is staring at me wide-eyed, panting as if she's in labour.

'Don't... Don't hy-hy-hyperventilate!' I stutter, wondering if my body has ever been this cold before in any of my forty-six years and why on earth anyone would do this more than once.

It's a comfort at least to hear the squeals from my fellow dippers while Peggy calls to us to remember to breathe and to just trust in our body's ability to adjust to the cold.

The squeals quickly quiet, replaced by laughter and chatter. When I glance to Laura she is smiling – still focusing on her breathing but thankfully at a more controlled rate.

Niamh has her eyes closed and is breathing hard, as if she is just about to go in for the home stretch and push a baby out.

'It's not so bad, is it?' Laura says.

'Dddde... pp... ends what you're comparing it to,' Niamh says.

I'm about to tell Laura she has to be having a laugh when I feel my body relax and that numbness Peggy promised start to take over.

Okay. This might actually be okay after all. I'm finally able to take my eyes from Laura, Niamh and the other swimmers and look around me. Here I am, this one person at the gateway to this vast ocean between Ireland and America. Yet in this second, bobbing up and down in the water, a smile now unexpectedly wide across my face, I feel a sense of belonging. I am part of something bigger. We all are. That's quite amazing, really.

'Okay, ladies,' Peggy shouts. 'Time to get out and get warmed up!'

'That's it?' asks Niamh, who has already pulled herself up to standing and thrust her hands back under her armpits, with incredulity.

'Yep. Any longer and we risk hypothermia kicking in, which is absolutely shite craic by all accounts!' Laura replies.

I stand up, the wind coming in off the ocean whipping around me as I walk back to shore. It's the strangest sensation. I do not feel cold. In fact, what I feel is something quite euphoric instead.

So of course I do what anyone in a state of euphoria would do – and I burst into tears.

24

BIG GIRLS DO CRY

'It's a release,' Peggy assures me as I sniff and blubber my way through getting out of my wet swimsuit and into something warm and cosy. I am incredibly grateful at this moment for changing robes and the advances that have been made in beach apparel, which allow us to fully strip off, dry and dress, under the protection of a big super-warm coat.

'It's existing in its purest form. We don't have the physical or mental capacity to carry the weight of our worries when our body is in survival mode. All our energy goes into controlling our breathing and our body temperature. The tension we are carrying on our shoulders – and us women carry a lot of tension – slides away even if just temporarily. That release can be powerful,' Peggy says, sagely.

I wonder how she knows this stuff. Who taught her? Is there a school for being a cool and chill human being? Whatever, she seems to have this Bean Feasa thing down pat. She's definitely not being forced to wipe her nose and dry her eyes on the edge of a towel anyway.

'It's incredible,' Laura says. 'I wasn't convinced to start with, but you know, sometimes you need to go down before you come back up, so I thought it was worth a shot. But I didn't expect it to be that good.'

Peggy smiles warmly at her. 'I'm so happy you got something positive from it.'

'You've no idea. That's the first time I have felt a sense of peace – proper peace – since my mum died. Probably even since before she got really sick. I felt as if I could breathe again.'

Laura doesn't cry as she says this, even though her words unleash a fresh torrent of tears from me. Instead she just seems happy. Younger even. It warms my heart.

'And what about you, Niamh?' Peggy asks. 'How did you find it?'

Niamh has already started to change into warm, dry clothes.

'Yeah, it was... well, it was an experience anyway.' There's about as much enthusiasm in her voice as there would be if she was next in the queue for a cervical smear test.

'Right, everyone, back to the meeting house for breakfast! Yoga with Eimear is in just over an hour!' Peggy calls, just as my stomach rumbles. I'd grabbed a banana first thing but it had done little to satiate my hunger. I was more than ready for breakfast.

'I'm ravenous,' Laura says. 'You'll have to stop me going full Cookie Monster with the croissants.'

'Bear in mind that yoga is next,' Niamh says. 'You might want to go easy on the heavy carbs. And most definitely no beans.'

Oh, God, I think. We're about to enter a room where twenty women, who have just been fed and had their morning coffee, are going to twist and stretch their bodies in ways that are guaranteed to get their guts rumbling.

* * *

It seems like we needn't have worried too much. The breakfast on offer was not a smorgasbord of flaky pastry delights, hot buttered toast or even a full Irish. Breakfast was, as declared on a whiteboard just inside the meeting house, a 'Refreshing and Detoxifying Super Smoothie, with Chia Seeds and Collagen Powder'. Someone had drawn smiley faces and flowers around the words in what I can only imagine was an attempt to soften the blow.

My stomach plunged. I knew before I even saw it that this was going to look, at best, like green sludge. It was likely to taste like green sludge too. I could feel Niamh tense up further beside me.

'Well... this will be interesting,' Laura says. 'At least we'll be filling our bodies with good, nourishing food.'

Personally I'd rather be filling my body with pain au chocolat, but I don't say a word – too concerned about what Niamh's response will be.

'Come on, girls,' she says after a pause. 'We might as well get this over and done with. I'm sure it won't be too bad.' I'd like to believe she means it, but there is a dullness to her voice that gives away her true feelings.

We sit down and Laura goes to very helpfully fetch our slop, leaving Niamh and me alone.

'Are you okay?' I ask her, knowing that it is a stupid question. The woman is very clearly not okay.

'Yeah,' she says. 'I'm just being a crabbit witch. It was a long week at school.'

'You want to talk about it?' I say, but she shakes her head immediately.

'Absolutely not. I'm here to get away from it all. Look, I'm sorry about yesterday. About last night. I handed my phone in while you and Laura were on the beach.'

I had wondered why I'd not seen her scrolling, but never

thought for a moment she had caved and handed it over. Still, I grab on to her apology in the hope we can make the most of the rest of the weekend. Sludge and all.

'I really appreciate you coming this weekend,' I tell her. 'I didn't know they would take our phones. Or that this would be our breakfast.' I spot Laura walking towards us with three tall glasses of something absolutely putrid-looking.

'It's a bit lumpy,' she says, as she sits down. 'I'd not use the straw if I were you. Mine is already clogged up.'

'Pretty sure the doctor can give you a tablet for that,' Niamh deadpans, and I snort, before staring at my drink suspiciously.

'I think we need to bring the big guns out,' Niamh says. 'Picture the scene. Derry, 1997. Henry J's cocktail bar. Your fifth piña colada of the night. It tastes like death but by God, you paid a fiver for it and you're going to get a fiver's worth out of it. Pinch your nose and down that bad boy.'

'Muskehounds style.'

Truth be told, I'm more scared of drinking this than I was of walking into the sea, and that's saying something. We glance at each other before Laura starts counting back from five and before I think about it too much more, I'm trying very much not to think about the texture and taste of this super-healthy vom-in-a-glass.

The silence that follows is deafening. We are, each of us, stunned by the sheer disgustingness of what we've just consumed. If the others are anything like me, they will also be trying very, very hard not to bring the contents of their stomach back up.

Eventually, Laura speaks. 'I don't think I have ever tasted anything as disgusting in my entire life. And Kitty told me I ate a slug when I was two. I'd put money on it still being nicer than that.'

'I'd take scrambled slug over that any day of the week,' Niamh says, and I feel my stomach start to turn.

'Please. Please. Let's change the subject. Anything. Anything at all,' I say, fighting to stop myself from being sick.

'Okay,' Laura says. 'I'm proud of us for doing this. This is exactly the kind of thing our sixteen-year-old selves would have wanted us to do. Feeling the fear and doing it anyway, etc.'

She's right, of course. 'Exactly!' I say.

'Hmmm,' Niamh says. 'I think sixteen-year-old me knew absolutely nothing. She certainly never thought about all the responsibilities we'd have on our shoulders when we reached this age. I think I'm too busy keeping the life I have afloat to be off chasing the dreams of a teenager. I've my yoga and that'll have to do me for now. Things have changed these past few weeks, Laura.'

She sounds so defeated that I'm not entirely sure what to say. Maybe she has a point. It was very easy to make all these promises to ourselves before the big baby bombshell hit. I feel my mood sink too – or maybe my body is just extremely sad that I made it consume the sludge. 'She has a point,' I say.

'My God, you two, you're going to be grannies. You're not dying. Your life isn't ending,' Laura protests. 'So we will have none of this defeatist nonsense. The situation doesn't have to change anything.'

'I beg to disagree.' Niamh sits up and leans forward. 'It changes everything. It's a whole mindset. Being someone's granny. Being married, in my case anyway, to someone's grandad. It just feels different. Even outside of the responsibility of it all.'

Laura shakes her head. 'But it doesn't have to change everything. It didn't for Kitty. She loved it. Every minute. She said she enjoyed Robyn being wee more than she did me and Conal. She was old enough to appreciate how fleeting those early years are, so she packed them with fun and love. But at the end of the day she was more than happy to hand my baby back to me and go on about her business. In those last years... before she got really sick, she packed in so much living. She even got a tattoo. And went on a few dates. Joined a salsa class. Bought far too many pairs of high heels, and enough handbags to sink a ship. She fell in love with herself.'

I can't believe that I did not know this about Kitty. Of course, I'd known she was always so very full of life and joy. But this? This version of Kitty was next level. I would've loved to have known this super-improved version of the woman I had loved and admired most of my life anyway.

Laura leans forward a little. 'Do you know what she called herself? Once, when she was half-cut on cocktails after we went out for a lunch that went on a little too long?'

My curiosity is piqued.

'Tell me,' Niamh says.

'A GILF,' Laura says in a stage whisper, her face colouring as she breaks into a wide smile.

'What's a GILF?' I ask. 'I mean, I know MILF, and DILF even, but GILF?' As I speak it clicks into place, my hand flies to my mouth, and my eyes widen with the realisation.

'Granny I'd Like to, you know... Fu...' Laura can't bring her to say the full word but just creases into giggles.

'Go on, Kitty! You absolute legend!' Niamh says, roaring with laughter loudly enough that we get a few strange looks from some of the other women. 'Oh, ladies, you'd be roaring laughing too if you knew this story!' she tells them before turning her attention back to us. 'I might start using that one myself. I imagine it would suitably horrify Jodie, and Paul for that matter. What about you, Becca? Are you going to go full GILF?'

I pause for a second to think. 'No. No. I don't think so. I'm going to stick with becoming an iceberg.'

She furrows her brow and looks at me, confused.

'Attagirl,' Laura says. 'Sure, that's almost the same thing.'

'Girls, did that cold water go to your brains? Or do either of you want to explain what on earth you're on about?'

At least, I think, at least Niamh is laughing again.

25

MY HEART BELONGS TO TROY BOLTON

Niamh

Niamh tells people she enjoys yoga. She tells herself she enjoys yoga too. But the truth is, she finds it an ordeal each and every time. Even as she feels her body get more flexible and can start to notice her wobbly bits tighten up, she thinks that the human body is not supposed to move in many of those positions.

However, while she finds it an ordeal each and every time, she is addicted to it like the sad little masochist she is. She's addicted to the hour spent trying not to fall down, fart or throw up so much that it blocks out all other thoughts and feelings.

And yes, she does feel a certain sense of zen afterwards – and pride in herself for not walking out halfway through when her muscles are screaming for the sweet relief of death.

She's never been the kind of person to actively enjoy exercise and is immediately suspicious of anyone who does. She's never fallen victim to any of the latest trends – be it Zumba, or joining a running club, or doing some HIIT with a trainer.

So she's surprised to find that, even though this weekend has been challenging so far, she is looking forward to this particular yoga session. Much more than Becca and Laura, who have discussed faking an illness to leave early. Given what they've just consumed, their current thought process is pretending they have a good old dose of the skitters.

Things are definitely bad when you're happy to tell people you have diarrhoea rather than complete a yoga class. But this is no ordinary yoga class, Niamh soon realises when they walk into the studio space to tropical temperatures that make a hot flush feel like an ice bath in comparison.

Still, she is not going to be defeated. She has been defeated enough recently and she needs, with every part of her, to be good at this.

Laura and Becca claim a spot close to the door – 'Perfect for a quick getaway if it gets too much,' Becca says. But yoga is Niamh's thing and she's not going to hide at the back of the class.

She's not a complete lunatic though, so she doesn't want to be at the front of the class either. She doesn't want to look like a wannabe teacher's pet.

Sitting down on the mat, and placing her water bottle at her side, she adopts a cross-legged position and tries to focus on her breathing while the room is still quiet. Already she has started to sweat, her forehead and back of her neck damp.

In front of her a full-height window reveals the rugged seascape ahead of them – windblown seagrass clinging onto the soft but remarkably durable dunes ahead of them. Just over the top of the dunes, Niamh can see the white foam of waves crashing to shore, set against the grey sky of a winter's day. It looks absolutely freezing outside and Niamh hopes this will trick her mind into believing it's just as cool inside. Already, however, she knows she is fighting a losing battle.

She will not give in to negative thought patterns though. As hard as it feels. She just needs to do what Peggy urged and open her mind to what this weekend might teach her. There's always the possibility her life isn't on some sort of collision course right now, after all.

She smiles when she remembers Laura telling them about Kitty O'Hagan – bold, beautiful and strong Kitty who had battled cancer so valiantly until she couldn't any more – calling herself a GILF. She'd wanted to text Paul then and share that story with him, maybe call him a Grandad I'd Like to Fu...

But then she'd remembered she doesn't have her phone, and she isn't sure, for the first time in their forever together, how Paul would react. She might be the one going through the menopause but he is showing as many grumpy symptoms as her.

She shakes her head as if trying to rid it of the thoughts flooding through her mind and smiles as the rest of the women file into the room and take their places.

'I've never done yoga before,' a tiny woman who looks to be in her early fifties, with a mass of dark curly hair, says to her before claiming the mat beside her. 'I'm sick with nerves!'

'You'll be fine. I think it's pitched at beginner level anyway, but the best thing you can do is just take things nice and slowly. And don't be afraid to ask for help.'

The woman smiles. 'I'd say that kind of advice could apply to almost every aspect of life. Take it slow and don't be afraid to ask for help.'

'True,' Niamh tells her.

'Is it warm, or is it just me?' the woman asks before taking a swig from her water bottle then removing a scrunchie from her wrist and tying her hair back. 'I never know these days. My thermostat's on the blink.'

'Mine too,' Niamh says. 'But it is warm. Very warm, in fact. I think they're going full hot yoga with us.'

The woman turns to look at her. 'I'm Deirdre,' she says. 'I'm hoping to save my sanity this weekend. But today is testing it a bit.'

'And I'm Niamh. I'm not sure my sanity can be saved at this stage but I'm willing to trust the process. I think.'

'Attagirl!' Deirdre says. 'Sure, all we can do is take it slow and not be afraid to ask for help.' She winks at Niamh and smiles.

'Advice for the ages,' Niamh replies.

'Indeed. We're all in this together, aren't we? Ah, great!' Deirdre says, throwing her hands up in frustration. 'I've gone and bloody done it now.'

'Done what?' Niamh has no idea what it is Deirdre has or hasn't done.

'Only gone and managed to get that bloody song from *High School Musical* stuck in my head!'

Niamh peals with laugher as Deirdre starts singing 'We're All in This Together', before joining in herself.

'My God, that song! All those songs! I don't think my daughter remembers any of them any more but I've PTSD from watching that movie on repeat when she was wee!'

'Same!' Deirdre says. 'Troy Bolton still lives in my heart!'

The two are still laughing when Eimear, yoga instructor, walks to the front of the class and claps her hands to signal the session is about to begin.

Niamh takes a deep breath and reminds herself that she doesn't have to get it done perfectly. She just has to do her best. Take it slow and not be afraid to ask for help, she thinks, before mentally adding, 'And don't beat yourself up when it isn't perfect.'

A sense of calm, and of not taking herself too seriously, descends on her as she winks at Deirdre and starts into her poses.

Maybe this break will be exactly what she needs to give her some sort of clarity, just as Peggy says it will.

* * *

Two hours later, Niamh feels like a new woman. The yoga class was everything she had hoped it could be and the body-positive meditation session had been surprisingly emotional.

Yes, she had found herself shedding more than one or two tears as she lay on her mat in the darkened room listening to the class leader talk her, and all the other women, through a meditation which made her stop and think of all her body has endured over the years and how her body 'is evolving into total maturity'. Niamh much preferred that description over any other she had heard about the ageing process.

'How lucky are we to be bringing our bodies to where they were always meant to be?' the class leader had said in a soft, almost whispered voice. 'The end goal was never to just reach adulthood. It was never simply to journey through the reproductive cycle of life, or about whether or not we became mothers, chose not to, or had that choice taken from us. Our bodies are not about the babies we have or haven't carried. Rest your hands on your lower stomach and focus on the very centre of what we are told defines our womanhood. Our wombs may be a part of our journey, but they are not our final destination. They are not who we are.'

Niamh had heard sniffles around the room and had felt comforted by them. There was something so incredibly freeing and unifying about crying in a safe space, in the comfort of a dark room surrounded by women who know what it is like to live in a changing body but not yet know how freeing it will feel once the changes have passed and the new chapters have begun.

Change, Niamh realised in the dark, as her tears joined the beads of sweat she was shedding, is inevitable and it's not always comfortable, but that doesn't mean it's bad.

She listened and cried as they journeyed through their bodies, accepting and thanking their stretch marks, their wrinkles, the grey hairs and, yes, even those rogue wee bastards that started to sprout on their chins once they hit forty and seem to be multiplying almost daily.

'In the spirit of this session, we can thank them,' the class leader had said with a hint of humour, 'but it's okay to tell them to take a day off every now and again. It probably won't work, but it might make you laugh and see our bodies seem to have an in-built sense of humour too.' Niamh could hear the smile in her voice.

'Our bodies were built to mature. Like fine wine. They were built to become softer, and rounder. Our hair to become greyer. Our wrinkles deeper. Our eyes more wizened. That they do all these things proves the one thing that really matters in this world – it proves we've lived. We're still living. We're embracing a body that is no longer tied to childbearing. We're embracing an era when we can pass our wisdom, and wit, onto others. Most of all, we can pass that on to other women. Our friends. Our daughters. Our granddaughters.'

That's when Niamh felt her heart contract just a little. A granddaughter. She knew, of course, on a logical level that she did not and could not know the gender of the baby her daughter was carrying, but in that moment in the quiet, empowering space of this retreat she suddenly felt it so very deeply in her bones that this baby would be a girl.

She's sitting now with Becca and Laura at lunch and it feels as if she has this little seed of hope in her. She doesn't want to say anything though. She's scared that if she opens her mouth and dares profess that she feels better, something will come along and whip that happiness right out from under her feet.

Her body – her nervous system – has made a fragile peace with itself for once.

For now she'll just hang on to it and enjoy listening to her friends talk about how much they too enjoyed the session. They have two hours now, to shower and then eat lunch, before they will take their group walk up to the waterfall later.

'Hark at us being all outdoorsy!' Laura grins. 'Who would've thought it?'

Niamh smiles. 'I kinda like it. But tell anyone and I'll deny I ever said it.'

'So no sneaky bottles of Fanta in your pocket on our walk, then?' Becca asks.

Niamh bristles but she's not sure if it's because she feels judged by her best friend, or because she feels judged by herself. She cringes when she thinks of the show she made of herself arriving here last night. 'No. No Fanta. You can check if you want.'

'No need,' Becca replies. 'I'm only teasing, as well you know.'

But Niamh doesn't know, she realises. Or at least every time she thinks she has a proper idea of what's happening something happens that makes her question it all again.

Just then, Niamh spots Deirdre carrying her tray of food and looking all around the room for a spare seat. Now that she thinks about it, she hasn't seen Deirdre talk to anyone else. It's possible she might just be here on her own, and if Niamh Cassidy is good at anything, it's at picking up waifs and strays.

'*Deirdre!*' Niamh stands up and waves until Deirdre notices her and smiles. 'Do you need someone to sit with? Come and sit here!'

She's rewarded with another bright smile and all three women sit and wait while Deirdre makes her way to their table. 'Sorry, I don't want to intrude. I can find a seat somewhere. Sure,

I'm only wee,' she says as she sits down in the empty seat beside Niamh.

'Well, you found one here and that's good enough and no, you're not intruding. Isn't she not?' Niamh asks.

Becca and Laura immediately jump in with a wealth of reassurance.

'So do you three know each other already?' Deirdre asks.

'We do. We've been friends since school. A very long time indeed! This is Becca and this is Laura. Full disclosure, Becca here is working on an article for *Northern People* about this retreat. She dragged us along for the craic.'

'Don't hold it against me!' Becca says. 'This is my first gig for *Northern People* and my nerves are wrecked over it all.'

'No need to be nervous,' Deirdre smiles. 'Tell me this. Have you ever seen *High School Musical*?'

26

LEAVE COLIN FOR PENELOPE

Becca

I am successfully managing not to worry about my mother, Daniel, Adam or Saul. Or Simon's reaction to the situation. Or whether or not my article on this retreat will be up to Grace's standards. I am blocking all negative thoughts – or at least most of them – and focusing on making the most of this experience.

The meditation at the end of the yoga class had been something else. I'd come dangerously close to doing a full, noisy ugly cry sob during it. And not just because I was sure I was about to expire from the heat. I don't think I have ever sweated so much in my life. Eimear made sure to tell us all to hydrate as much as possible and that had made me nervous. I feared when we had showered and gathered for lunch we would be 'treated' to another variety of smoothie, or something that was 70 per cent edamame beans, 15 per cent quinoa and the rest a mix of chickpeas and seeds.

It was, as my mother would say, 'far from chickpeas and quinoa I was reared', and as much as I have tried to embrace healthier eating, my idea of a salad still mostly revolves around lettuce, tomato, spring onions, a boiled egg cut in half and a slice of ham. A good old Irish salad.

Thankfully when we arrived for lunch we were greeted instead by the smell of a delicious leek and potato soup, complete with freshly baked wheaten bread right out of the oven. I don't think I have ever tasted anything quite like it in my life before. Although I'm willing to accept my appreciation for it might be heightened by the experiences of the morning. In the space of a few hours we had been almost frozen to death, fed lumpy smoothies and then parboiled in our own sweat for almost two hours. We were hungry, a little achy and desperate for carbs.

But I don't regret coming here. I'm drinking in this experience. Trying to consign it all to my memory, which is no easy task given the brain fog that was swept in with the menopause. Yet I am determined to not only write a kick-arse article but also to hold on to this feeling. Being surrounded by other women, all of whom are here making each other feel like we are superheroes, is quite intoxicating.

Negative self-talk is verboten, but I'm also finding I'm just not in my usual self-deprecating frame of mind. I feel as if we're all in a big bubble of sisterhood – a maxed-out version of the ladies' loos in a nightclub after midnight. The vibe is all mutual appreciation and support. But with no worries about a hangover in the morning.

Even Niamh seems to be in better form than she was yesterday, or even this morning. She's chatting animatedly to her newfound friend, Deirdre, and it's nice to see her smiling and laughing. I'm coming to realise she'd been doing less of that recently.

I find myself thinking it would be amazing to do this *every* weekend. Or live in a community just like this full time. A place that can pull us out of our low mood. A community of women of a certain age, celebrating ourselves just as we are, being creative and open to new friendships. A communing of spirits.

A bit like a cult, I realise.

Maybe I'm getting a little carried away with myself.

Then again, are cults always bad? Surely there must be some good ones out there?

'Penny for them?' Niamh asks as she and Deirdre come level with me. We're walking uphill towards Glenevin Waterfall, and we're now on the final stretch, having hiked up from the glamping site, along the twisty country roads and now into the woods. The rumble of the waterfall in the distance lets us know we're close and I can finally stop calling Niamh and Laura 'Papa Smurf' and asking them 'how much further'.

'Oh, God, they're not even worth a penny.' I smile. 'Mostly thinking about the Smurfs and where they came from.'

'Duh!' Niamh says. 'They come from Smurf Village, which is in the Smurf Forest. Call yourself a fan!' She rolls her eyes in mock disgust then laughs.

'I know that!' I protest. 'That's not what I meant though. I meant... how they come about? Like if Smurfette is the only girl Smurf, who births them? She's a young Smurf – certainly younger than Papa Smurf. So she can't have birthed them all. And even if she did, that would mean either her "papa" or one of her own children would have to have impregnated her... unless... this is some kind of Smurf miracle and the Smurf Angel Gabriel came down from on high and—'

'I beg you please don't continue with this story. I'm not sure I've ever been more disturbed in my life. I knew you'd a sick mind.' She smiles.

'I'm just curious!'

'Do you not remember? The Smurfs are delivered to the

Smurf Village by a stork. No immaculate conception needed,' Deirdre chimes in.

'You deserve a prize for remembering that,' Laura says. 'There's days I swear I can't remember my own name.'

'You and me both.' Deirdre laughs, and she and Laura walk ahead, falling into their own conversation.

Now it's just Niamh and me. Maybe it's time to really check in with her.

'So what about you, Niamh? A penny for yours? If you don't mind me saying, you've really not been yourself lately.'

'I'm fine,' she says, but it's clear she's not fine. My even asking the question has brought the shutters down. I can sense a full change in her demeanour.

'Niamh, we can't support you if you don't tell us.' I try and say it as gently as I can, and bearing in mind all Laura's wise words at the bonfire last night, but I feel so frustrated with her.

If things have been going wrong for her, why hasn't she spoken to me about it? We tell each other everything. Or at least, I thought we did.

There's a pause before she replies. 'It was just a long week at work. And you know, with everything else with the kids. And it's January and the SAD is at me like a bastard. Combined with this perimenopause horror show... But I'm fine. I'm honestly fine.'

She sounds as if she is trying to convince herself. I have to tread carefully here because I know that, for all her over-sharing and boisterousness, Niamh can be quite a private person. Especially when it comes to things she finds more challenging. In fact, she can even be an occasionally prickly person if she feels she's being pushed.

'At least the winter solstice has passed. The days are starting to get longer once again. The end is definitely in sight for these bleak long nights,' I offer.

'Aye. I imagine my form will be better come March, or maybe April,' she says and walks on a few steps ahead of me, signalling the conversation is over even though I don't think we're any further forward, not at all. Even though there is the chatter of the women around us, there is no escaping the depth of the awkward silence between us.

As if it can sense the darkness of our mood, the sky seems to cloud over – heavy, dark clouds gathering above us.

We walk on for another couple of minutes, me trying to match Niamh's pace as she angry stomps towards the site of natural beauty that is normally so peaceful and serene.

Until she stops, suddenly, and turns back to look at me. 'Actually, you know what? If you want the truth, I am... fed up. To the very back teeth. And it's not just all those things I've just listed, or that I need someone to look at my HRT dose – although I do very much want that to be looked at because what the actual fuck, Becca? How do women go through this every day and just keep going as if their body and mind isn't trying to kill them or strip whatever sanity they have left from their bones? I am constantly stuck in my own head, thinking about, you know, everything. How it's all changing. How Paul is being a grumpy shite and I don't know how to get through to him.' She starts walking again and I set off alongside her, determined to keep up and to listen and be a good friend.

'You know what the pair of us are like,' she says of her marriage as she walks. 'We balance each other out. If one of us is down, the other does the lifting. We've managed to maintain a pretty healthy balance doing just that. But when both of us are down it's just... pure shite if I'm being honest. Neither of us seems to be in the right place to lift each other up much. In fact, if anything, he's just irritating the life out of me at the moment. I'd go as far as to say I don't bloody like him at the moment. What if we're going to fall apart?' I can see her start to well up, but she roughly wipes her eyes and just walks faster.

I feel uncomfortable when Niamh expresses any discontent in her marriage. Not that it happens very often. But she and Paul are my living proof that good, strong marriages exist still in this day and age. And in my generation. The generation the world tells us is all too happy to call it a day on their lifelong commitment and head for the divorce courts. Like Simon and I did. Even if that was not a quick or easy decision to make.

Niamh and Paul have not only always been miles away from the divorce courts, but also very obviously still very much in love with each other. They are everything Simon and I were not. And I need them to still be that.

'Don't look at me that way,' Niamh chides. 'I can read you like a book, Becca Burnside. I'm not saying I've fallen out of love with him. Or I want to run away with a younger man – although, if that fella from *Bridgerton* was available...'

'Which one?' I ask, in a very pathetic attempt to lighten the mood because, if I'm being honest, I have no idea what to say to her.

'Oh, God... does it matter? Any of them would do. Except maybe Colin,' she says, her expression perfectly serious. 'But anyway... I'm not saying it's all over, just that he is so infuriating at the moment. He's so concerned about Jodie and worried she's throwing away her young and free years that, well, it makes me wonder, does he regret settling down? With me? We were still young. Not as young as Jodie and Adam, obviously, but young all the same. I'm not sure what had us in such a rush to grab hold of as many responsibilities as possible.'

She looks so sad that I do the only thing I can think of to do, which is to immediately pull her into a hug. Thankfully she lets me and doesn't push me to the ground for aggressively hugging her too tight.

'He loves you, Niamh,' I say. 'I think it's just... well... men don't really get it. Do they? This whole menopause thing and how it effs with our emotions and our very sense of sanity. And I don't want to generalise,' I begin, knowing full well I am absolutely about to walk headfirst into a massive generalisation, 'but men tend to not think before they speak. I'm not saying they lack empathy, but they absolutely and definitely lack the ability to read the room at times. Of course, I'm no expert, being a single woman who hasn't lived with a man in a decade.'

'Your boys are men!' Niamh protests.

'They don't count. They are duty bound to listen to me as their mother. I mean, they don't always do it but...'

'No, I understand. And yeah, I think there's some truth in that, but I also wonder if it's just that I have become some sort of ginormous bitch or something? My patience is definitely not what it used to be.'

Niamh can occasionally be a bit scary. She is a very determined woman who very much likes to take control. But given that I am a very passive person who often struggles to make decisions and has a serious people-pleaser problem, I have been only too happy to let her make key decisions in our friendship. Be that where we go for dinner, or any plans we make surrounding going to concerts, or days out with the kids. She's good at it. Why would we not play to her strengths?

But even at her scariest, I would never – could never – think of her as some sort of ginormous bitch. I shake my head. 'Not possible,' I tell her.

'But you would say that! I love you very, very much, Becca. Like insanely a lot. But you are the kind of person who sees the good in everyone, and while that's all very admirable, it does sometimes blind you to days when I am in fact a complete bitch. Or grumpy in any regards. I've become so snappy lately. And Paul has become snappy too.'

'You've had a lot on your plate,' I say, trying not to let my mind run away with her statement that I can be blind to bad behaviour in others. Is that true? How can it be when I can very clearly see the more annoying qualities in Simon? Not to mention it was me who led a ten-year Cold War with Laura after my marriage broke down and she welcomed Simon to her home. I can be a badass when I want to be.

'We're in our late forties, Becs. There is always a lot on our plates. You know that. We're dragged from pillar to post doing all the things we're supposed to be doing and having next to no time to do things we actually want to be doing. And we're doing it all with hot flushes and the return of acne in some twisted sequel to puberty.' She makes quote marks with her fingers and in a deep voice, as if she's doing a voiceover for a movie trailer, she says, 'Return of the Acne: This Time It's Serious.'

I snort.

'And our periods... dear God... I fear I'll give birth to my own womb one of these days. Then the brain fog, and the thinning skin and... and... itchy nipples! Jesus Christ, Becca! Why did no one tell us that itchy nipples are a thing in menopause? Do you know how absolutely horrific it is to have your nips itching like you've just dipped them in itching powder while you're standing in front of a class of twenty-five teenagers? There is nowhere to run! And trust me, there is no discreet way to scratch them!' Her voice has reached fever pitch now and a few other walkers have stopped to listen.

Thankfully on this cold January afternoon the walk is relatively quiet and the only people who hear her outburst are our fellow group members.

'E45,' one of them says. 'Or any type of unperfumed mois-turiser or emollient. Rub some in after your shower each day. It really helps.'

'A shower definitely helps take the itch away, at least for as long as you're under the water,' another woman says.

'Can we permanently stay under the shower? It can take away the itchiness and the sweatiness. I swear as soon as I get out of the shower, I start sweating all over again and want to get right back in.' This time it's Deirdre speaking, and she is smiling sympa-thetically.

'These are great ideas,' Niamh says. 'I'll definitely try them.'

'We didn't mean to jump into your conversation,' Deirdre says, all of a sudden colouring.

'Oh, God, please don't apologise,' Niamh says. 'I wasn't exactly being discreet, was I? I'd have listened in too if I heard someone mention their itchy nipples. Plus haven't we already bonded over Troy Bolton and his abs?'

Deirdre breathes a sigh of relief, just as Peggy catches up with us.

'All good, ladies?' Peggy asks upon seeing us huddle together having what my mum would no doubt call a 'Mother's Meeting'.

'Yeah,' Niamh says cheerily. I know immediately that her big chat about her big feelings is over for now. Niamh is back to doing what Niamh does best – enthusiastically leading everyone on. 'We were just perving over Zac Efron.'

'Great!' Peggy says, enthusiastically. 'Although he's a bit too young for me. I like an older man. A Harrison Ford, for example. Now there's someone I could perv over from morning till night.'

27

SUCH A HOO-HA!

There's an air of trepidation in the campsite this afternoon. The details offered about the 'Locating Your Inner Goddess' workshop have been scant.

I can't help but worry that I might not be able to find mine. It's entirely possible I've left her somewhere by accident. Maybe down the back of the sofa or on top of the microwave. Nine times out of ten I can only find my keys and purse because I have Tile trackers on them. I'm not sure it's possible to attach a Bluetooth tracking device to an inner goddess.

At least, I think... at least Niamh seems to have let out a lot of her worry and frustration. I don't think we've found a solution to any of it but I'm hoping that just talking about it will help a little. A problem shared and all that...

Deirdre meets with us as we leave our yurt and walk across the site. Her face is flushed. 'Girls, they were talking in our yurt and one of the ladies – Ciara, I think her name is – said she'd heard it was going to involve hand mirrors and looking at our bits.'

My heart sinks and my 'bits' cringe so tightly that it's hard to imagine anyone will ever get sight of them ever again. 'I'm not doing that,' I say. 'Magazine article or not. I have to draw the line somewhere. Can you imagine my boys reading about the time I examined my hoo-ha in a room full of other women?'

My face is blazing red, while Niamh laughs at the horror on my face. 'Oh, love, it's only a hoo-ha, or a vulva as us adults like to call them. I don't know, maybe it's because I've birthed four babies, and I've taught GCSE biology, but I'm not horrified at the thought. Enough people have seen mine already, I suppose it's probably about time I had a look at it myself.'

'Niamh,' Laura says, stopping stock still. 'Please tell me you haven't shown your GCSE students your vulva, because I'm pretty sure that could get you in trouble.' It's my turn to laugh while Niamh realises her wording might have just been a little off.

'Oh, for God's sake! Of course I've not shown my students... I meant my doctors. And nurses. Four babies equals a lot of time on display.'

'I'm only teasing,' Laura says, laughing. 'But honestly though – you've never had a look at it yourself?'

'Why would I?' Niamh asks.

'Yeah, why would she?' I jump in. 'I know it's there and it's doing what it needs to do. I've no need to go hoking and poking at it.'

Laura's eyes are wide. 'But it's only your body. Why would you not want to know what your own body looks like?'

'Because not all of our bodies are necessarily pleasing to the eye,' I tell her. 'Especially down in that general area.' I wave my hand vaguely towards my genital area, feeling weird to even do that.

'Wait,' Niamh interrupts, while Deirdre just watches, fascinated at the quick back and forth of our conversation. 'Laura, does this mean you *have* had a good old look down there?'

'Yeah. I don't see why I wouldn't. Like, I wanted to see how it changed after childbirth.'

Niamh visibly pales. 'Oh, God, no. There's no need for that. After I had Jodie, they were stitching me up and I got the quickest glance in the reflection on a lamp and I'm still not the better for it.'

'It is only a rumour,' Deirdre says, nervously. 'It might not be true.'

'Tell me you've at least had a look at yours before?' Laura asks her, and I feel immediately sorry for Deirdre, who is by now, no doubt, sorry she ever came and sat beside us at lunch.

'Ah, no. Well, not on purpose anyway. And I suppose it depends on how much of it you're talking about.' Her face is bright red.

'Laura, would you leave the poor woman alone. Just because you're best friends with your hoo-ha.'

'Vulva,' Niamh interjects. 'We can be mature about it.'

'That's rich coming from a woman who's never so much as looked at her own,' Laura retorts.

'My body, my choice!' Niamh retorts.

'I don't think that's about looking at your own genitals, Niamh.'

I mouth a sorry to Deirdre and link arms with her, leaving the other two women to work through their vulva-related issues themselves.

'I didn't mean to upset anyone,' Deirdre says as she joins me on a yoga mat halfway up the room. She turns her head away to take a drink from her water bottle.

'You didn't! It's banter. They love each other to bits. And yeah, Niamh can be a bit prickly at the moment, but absolutely don't worry about it.'

Deirdre smiles. 'You three have a great bond, you know. I can see that. Cherish that. It's so special.'

'I do,' I say. 'I will.'

* * *

To my surprise, it is Peggy, dressed in loose linen trousers and an oversized linen shirt, who walks to the front of the class and announces she will be leading the workshop. She is barefoot, and her hair is still in perfect curls despite the swimming and yoga and walk in the cold outdoors. The woman is glowing and yet it's clear she's not wearing make-up. Whatever method this woman has found to look and feel this good, I'm here for it.

'Good evening, everyone,' she says in her lilting Donegal accent. 'I know we have this room set up in rows, but can I ask that you shift yourself around so that we're all in a circle.'

'Leave a space for me too,' she says as we start to do what she asked. It's four in the afternoon, and the light is fading quickly now. Our reflections shine back at us from the floor-to-ceiling window, now speckled with rain, and I make sure to take a place in the circle where my back is towards the window and I am unable to see any part of myself and become self-conscious. I want to tell Laura this proves it's not just my genital area that I don't want to look at. I don't want to watch how my body moves, or even, I realise, how I look. I'd quite happily ban mirrors and selfie-taking cameras from the universe if I were in power.

God, I really, really hope no one is going to start handing hand mirrors out. Surely I can locate my inner goddess without having to go cave diving for my uterus?

'First of all, friends... fellow goddesses,' Peggy says, 'I've been made aware there has been some chatter about an exercise honouring the yoni – which, to you and me, is probably better known as your vulva or any other manner of interesting words for it.'

The room falls silent. We are hanging on her every word. I wonder how many people, if any, gathered here are hoping it's going to happen. From the expressions of the other women in the room, I'd guess a relatively small amount.

'Let me reassure you before we get going that such an exercise, while valid and empowering, is not part of this weekend's proceedings.'

There is a collective sigh of relief, which quickly turns into a ripple of laughter spreading around the room.

'Thank God for that,' a woman I don't know calls. 'I haven't waxed since before the pandemic and it would take more than a mirror to find mine. I'd need a garden trimmer and some safety goggles!'

More laughter ensues.

'Laugh all you want,' Peggy says. 'When I tell you what we will be doing you might be wishing we handed round the mirrors and the strimmers after all.'

Niamh and I look at each other, fear on our faces. What could be worse than such an intimate level of self-inspection?

The answer, it seems, as Peggy lifts a box of coloured scarves onto a table at the back of the room, instructing us to go and take two each from the box, is dancing.

Dancing and I are not good friends. I've never been blessed with a good sense of rhythm. Mum tried to take me to Irish dancing classes when I was five or six. As legend tells it, I survived all of two lessons before the teacher very gently took my mother aside and suggested she may want to look at speech and drama lessons instead.

As I have aged, I have been known to substitute skill with enthusiasm and I do enjoy a good bop around the kitchen. But dancing, with scarves, in a well-lit, populated setting, without the assistance of alcohol to make me think I could be the next Beyoncé, is not something that generally floats my boat.

Still, in the spirit of writing this article as authentically as possible, I know that I should, and I will go along with it. Looking across at Niamh, I can see that if I'm feeling uncomfortable at the thought of dancing in front of other people and waving scarves around, she is positively wanting to crawl inside her own body and die.

Laura, funnily enough, has practically elbowed her way to the front of the queue and has already selected her scarves and is waving them around as if she's directing the traffic at Belfast City Airport.

'I'm not sure about this,' Deirdre says. 'I'm not much of a dancer. Two left feet, and neither of them good for anything.'

'Listen, I'm the same if not worse,' I tell her. 'Niamh's not a bad mover – or she wasn't before her left knee started playing up. Laura there did ballet for two years in primary school and thinks she's Darcey Bussell, but I can assure you that she isn't. All three of us do a mean Macarena though, so how about we put that energy into it?'

Deirdre laughs and nods – and I even manage to feel a whole lot better about what we are about to do.

Peggy dims the lights and I immediately feel more relaxed and then, just as with this morning's meditation, she guides us through a movement class where we start slowly at first, swaying to and fro with our eyes closed. It reminds me of when the boys were little and I would spend endless hours rocking them to try and settle them down, and ease their colic. It's astounding how much of a muscle memory that becomes. I could almost be in their bedroom, 'The Blower's Daughter' by Damien Rice playing softly in the background. Even as babies, Simon insisted that they would be introduced to the classics instead of nursery rhymes. My children were raised to a soundtrack of angsty singer-songwriters.

There is something about this gentle swaying that evokes those feelings of motherhood. Of youth. Of fertility. Of nurturing. I want to keep my arms wrapped around my centre and hold that part of me inside, stop it from moving on from where it has been such a huge part of my last two decades. I am not ready to let it fly or accept that the young mother version of me is no more. Or that the new generation of us is getting ready to embrace that stage themselves.

But as Peggy talks and encourages small movements at first – the extension of our arms away from our bodies inch by inch, turning slowly in a circle, throwing our heads back, reaching upwards – once again taking ownership of each part of our bodies and our souls, my fears lessen.

The movements become bigger. The music becomes louder. The rain starts to fall heavier outside, beating off the roof, adding a percussion to our movement. I swear I feel it in my very soul. The scarves become an extension of our arms, and those parts of me that I have been holding so very tight to all these years seem to move and change. They adapt to fit the person I am now. It's as if they change colour and shape, as the energy within shifts and swells.

This is a dance shared by the woman I am now and the woman I am becoming.

Before I know it, I'm dancing and crying and thinking that I didn't need a GPS tracker after all to locate my inner goddess. She was always here. She was just hiding.

28

TRAINERS, SLIPPERS AND CROCS, OH MY!

'I am absolutely pooped,' Laura says, flopping down on the sofa bed. 'Between the sea air and all this activity my body doesn't know what's hit it.'

I know exactly what she means. I ache in places I forgot I had. My skin feels scrubbed raw by the salty sea water. My soul feels scrubbed raw by all the introspection. My face is windblown. My arms ache from all the scarf waving and goddess finding. I could lie down right now on this bed and be asleep within seconds. I don't even think I'd have to close my eyes before unconsciousness took over. In fact, I'm that tired I'm not actually sure if I'm awake at all right now and not just dreaming all of this.

'Well, you girls better get a Red Bull or something down your neck because the night is young and you absolutely cannot nope out of the silent disco,' Niamh says, searching through her weekend bag until she finds her 'All Panic, No Disco' T-shirt. 'I've been looking forward to this in the way you complete madzers had been looking forward to the sea swimming and the goddess hunting, and if I had to do those for you, then you have to do this for me.'

I groan. My feet cramp in protest. 'Really? But I'm tired! Surely you can just pop in your earbuds and dance here? Laura and I will sleep and you can go for your life.'

It's always worth testing the waters with Niamh. There's always the chance she'll surprise you. For example, she could just as easily turn around now and say, 'You know what? I never thought of that! By jiminy, I think I'll give that a go and have a jolly good time!'

Of course, that's not what she says. 'You owe me. You made me worry about whether or not I was going to have to flash my fandango...'

'Vulva!' Laura says, in her best teasing voice, hoisting Niamh by her own petard. 'Mrs Cassidy, you're a science teacher, you should be using the proper anatomical terms!'

'You're absolutely right,' Niamh replies. 'I'm sorry. I should be using the correct anatomical terms and I will do so going forward. So when I tell you that you are risking a kick up the rectum, you'll know exactly what I mean!' She sticks her tongue out, thankfully proving she is only teasing too and I'm not going to have pull them apart from a cat fight in the very near future.

'But that aside – girls, come on!' Niamh pleads. 'It's Saturday night. I have my disco T-shirt. There are no children nearby. No adult responsibilities. There's just the chance to let our hair down a little and enjoy the silent disco. I've always wanted to try one!'

The concept is fun, I suppose. Everyone wearing earphones, simultaneously listening to the same music and having a boogie. Or if the playlist isn't to your liking, you press a button and move on to something else. They could be breaking it down to 'Bootylicious' while you are enjoying the Nolan Sisters sing about being in the mood for dancing, and nobody needs to know.

Everyone's happy. The neighbours – in this case the sheep in the nearby field – aren't troubled by noise pollution and you get to dance without judgement. What could be better than that?

Except some sleep, I suppose.

'Can I wear my trainers though?' I ask. 'Because there's no way I'm putting on my heels.'

'I'm wearing my Crocs,' Niamh says. 'And I don't give a damn what anyone says, because they're comfy.'

'Do you think I could wear my slippers?' Laura asks, glancing down to her feet where she is already wearing her pink fluffy mules.

'I think you can wear whatever you want. Whatever makes you comfortable. Peggy said she doesn't care if we land in our pyjamas if that's what floats our boats.'

Oooh... the thought of having a dance in my slippers and jammies does sound appealing. A quick boogie then back home and straight to bed. Perfect!

'Grand so,' Laura says. 'I'll wear my slippers and my joggers.'

'Good woman!' Niamh says, turning her gaze towards me. 'And you? Becs? Come on! Say you will! Even for a couple of songs? We don't have to go crazy but we'd be raging if we missed it altogether.'

She has a point. This is our last night here – and even though we have packed as much as possible into the day, it does feel as if we would be letting the side down to disappear.

'Okay then,' I tell Niamh, to a whoop of delight.

'Comfy shoes to the ready! Write that in your column for *Northern People*. Let's normalise comfy footwear! Heels are gorgeous and all, but dear God, life is tough enough without feeling as if the balls of your feet are ablaze by the end of the night. Not to mention I'm pretty sure the heels I wore in my twenties are the reason my knee is absolutely fecked now.'

'Noted,' I say with a smile. 'I'm on it! Comfy shoes and elasticated waists for the win!'

'You get my vote,' Laura says, as she hauls herself back to a sitting position and raises an imaginary glass to us both. 'That and celebrating the beauty of a good cardigan.'

'I do love a cardigan,' I agree, as I start looking through my limited selection of clothes to decide what to wear.

29

'DANCING QUEEN'

Niamh

It's a bit like poking a bruise, Niamh thinks, as she tries to assess her emotional state without allowing herself to dig too deeply into her feelings. What she's pretty sure of is that she is starting to truly, really, understand the power of mood swings.

Today has been interesting. Challenging. A lot. But cathartic too. She feels relieved to have told Becca the truth of what is happening with Paul. She'd been so afraid that giving her feelings a voice would make them seem real. Which was, she knows, ridiculous because they already were real and keeping them bottled up was simply driving her mad.

At the same time, she feels guilty for expressing her worries about her relationship and just how much Paul Cassidy's very existence is winding her up at the moment. Has she been disloyal in some way? Or has talking about her stresses and worries stopped her from losing her mind completely with Paul and saying things to him that neither of them will forget in a hurry?

She feels good for expressing just how much this menopause

business is messing with her body and her head. Since going on HRT, Becca has seemed to be doing really well. Niamh couldn't help but think there was something inside her that was broken. One of the older teachers at school had launched into a diatribe on how 'women these days think they deserve a medal for going through the menopause'.

'What happened to just getting on with it? I didn't go about complaining about hot flushes, or heavy *periods*.' She'd whispered the word periods, of course. Niamh had only just managed to stop herself from rolling her eyes. 'There are things best kept to ourselves. You can't go anywhere now but you see books about it, magazine articles about it, support groups, TV programmes. I saw an ad on the TV the other day and I will not tell you what it was but it was indecent. And it was during the daytime!'

Probably the ad that's doing the rounds for 'intimate mois-turiser', Niamh thought, making a mental note to pop into Boots on the way home to get some.

'How generations of us got through it without all this fuss, I'll never know. Now you young ones seem to have no qualms at all about talking about your private affairs. Even in polite company. It's a madness, and next thing you know, the school will be appointing a Menopause Officer.'

Niamh has always struggled to understand the mentality of older generations who cling on to the belief that just as they had to struggle, so should everyone else. It doesn't matter that research has moved on. That we know now just how debilitating menopause can be for some women. They suffered in silence and so should all future generations.

'Well, maybe they should,' Niamh had snapped. 'The majority of teaching staff here are female. We will all go through menopause. Some of us will sail through it and some of us won't.

Some of us need support and treating it like some dirty little secret to be whispered about in corners doesn't help anyone.'

The older teacher had looked most put out, but Niamh hadn't cared. She just got up, taking her coffee cup with her, left the staffroom and went back to her classroom.

The conversation has stayed with her though. She's asked herself a thousand times if she is just being overly dramatic. Is she using menopause as an excuse to be short tempered and tearful? If she can really be sure it's menopause causing all her symptoms and not just a common-or-garden mental breakdown instead. Even though she had Becca and Laura, she still felt out on her own. But today... today has helped her. Simply by being in a space with other women who have been expressing their distress and offering solutions. It has made her feel less mad. It has given her hope that she can come through this and pull herself out the other side. She's not quite sure what the other side will look like.

She needs to talk to Paul. Properly talk to him. And not just about Jodie, but about how she feels she has lost her connection with him. Surely he must feel it too? She has to tell him how stressful she is finding work and how that's having a knock-on effect to almost every other aspect of her life. She needs to tell him she's hanging on by a thread. But at least, after this weekend, she's starting to feel as if that thread isn't fraying after all.

That, she decides, is more than enough of a reason to slick on some lip gloss, backcomb her hair and get ready to dance her socks off. She can't remember the last time she danced. When she was younger she would've been the first to the dance floor on almost every occasion. She lived for her Friday and Saturday nights out clubbing, hands in the air, letting the music pulse through her as if nothing else mattered.

For the first time in weeks, she feels a buzz of excitement building within her and she can't wait to start dancing.

30

WHEN I GROW UP

Becca

Once the music has started, I'm glad we came and didn't just fall into bed as I had wanted.

The lights are dimmed in the room, we're all wearing our headsets and Peggy has provided us all with glow sticks, which we've fashioned into bracelets and necklaces. It's not quite a rave atmosphere. We're not sweaty enough to really get that vibe, because thank God Peggy knows what it's like to be menopausal and has switched on the aircon. But it is a fun vibe. I'm not sure when I ever forgot that having a good old throw around on the dance floor was a brilliant way to boost my dopamine levels, but I'm glad to be experiencing it all the same now.

We've been joined, once again, by Deirdre, who is as hyped up as Niamh for what's to come. I did wonder if Niamh had been at the Grey Goose again – her mood being so improved from this morning – but she smiled and said she was just 'high on life'.

'Enjoy it while you can,' she'd grinned. 'No doubt the next mood swing is just around the corner!' She'd then linked arms with Deirdre and the pair of them had rushed to the front of the queue to grab their headsets.

Peggy has put together a couple of playlists – absolute bangers from the eighties, nineties and early 2000s. There's even a choice of angsty emo teen music from the nineties for the women who were cool enough to follow Pearl Jam, Nirvana and REM back in the day.

I was more of a Backstreet Boys/Spice Girls fan so I'm happy enough to throw some moves around to 'I Want It That Way' and 'Stop' instead. I do enjoy a minor segue into some of the dance classics from my uni days though, and even though I am so not nineteen any more, I jump around to 'Set You Free' by N-Trance as if my pelvic floor has never been pummelled on the inside by twins.

Even though I was sure I was only popping along here for a couple of songs, I'm shocked when the lights come back up and we're told that's us until morning – when there will be another sea swim for anyone feeling brave enough, before a session on supporting your menopause from a holistic perspective, whatever that entails.

My feet ache, despite wearing my trainers, but I don't care. I don't think I've had as much fun in years. Sixteen-year-old Becki would have loved this. She would've loved that I was dancing until midnight with our best friends on a weekend away. She would love that I'm going to write about this once I get home. I can almost imagine her giving me a big thumbs up of approval – probably before ruining it all by asking me how our marriage to David Duchovny is going.

'Thank you so much for letting me be your fourth wheel,' Deirdre says, her arm linked in Niamh's as we walk back to the yurts. 'You've no idea how much it means. I was absolutely sick with nerves coming here, but you all have made it so easy for me.'

'You're very welcome to be part of our crew any time,' Laura says. 'Why so nervous though? I think you're amazing coming to the retreat on your own. It takes real courage.'

'Do you really think so?' Deirdre asks, and of course we all turn around and tell her that of course we bloody do.

She shrugs, but even in the darkness I see that she is smiling. 'You're all very kind,' she says. 'And maybe you're right. I just… well, I'm not one of those girls who has bucketloads of friends waiting to hang out with them. My friends from school have all moved on or moved away. We've all just drifted apart and no one really warns you how hard it is to make friends when you're a proper grown-up doing proper grown-up things.'

'There's the truth,' I say, acutely aware that I would be lost without the girls, and especially without Niamh, who has consistently been there for me and with me through my life. Yes, I have a few acquaintances but not a whole lot of people I'd class as ride-or-die friends. My mum always told me it was quality that mattered, not quantity, and I happen to believe she's right. Sensing that Deirdre may want to talk more, I don't share my own experiences, wanting to leave room for her to talk.

'I've never had children,' she says. 'And my friends did. Their children became the centre of their lives, and I totally get that, but it became difficult for me. I started turning down invitations and then, perhaps not surprisingly, they stopped inviting me.'

'That sounds difficult,' I say.

'Yeah, it wasn't great. It isn't great, to be honest. Feeling like I didn't belong simply because I'm not a mother. It was even more painful because I desperately wanted to be a mum but it just never happened. It was never the right time, or it was never the right man and then by the time I finally met the man I thought would be a great father I just never managed to get pregnant. I imagined it was down to my age.'

'You don't know for certain what the problem was?' Laura asks gently.

Deirdre shakes her head. 'There's a whole story there. He didn't want to get tested. Said if it was meant to be, it would happen. He said we should leave it to fate and sure, hadn't fate brought us together. Then he said he was scared that if we *did* find out, it might be very difficult for the problematic partner to deal with. And, as he said, age wasn't in my favour; he was confident the problem would be with me and he didn't want to put me through that pain.'

I can hardly believe what I'm hearing. What an absolute shed-load of fuckery disguised as concern for her wellbeing.

'Ooof!' Niamh says. 'I'm sorry. He sounds like an absolute dick.'

I freeze. We don't know Deirdre. Not enough to know that she will be comfortable with one of us calling her partner – hopefully her ex-partner – a dick. Even if he is very clearly a ginormous dick. It's possible Niamh has just said something that will upset her and that's the last thing I want. Imagine coming away for a weekend on your own, finally being delighted to have met some nice people, only to have one of them insult your partner outright.

'He is an absolute dick,' Deirdre says, and I breathe a sigh of relief. 'Because the absolute plot twist in all of it is that I found out he'd had a vasectomy five years before we met. He just didn't think he owed it to me to let me know. Thankfully he's no longer *my* absolute dick.'

My jaw drops so far I imagine I look like one of those cartoon characters whose jaws hit the floor.

'That absolute mother-fudger!' I say.

'Becs, you're among the grown-ups now. You can say the actual word,' Niamh says.

'Well then, he's a fucking big fucker!' I say with a level of enthusiasm usually reserved for children swearing out of earshot of their parents and getting high on the thrill of speaking the forbidden words.

Deirdre laughs. 'Yes. Yes, he is a fucking big fucker. But it's okay. I can laugh about it now. I couldn't for a long time, but then I realised I could be angry, or continue waiting for the right man, or the right friends, or whatever to come along before I started doing the things I always wanted... or I could just do them anyway. It's been really freeing actually. I've been to concerts by myself. It doesn't take a fizz out of me to go to the cinema or out to lunch on my own now. I even have a holiday to Italy booked for this summer. Just me. I can't wait.'

I am actually in awe of this woman. She has grabbed onto life and is living it even if it's sometimes a little scary, or she knows no one at all. It takes courage to do these things as a lone woman in this world. It takes courage to live your life.

'I want to be just like you when I grow up,' I say.

'Ah, stop it! Sure, look at you three! You're here, aren't you? Living your best lives? Having each other to hang on to? We don't all have to do the same thing to be doing great things. If that doesn't sound too cheesy?'

'We're all about the cheesy,' Niamh tells her, and we start walking towards the yurts, where we invite Deirdre to come in and join us for an absolutely rock-and-roll cup of tea before bed, since it seems the drugs orgy is off the table.

31

THE FABULOUS FORTIES CLUB

I'm sitting outside the yurt, drinking a cup of tea as the sun is starting to rise. It's so incredibly life-affirming to watch the sky turn from the darkest black to navy streaked with pink, orange and red before the day arrives in all its dry and bright glory.

It's freezing though – frost lies thick on the ground, glinting and sparkling in the early-morning light. My breath plumes and rises in front of my face and I can feel the cold pinch at my nose and cheeks.

I feel amazing though, even though the cold and I are not usually friends. That's the power of a good dryrobe, I suppose. And the thermal leggings and socks I'm wearing, along with my thickest, most oversized and insanely comfortable hoodie. Do I look good? Absolutely not. I look three times my normal size and I haven't bothered to brush my hair yet. I've simply popped my pink bobble hat on top of my head instead.

The truth is I don't feel the need to make an effort here. I don't feel I need to put on any make-up, or make sure my clothes are designer. I don't feel the need to straighten, curl or even brush my hair. I'm maintaining basic levels of hygiene because I'm not a total dirt-bird but that aside, I'm just enjoying being me.

Ideas for my article are dancing around in my head and I am already so excited to sit down and write it. It's the most excited I've been about writing anything in years – leaving all those listicles and industry updates cold in the dust.

I think of how Deirdre – lovely, amazing Deirdre – is finding her voice and I think that she was quite right when she said we are all allowed to live our lives in our own way. I'm finding my voice too. Yes, I'm shit-scared, but I'm still doing it. Because deep down inside I believe that I have something to say that people might want to hear – or read. Maybe that makes me sound full of a sense of my own self-importance. Who am I to think people will want to read what I write? But if the experiences of the last two days have taught me anything it's that we have more that unites us than divides us.

Or maybe I'm just buzzing off the feeling of being with friends, in the fresh air and just getting to put myself first for a bit.

The flap to the yurt lifts and Laura creeps out, wrapped up as much as I am and with a coffee cup nestled between her hands. 'It's a cold one,' she says.

'Yeah, but it's absolutely gorgeous. Look at that sunrise!'

'Yeah,' she agrees and sits down on the wooden bench just outside the entrance way. 'It's breathtaking. And speaking of breathtaking... Becca, I love you very much and I'm absolutely so proud that we did the sea swimming yesterday. Honestly. I'll probably do it again sometime. But please don't make me do it today. It's Arctic out here and I don't think my nipples would survive the challenge.'

I honk with laughter, mixed with relief. 'You're safe,' I tell her. 'I just can't imagine willingly walking into the sea in that. I might go and walk down to the beach though – cheer those mad women on and get a little fresh air before breakfast.'

'While wrapped up nice and warm?'

'While wrapped up very nicely and very warmly.' I raise my cup to clink it against hers.

'Sounds like a plan,' she says.

'Are the others still sleeping?' I ask and Laura nods.

'Completely out of it. I think they sat talking for a while last night after we went to sleep.'

It's not really a surprise to me that Deirdre ended up bunking in with us last night. All four of us had sat around the wood-burner until the early hours when Laura and I could no longer even try to keep our eyes open. I'd heard Niamh and Deirdre still talking as I drifted off to sleep. Just nice easy chatter about nothing and everything, and making plans to meet up again after the weekend. Niamh has invited Deirdre to go to yoga with her and I'm perfectly happy about that. Anything that gives me an excuse to avoid the zero-craic version of Twister is fine by me.

'She seems really lovely,' I say.

'Doesn't she? It's heartbreaking she was so lonely, although I admire the hell out of her for getting on doing things anyway on her own.'

'I imagine there's a lot of women in her position,' I say. 'Not necessarily single, like, but women who are having to redefine their lives at our age. Maybe their marriages have ended, or their kids have left home, or they've just drifted away from their friends. It's not easy to make new friends. Options are limited, aren't they? Night classes and joining a club.'

Laura pulls a face. 'I've never been one for clubs.'

'Me neither. But maybe we've just not found one we'd really like. I've been thinking about it, you see. Being away this weekend has been so good, and so empowering, but when we go home later today that will be it. We'll have our memories and we'll talk about the cold water, or the body-positive yoga or surviving the green sludge of doom, and for a while we'll feel great – and empowered. Then life will take over again and we'll just go back to the way things were...'

'God, I hope it's not more green sludge for breakfast today. I don't think my stomach could take it.' Laura grimaces. 'But sorry, back to the point... are you talking about forming some sort of club?' She raises one eyebrow in suspicion. I don't blame her. I haven't formed a club since the informal David Duchovny Appreciation Society when I was fifteen. And I was the only member.

'I don't really know,' I say. 'Maybe. Don't you think it would be a good idea to have a regular date in the diary to meet for these things – things you might not want to try on your own but you'd give a go if you knew you were going to be there with like-minded—'

'—equally hormonal—'

'—equally hormonal, yes! Exactly!' I say. 'The Fabulous Forties Club... or something less cheesy. I don't know. But wouldn't it be good?'

'I think you might be on to something there,' Laura says, as she takes another drink from her coffee before turning her face towards the sky and closing her eyes.

'It's nice here, isn't it? Even with the cold. It's nice to sit and feel the hint of sun on your face and the cold nipping at your ears. Mum would've loved this.'

There's a moment or two of silence. There is no doubt that Kitty O'Hagan – a woman determined to enjoy her life no matter what it threw at her – would've enjoyed this very, very much.

32

UBER FOR MRS BISHOP!

Daniel the Spaniel is in the biggest huff known to dog-dom. He has refused to so much as wag his tail or jump up on me since I arrived back. Instead he has been lying on his favourite spot in front of the fire giving me the mega side-eye roughly every five minutes.

'Do you think he might be sick?' I ask Adam, worried to see the usually enthusiastically affectionate dog so glum.

'There's not one thing wrong with that dog other than him being raging at you for going away for two nights. He's been having the time of his life. Jodie fed him cooked chicken breast and rice for his dinner on Friday. Conal took him out to the beach yesterday where, by all accounts, he tired himself out with a bout of the mega zoomies and—'

'Wait! Conal took him out yesterday?' My heart flip-flops.

'Yeah, he called in yesterday morning. He was taking Lazlo for a run down at Lisfannon and thought Daniel would love it too. He said he would've messaged you but, obviously, you'd handed your phone in. It was really cute, actually. Dan the Man here was so excited to see Lazlo. He was wagging his tail so hard it's a wonder he didn't take off helicopter style.'

I can't help but smile and vow to message Conal, or maybe even phone him, at the first opportunity I get. I have to start laying the foundations for my iceberg, after all.

'...And then Granny called in and she brought some treats,' Adam continues.

'Your granny called in here? With treats. For the dog?' I ask – nothing about that whole scenario making sense to my ears. First of all, my mother does not just call in here. She rarely visits here at all, and when she does it is only when I beg her to do so and offer to drive her here and back.

Second of all, my mother does not ever get treats for Daniel – who she still insists on calling 'that dog', even though he is ten years old and I love him as much as if I birthed him from my own body. That she would willingly call here, without my bringing her, and bring treats... I'm starting to wonder if there has been some sort of alien abduction and replacement situation.

'Are you sure you're not on drugs, son, and you didn't hallucinate that?'

He laughs. 'I'm pretty sure. I have proof, actually!' He reaches down the side of the sofa and lifts up a bag containing two exceptionally beautiful and intricate crocheted cardigans in a soft cream yarn. Tears immediately prick at my eyes.

'She wanted to leave over these cardigans that she knitted—'

'Adam – it's crochet. I've warned you to get it right or you'll end up written out of Granny's will.'

He rolls his eye. 'Sorry, Mum. These cardigans she *crocheted*, then. Jodie absolutely loves them.'

I take one of the cardigans in my hands and feel the soft, warm wool. I admire each and every stitch, knowing how painstaking this work is, especially given the developing arthritis in my mother's hands. I am struck by such a huge wave of love for her that I almost forget that Daniel is still giving me the evil eye from the rug.

'How did she get here?' I ask.

'She got an Uber,' he says. 'Mrs Bishop downloaded the app and they are absolutely thrilled with the whole thing. Mrs Bishop came with her, by the way. Did you know she used to sing in nightclubs around town? Caused quite a stir with her short skirts and big hair apparently.'

I think of tiny Mrs Bishop, short in stature, skinny as a twig and who looks as if a good breeze would send her flying and try to think of her mini-skirted, with bouffant hair and causing a scene in the dance hall. Yes, I'm shocked, but I'm also exceptionally impressed. Just as I am that she can get my mother out and about in an Uber, and to be nice to Daniel.

'That's mad,' I say, the tiny cardigan still in my hand. 'Brilliant, but mad. Go Mrs Bishop! Who'd have thought she had that in her!'

'She seems like great craic,' Adam says. 'She has some stories to tell.'

I can't help but feel a little ashamed that I have never given her the chance to tell me her stories. Yes, I've run a few errands for her, and made tea for her and my mother, but I've never really sat down to listen. Maybe it's because I've been too busy, or stressed or just didn't think to do it, but I still feel bad about it.

'I must get chatting to her the next time I'm over in your granny's,' I say, and hand my big son back the tiny cardigan, trying not to think about the tiny cardigans he once wore himself or the fact that in seven and a half months there will be a little person in their lives small enough to fit in it. The exhaustion after a week well spent is definitely making me more emotional than usual.

He folds it carefully and places it back in the bag. 'I'm going to get a storage box for my room so I can start collecting things for the baby. I want to make sure I have everything he or she will need. I definitely want to take extra good care of Granny's gifts.'

'You're a good man,' I tell him. 'I'm very proud to call you my son.'

He blushes and I give him a quick hug before he escapes my grasp with the excuse of going to make me a cup of tea.

Soon it is just Daniel and me in the room. A stand-off to end all stand-offs.

'It was only two nights, Daniel,' I say.

I am rewarded with the most expressive side-eye I've ever seen – one that screams of not being one bit impressed with me.

'And you had Adam, and Jodie, and didn't you get out to the beach with Lazlo?'

There is the tiniest flick of his tail at the mention of Conal's dog, before he remembers he's officially huffing and returns to side-eye mode.

'And Granny came round with treats. I hear you got chicken for your tea.'

Normally the very hint of the word chicken would set his tail in major helicopter wags, but no. He's being what my mother would lovingly call 'a stubborn wee shite'.

I'm not sure what he wants me to do to make amends. Some self-flagellation perhaps? The promise of the noisiest, squeakiest, most annoying toys the pet shop can sell? Extra walks at whatever hour he decides?

'C'mon, pup,' I plead, patting the sofa beside me. 'Come and get a cuddle. Can we be friends again?'

Slowly, his head still low as if he has been wronged in this life and the last to an egregious level, he stands and plods over towards me before jumping onto the sofa and lying down with a sorrowful 'boof'.

'And the Oscar for best dog in a dramatic role goes to...' I start, as I begin petting him, only to be interrupted by Adam coming back into the room, his face ashen.

It's amazing how the atmosphere of a room can change in a heartbeat. How a room warmed by the glow of the fire and a loving chat between mother and son can so quickly become icy cold. As if sensing the shift, and the immediate thudding of my heart, Daniel lifts his head and lays it on my lap, staring up at me, before pawing at my arm as if to comfort me.

'Adam, love. What is it?'

'Mum, it's Jodie. She's started bleeding.'

My son. My big man of six foot tall, with the makings of a beard and a solid jawline, crumples in front of my eyes.

33

A WHITE COTTON HANKIE

Niamh

Niamh is holding onto Jodie's hand in the back seat of Paul's car as they drive to the hospital. She's not sure whether it is her, or her daughter, who is squeezing most tightly. Jodie is remarkably stoic – more stoic than Niamh managed to be that time she was the one being rushed to hospital only to find there was nothing to be done.

She had sobbed and gulped while Laura drove and Becca held her hand. She'd been desperately trying to get hold of Paul but, given that he'd been on a flight from London to Belfast, she'd been unable to speak to him.

'He's going to be so disappointed,' she'd sobbed into Becca's shoulder.

'We don't know what's happening yet,' Becca had told her. 'It might be nothing. Try to keep calm.'

Niamh had failed, spectacularly, at keeping calm. Afterwards she'd look back on it and come to realise it was because she knew.

Deep in her heart, she knew. She didn't have all the same symptoms she'd had when she had been pregnant with Jodie. Her boobs didn't hurt. She didn't wake up each morning and immediately throw up. Yes, she was maybe a little more tired than normal but she was a mother to a two-year-old and was also working full time. Her husband had been away on business for the past week. She was bound to be more tired – but she was nowhere near the bone-crushingly exhausted horror of her first trimester with Jodie when she struggled to stay awake even in front of a class of rowdy teenagers.

Still, even though she had suspected that something was not right, she still felt shocked to see the streak of red in her knickers when she went to the loo. How strange, she'd thought, to suddenly find it so alarming when it had been a monthly occurrence ever since she turned twelve. Annoying, yes. Inconvenient? Abso-bloody-lutely (no pun intended). But not alarming.

Suddenly, though, it was a signal that something had gone wrong inside her body. That her body had let her down. Was it something she had done? Had she not been excited enough? This had been a surprise pregnancy, unlike that with Jodie, which they had planned for. She had already been struggling with Jodie in the terrible twos and Paul's work requiring long spells away. She'd cried when the test had turned positive. So was that her fault? Had she wished the baby away?

Sitting now, beside her daughter who is staring, face expressionless, out of the car window, she wonders what thoughts are running through her mind. Looking at the back of Paul's head as he drives, she wonders what he's thinking. Is he relieved? Worried? Scared?

She wonders if he feels the way she does right now – that she hates that there is nothing she can do to influence the outcome of the next few hours. There is no way she can take whatever pain –

physical or emotional – her child will be experiencing and carry it on her own shoulders. Yes, she'll feel it because, God knows, a mother feels the pain of their child on some instinctual, deeply rooted biological level – but it won't be as sharp. It won't ease what Jodie is going to go through.

If the worst happens. She tries to remind herself that it's not always bad news. It might all work out.

Jodie winces, her hand shaking free from Niamh's and going straight to her middle, and Niamh feels a lump form in her throat.

'You okay, love?' Paul asks, glancing up to the rearview mirror.

'Aye, Daddy,' Jodie says, but her voice sounds small and scared.

'We're almost there,' he says. 'I'll drop you and your mum at the door and then go and get parked. Is Adam meeting you there?'

'He is,' Jodie says. 'Becca is bringing him.'

'Maybe I'll just wait outside. There will be enough of you in there. I don't want to be getting in the way.'

Niamh bristles. She wants to tell Paul he should be there with them but at the same time she doesn't want to upset Jodie further by letting her know that she's cross.

'Okay, Daddy,' Jodie says as they turn into the grounds of the hospital. She takes her mother's hand again and Niamh feels that she is shaking.

'It's okay, love. I'll be with you, and Adam too. And Becca.'

Jodie nods.

'And I'll be here. I'll not move from this car park. You need anything, you let me know. I'll be right here,' Paul says, as they pull up at the doors of the Emergency Department. 'I love you, Jodie.'

Niamh can hear the emotion in his voice and, if she's not

mistaken, a little bit of fear there too. That's when she notices that his knuckles are white against the steering wheel – his grip being so tight. Maybe, she thinks, he does feel some of the pain too.

She guides her daughter into the Emergency Department and in a voice she doesn't quite recognise she fills the receptionist in on what is happening. The young woman, probably not much older than Jodie, taps on her keyboard and directs them to sit down while showing no emotion or empathy on her face. Niamh supposes she sees this, and worse, every day but still, it wouldn't hurt her to give a sympathetic nod.

'When will she be called in?' Niamh asks.

The woman scans her computer screen and shrugs. 'It's hard to tell but it's not too busy tonight. You're lucky.'

Niamh raises an eyebrow and gives her very best withering glare. The kind of glare that she normally only reserves for her very worst-behaved pupils. It's the glare that says their cards are marked, their parents are being called and the detentions are being piled up. 'Lucky' is not the word she would use. Far from it.

'I... I mean... it shouldn't be long. The triage nurse should call you through in the next ten minutes,' the receptionist says, wilting under her stare.

'Thank you,' Niamh says, tersely, tension thrumming through her body as she guides Jodie to her seat.

'What if the baby is gone, Mum?' Jodie says in a small, scared voice.

'Let's wait and see what the doctors say,' Niamh tells her. 'You never know.'

'I know we're young... and it wasn't planned...'

'I know, darling. It doesn't make it any less scary.'

The double doors to the waiting room swoosh open and when Niamh and Jodie glance up they see Adam and Becca scanning the room. Adam is almost as pale as Jodie is, Niamh thinks. Becca has the same look on her face that she did that day eighteen years ago when she had brought Niamh to the hospital to hear that her pregnancy was lost.

It's incredible to Niamh that even now, all these years later, she can so quickly recall almost every detail of that visit. She can feel the same feelings taking hold today and she wants to cry. But she knows it's not her place to cry. Not now. Not here. Here, it is up to her and Becca to put on a brave face to guide their children through this. Children who just two weeks ago were living their best lives, falling in love and doing all the things that students with no real-world responsibilities did. Things have changed so quickly, and so completely and now it could all change again.

She raises her hand and waves to attract the attention of Becca and Adam. Within seconds, Jodie and Adam are hugging, Jodie finally sobbing, and Niamh finds herself just looking at Becca – both of them not sure what to say. Maybe, Niamh wonders, there just isn't anything to say. She can hardly believe it's only a matter of hours since they were walking along the beach in Donegal feeling reinvigorated and reinvented. It's just a couple of days since they were joking about being GILFs. And yet all of it could be over already. For now.

When the triage nurse calls Jodie's name, she makes to stand up to accompany her daughter in for assessment. But as Adam stands up too, Jodie says, 'It's okay, Mum. Adam is going to come in with me. Is that okay? It's his baby too.'

She has to fight the urge to say that of course it's not okay. She is her mother. She has been accompanying Jodie to every medical appointment her entire life and up until very recently she has still been subjected to Jodie turning to her and pleading with her eyes for her mother to answer every question the doctor asked. But now she wants to go with Adam and leave her outside, unaware of what the hell is happening now? Oh, she is so not ready for this, but she realises she doesn't really have a choice. Now is not the time to have a meltdown about her child's growing independence.

She feels Becca's hand lightly on her arm. A gesture in solidarity of 'this is not about us even if we feel that it is very much about us'.

Niamh nods. 'Of course, love. Of course. I'll be here with Becca, and we will be doubling up on giving the receptionist the evil eye.'

'What's that about?' Becca asks, as Jodie gives a watery, nervous smile and – taking Adam's hand – follows the nurse through for assessment.

Niamh can't take her eyes off her. She can't quite believe this is a grown woman walking away from her and not just her little girl. How can they be here already in this life? She is not ready for this. The next sound from her mouth is a sob – one so loud that the elderly gentleman in the row in front of her turns and offers her a hankie. It's not just any hankie either. It's a cotton one. Pristine white. 'You hang on to that, love,' he says. 'I'll say a wee prayer for your troubles.'

She sobs a little more while Becca thanks the gentleman for his kindness and asks him if he is waiting to be seen. He's not, as it happens. But his wife is through getting a sprained wrist strapped. 'Silly woman – does too much. I'm always telling her she needs to take it easy and sure, haven't we seven grown-up children can come and do her errands for her, but... well. You know what you Derry women are like. Stubborn as goats.'

Niamh is embarrassed that she can't find it in her to join in the conversation, but she is somewhere between worried sick for her daughter and in some weird PTSD replay of her own long-buried miscarriage.

It's really only the firm grip of Becca's hand that is keeping her grounded in this moment.

'They'll be okay,' Becca says.

'Do you really think so?'

Becca nods as if trying to convince herself. 'I really hope so.'

34

JELLYBEAN

Becca

Niamh and I were eventually called through to a curtained-off bay where Jodie and Adam sat, eyes red-rimmed. My heart, which I'd thought could not possibly get any lower, sank even more. The ultrasound scanner was still there with them, the image on the screen frozen, a small, grainy jellybean-shaped blob at its centre. A jellybean that had changed everything already.

I heard Niamh gasp, was aware her hand was flying to her mouth, but I didn't look directly at her. All I could do was look at the shape on the screen.

'Oh, love,' I say, as Niamh moves directly towards Jodie.

Adam looks up at me, the eyelashes I always said were wasted on a boy blinking back at me filled with tears. 'That's our baby, Mum,' he says, and I notice he is gripping Jodie's hand.

'I know, love,' I tell him. 'And it will always be your baby. You will keep him or her in your hearts.'

'No... no,' Jodie says as Niamh stands up. 'It's our *baby*.'

I notice a hint of a smile on her face, and look back to Adam, who is smiling, and for a second I can't make sense of it.

'We heard the heartbeat,' Adam says, and suddenly I finally understand what it means when an author writes 'she released a breath she didn't know she was holding' as a rush of relief is accompanied by a shaky exhalation.

'The baby's okay?' I ask, hardly able to believe what I'm hearing. I can't quite allow myself to believe it.

'Perfect,' Jodie says, her voice thick with tears.

'And the bleeding, what did they say about the bleeding?' Niamh asks.

'They think it's just some spotting.'

At that the curtain is pulled back and an impossibly young female doctor walks in. 'Okay, Jodie. I've arranged for you to come back in a week to the Early Pregnancy Unit just to keep an eye on baby and what he or she is up to. In the meantime, lots of rest. No heavy lifting. If the bleeding gets any heavier, or is accompanied with cramping, then do, of course, come back.'

'Excuse me,' Niamh says before introducing herself. 'So what might have caused the bleeding?'

The doctor looks from Niamh to Jodie, presumably looking for some clue as to who this woman is asking questions.

'Dr Harkin, this is my mum, Niamh. And Adam's mum, Becca.'

Dr Harkin nods a quick hello. 'The truth is we might never know. Up to one in four women can experience some form of bleeding in the first twelve weeks of pregnancy. For some of them it is the first sign that something is going wrong, but in this case it all looks as it should. There's a lovely strong heartbeat in there, which is always a good sign. It doesn't mean we're out of the woods, but we're a bit closer to the exit than we were. So, as I said, my recommendation is rest and relaxing as much as possible. Oh, and to try and manage your sickness a little better; I recommend staying hydrated and eating little and often as opposed to sitting down to big meals.'

I'm listening. I swear I'm listening. But I also can't keep my eyes from wandering back to the screen and the jellybean.

'Look,' Dr Harkin says, 'I'm not really supposed to do this but if the two grannies would like to hear the heartbeat – we can do another quick scan. Entirely up to you, Jodie, of course.'

'That would be great,' Jodie says as she lifts up her top ready to smear on the cold transducing jelly.

Niamh and I catch each other's gaze and we don't need to speak. To be honest, I'm not sure I could if my life depended on it. My need, suddenly, to hear this heartbeat is overwhelming.

I startle a little as I feel a hand reaching out for mine. It's not Adam, however. It's my friend. My soul sister. My fellow granny-in-waiting. The only other woman in this world who will understand how much this moment, in this space, with these two other people, could ever mean.

Dr Harkin presses down on Jodie's stomach and starts to move the probe around. My eyes go back, once again, to the screen, which is no longer static. There is movement. And there I see it, that little jellybean again. Dr Harkin taps something on the keyboard in front of the monitor and we zoom in just slightly. It's not the clearest of pictures but I think I can make out the little buds of arms and legs and, yes, I see that super tiny flickering dot.

'And that,' Dr Harkin says, 'is baby's heartbeat. Let me put the volume on.'

She taps another button and a soft but remarkably fast 'whomp whomp' sound fills the cubicle. 'Baby's heart is currently beating at around one hundred and sixty beats per minute, which is exactly where we want it to be.'

I think she keeps talking. I'm vaguely aware of the drone of her voice, but I can't hear anything except for the rhythm of that heartbeat, and I can't feel anything but the tight squeeze of my friend's hand.

There he or she is. This tiny little thing that will be such a big part of our lives. This tiny little thing who I have worried about already. The cause of my concerns that Adam and Jodie are tying themselves down. The reason I've woken up in the night after a dream I am left holding the baby while trying to meet my deadlines and walk Daniel and care for my mother. There he or she is, and those concerns, while not silly, don't seem to matter as much in this moment. We'll make it work. We'll cope and manage because we always do. And because this little jellybean has just stolen my heart.

35

TWO HAPPY MEALS

Niamh

The house is silent. It's not something Niamh usually gets the opportunity to experience. She's normally fast asleep by ten these days – and Fiadh is usually the only one of her children to be asleep before her.

Normally she has to shove earplugs into her ears to drown out the shouts of her boys over their PS5 to their friends. And yes, she and Paul have both asked them, many, many times to keep the noise down and they do try. For a bit. But inevitably some big drama unfolds in whatever game they are currently obsessed with and they start to get louder and louder again. Niamh believes that anyone who thinks women are emotional and irrational has clearly never listened to teenage boys playing *Fortnite* with their friends online.

Paul tends to come to bed between eleven and twelve. Somewhere along the line – maybe in the last year – she started to see it as a mega bonus if he managed to not wake her up when he did. Even though she used to love those half-asleep moments with him. Those seconds or minutes when he would climb into bed, give her a cuddle and whisper that he loved her were among her favourite of the day, and she would fall back asleep a very contented woman.

But that was before the night sweats and the hot flushes and the not-hot-flushes-so-much-as-thermostat-malfunctions that now seemed to hit around eight every evening kicked in.

The nightly spontaneous combustion is so reliable now, she could almost set her watch by it. One moment she'll be relaxed and feeling perfectly comfortable with a normal body temperature and the next, as the clock strikes eight, something switches and she becomes almost radioactive with heat. If she had a thermal camera pointed at her, she is sure she would look like someone from one of the old Ready Brek ads in the eighties. When she looks in a mirror during one of these episodes she is always surprised to see that her face is not ablaze and her skin not a fetching shade of 'Serious Sun Burn'.

She hasn't found a way to cool herself down when that surge hits – not one that works to any truly effective level anyway. Unlike a flush – or a flash if you happen to be American – this particular form of torture does not pass in a minute or two. It stays, and it builds and builds until Niamh finds herself with no other option than to lie with the bedroom heating off, the window wide open, in her lightest PJ shorts set and on top of her duvet to try to sleep. It's horrendous enough in January. During the summer months it was sheer torture. No amount of cooling spray or ice-cold water would stop the feeling that her blood was literally boiling inside her.

Recently, she tried blasting a fan directly at her body, but Paul had begged for mercy. He was freezing, he said, as he lay shivering in bed, duvet pulled up under his chin, and – on occasion – wearing a hoodie with the hood up. A fan is a step too far, so she puts up with lying, sweltered, on top of the bed, feeling as if she is baking like a Christmas ham.

Given those nightly horrors, she very much has not wanted to cuddle. The last thing she needs is an additional heat source. The only spooning she's interested in these days involves a giant carton of Ben & Jerry's and her open mouth.

But tonight, she doesn't care that she is too hot. She doesn't care that Paul feels like a nuclear reactor pumping heat in her direction. She needs to feel the weight of his arm around her waist and the security of him behind her. The familiarity of his touch and his smell. The knowledge that there is nothing in this world that he can't make just that little bit more bearable.

Tonight she needs that comfort so much that not even the changing of his breathing into soft snores, right in her ear, annoys her.

Because tonight he needs her as much as she needs him. And she does *need* him. Tonight, even though they have yet to talk it out between each other, they both know they have dodged a bullet. Fear walked in and rearranged their priorities entirely. Niamh got a tiny glimpse of what it would feel like to lose something you couldn't help but love.

She thinks, from how he has acted since, that Paul might just have got the same glimpse.

Just as he said he would, he had waited outside the hospital in the car park, messaging Niamh approximately every nine minutes to see if there was any news.

There was none, of course, until there was not only news, but pictures and a sound which Niamh had very quickly recorded on her phone to share with him.

She didn't expect him to react quite the way he did. She certainly was not expecting that as they walked out of the doors of the hospital, he would be standing, shivering, in the cold, waiting to pull his daughter into a tight hug and cry.

'I'm so glad everything is okay, love,' he said, his voice dripping with sincerity. He had teared up when Niamh showed him the video before hugging Jodie again, and then Adam.

In fact, it was Paul who had suggested that Adam come back to their house for the night, if he wanted to. He had squeezed Niamh's hand tightly when they had all climbed into the car and for the first time in weeks she realised the feeling that was now bubbling away inside her was hope. That squeeze of her hand said more than words ever could. He was undone. Paul, who had been like a bear with a sore head – just as she had been like a bear with a sore head herself – was mellowing. Of course he didn't want to see Jodie in pain. It was clear to him now that she needed her dad and his support. And that soon there would be another person who needed him. Niamh had no doubt that was why there was a shake in his voice and a glimmer of tears in his eyes.

Once he'd had time to compose himself, Paul had switched into super-dad mode. He stopped at the McDonald's drive-thru on the way home, insisting that both Jodie and Adam needed to eat something. And no, it didn't matter that neither were hungry. They needed food. The baby needed food. Yes, he may have panic ordered much too much food including, for some bizarre reason, two Happy Meals. But he'd been right. Both Jodie and Adam had eaten when they got back to the house – both going straight for the Happy Meals. Then he had set out again, his body fizzing with unspent emotion, coming back half an hour later with ice cream, chocolate and a bunch of slightly wilted garage-forecourt flowers. 'They were the best I could do on a Sunday night,' he'd told Niamh as she'd tried to make them look presentable in one of their vases. 'I should've got her flowers before. We should've celebrated this baby before. Imagine it had been gone and we'd not showed it our love.'

'It's okay to have mixed feelings,' she'd told him. 'I have so many. Less now, maybe, that I've seen the wee mite wriggle on the screen.'

'You have mixed feelings?' he'd asked, genuinely surprised. Niamh had once again wondered how men can so often be so bad at reading the feelings of their lifelong partners.

'Of course I do. I've told you that I'm concerned about their age and how we'll manage with a baby in the house. Admittedly there's a lot I have kept to myself,' she conceded. 'Because ultimately when it comes to this situation, it's not our decision to make. It never was. Being annoyed with Jodie was never going to change that and, to be honest, if us being annoyed was the reason she decided to end the pregnancy I'd not be much of a fan of us anyway.'

He looked at her, a little shamefaced. 'I just wanted more for her.'

'This isn't the 1800s, or even the 1960s or 1970s. There is no reason that she can't have more!' Niamh had said. 'The timescale may change, or she might take a different route, but it's not the end of the world.'

'I suppose,' he said. 'There's no reason she can't still build her career and go on to have the teaching position of her dreams. Just like her mum.'

That's when Niamh's voice had cracked. 'I think I need to talk to you about that,' she said.

He'd been so confused as she'd started to outline just how she felt about teaching at the moment. How she felt she was losing herself. Losing her love for the classroom. Losing her love for... well... everything, and she didn't know how to cope with it all.

'You should've told me sooner,' he said, pulling her into a tight embrace.

'You were being a bit of a grumpy shite,' she sniffed through her tears. 'I was afraid to open my mouth.'

'I'm so sorry,' he said. 'I know I've been a bit out of sorts.'

She waited for him to tell her that she was a grumpy shite too, but he didn't. She'd like to think this was because she really hadn't been and she was just being extra hard on herself. But of course, she knew she had been on a hair trigger lately. So she apologised anyway.

And for the first time in weeks, she made sure to still be awake when he came to bed because she so desperately needed to feel his arms around her.

36

THESE ARMS OF MINE

Becca

I'm stuck to the sofa, exhaustion having taken over. Between the weekend away and the drama at the hospital, I am completely, and totally, worn out.

I know I should haul myself up, go and wash my face, brush my teeth and slip into my pyjamas and my bed, but my body does not want to comply. So I sit with Daniel and we stare at the cold embers of the fire together, his head resting on my lap.

At least, I think, at least it is a happy kind of exhausted. A relieved kind. I can still hear the thump thump of that little heartbeat that promised so much.

My finger is hovering over my phone as I try to think of what message I could possibly send to Adam to let him know how much I love him and how proud I am of how he supported Jodie this evening. I saw the fear in his face. I knew what was running through his mind, but he had shown maturity and compassion and had done himself proud. My boy – now a man, I realise – is growing up.

My doorbell rings – the noise making both Daniel and me jump. Unlike Daniel, however, I don't immediately break into a volley of excited barks in response. It's almost eleven and no one ever calls to my house at this time. Ever. Unless there is some sort of awful emergency. My heart plummets once again, as my brain scans for all possible awful outcomes to find the one I will worry about most until I'm brave enough to open the door and see who it is. I know it can't be Adam or Jodie. I know they are safe and sleeping at Niamh's.

Saul is my first thought. Because Saul is a walking disaster. The doctors in A&E used to joke they'd name a bay after him as he was such a frequent flier. Sprained ankles, broken fingers, on one particularly memorable occasion an arm fractured in three places due to his belief he could perform stunts on his BMX without any practice. But no, I remind myself, Saul has just messaged me and he is fine.

Which brings me swiftly to my biggest, most enduring worry – that something has happened to my mother. Could it be the police at my door? Or my brother Ruairi, pale faced and bearing grim tidings? Could it even be Mrs Bishop, who has zipped over here in an Uber to break some awful news?

That, I think, as I get up to walk through to the hall, would just take the bloody biscuit. Just as I find a sense of inner calm and purpose, something huge would come snowballing into my life to knock me for six. But not in one clean sweep, of course. That would be too easy. This would come in stages – one strike just strong enough to almost but not quite knock me off my feet followed by a dirty big hallion of a strike that would floor me like no other. Please God, I beg, please let my mother be okay.

A big part of me wants to ignore the door. I could pretend I didn't hear it ring. Or tell myself it was just a hallucination. Surely then whatever was waiting for me on the other side would take the hint and simply go away. I'll go to bed – since I'm already up on my feet I might as well – and when I wake in the morning it will be like *The Wizard of Oz* and today will just have been a dream.

Maybe I'll be back in the yurt and I can decide to swim in the sea after all and that will change everything. (I've no idea why it would change anything, let alone everything, but I'm happy to cling on to whatever hope I can at this stage, if we're being real.)

There's a shadow of a person through the glass at the side of the door. It's definitely too big to be Mrs Bishop. She's all of five foot on a good day and bird-like in physique. This figure is tall and broad. Definitely man-like. Should I be scared? What if this is some psychopathic serial killer hunting his next victim? Well, God love him if it is, I think. Because I could probably use someone to take out all my frustration and hurt on. This mother-fudger won't know what's hit him.

I'm just getting ready to grab the lamp from the hall table to act as a makeshift weapon when the bell rings again, Daniel barks again and I feel my blood pressure start to skyrocket. I do not need this now.

I'm on the very, very verge of going full Hulk when the figure behind the door calls out and I can hear a muffled, yet familiar, voice.

'Becs! It's only me. Let me in, will you, it's bloody Baltic out here!'

Conal.

Conal is here.

'I heard about what happened with Adam and Jodie. I wanted to check on you,' he calls.

Laura, who I had sent a garbled voice note to as I left the hospital, must've told him. I would, of course, have told him myself but Laura was the first person who came to mind. It was only natural for me to call my best friend.

Putting the lamp down, relieved I won't have to use it to batter the head off a random serial killer, I open the door and there stands this handsome, caring man with an expression of sympathy so genuine that my resolve finally falters and I disintegrate into a mess of tears as he wraps his arms around me and pulls me in tight for a hug.

I let him hold me and feel him kiss the top of my head softly.

'You must've got an awful fright. All of you.'

I nod, allowing him to comfort me. Although ultimately the news had been good, I'd had a moment of feeling so very sorry for myself as we'd left the hospital. Paul had hurried to hug Jodie and then wrap his arms around Niamh. Adam had stayed almost attached to his girlfriend and I had found myself standing alone, desperate for a hug – desperate for someone to share this news with. It was too late to call my mother – who is of the very, very firm belief that only sociopaths call people after nine at night. I didn't know if Conal and I were at the stage in which we could call each other in a crisis yet and very obviously I was not going to call Simon. So I'd sent a voice note to Laura and walked back to my car alone, hands thrust into my pockets, like the saddo I am.

Or was.

It might not seem like much to some people. He is doing nothing more, after all, than hugging me and letting me cry, as we stand on my doorstep with the bitter chill of the January night swirling around us, but it feels in this moment as if he is doing everything.

He is letting me feel my feelings without judgement or comment. He isn't trying to minimise the multitude of emotions running through my body. He is caring for me – in a way that no man has in over a decade, if not longer. Simon was never really the hold-you-while-you-cry kind of a person. He tried, but he tended to get a little embarrassed by shows of emotion, especially any on a scale as big as this.

I can feel Conal sway just slightly, as if he is rocking me to soothe me. And I'm back in the workshop as those feelings of empowerment and safety rose up in me, and I'm back in my boys' nursery as I rocked them to sleep and 'The Blower's Daughter' played again and I am not embarrassed. I am not urging myself to get it together in front of this man. I am not worried that he will see me, and judge me, as an emotional woman. I'm not concerned he might think I'm overreacting. That I have nothing to cry about.

I am just feeling my feelings and I know with this man – this man who teased me relentlessly through my teenage years – I am safe.

He continues to hold me, and I breathe in the warm scent of him, revelling in the warmth of his body against mine. When the worst of my sobs have subsided, he pulls me just a little closer.

'Becs,' he says, and I can feel his breath on my ear. 'Can we go inside now? It's bloody freezing!'

That's when I look up at him and see his warm caring face looking back me. I take a step back and another, and he follows me into the house, but we don't take our eyes off each other.

He kicks the front door closed behind him, and to be honest, if I wasn't absolutely emotionally drained in this very second, it would be the sexiest thing I've ever seen. Or at least it would be until he cradles my face in his hands and tips my head up towards his.

'I'm so glad everything is okay. I'm so glad you're okay,' he says before bringing his lips to mine. It's a kiss that speaks a thousand words. Words that mean so much more than 'I want to have sex with you very much right now thank you very much'. It's a kiss that makes me believe, to my very core, that when he says he's glad I'm okay, he means it with every cell in his body.

As he pulls back, and drops his hands, and leads me back through the living room where Daniel is patiently waiting for some attention, the only thing I can think of to say is, 'You're not supposed to be the iceberg. I am.'

* * *

For a moment, when I wake up, I am confused. Daniel is staring at me, wide-eyed, from where he stands beside my bed. And yet I can feel that I am not alone *in* my bed. There is definitely something – someone – in the space Daniel normally tries to commandeer until I chase him off into his dog bed.

Daniel doesn't seem too distressed by the presence of someone other than me in the room. This isn't necessarily reassuring. Daniel the Spaniel is easily bought. A slice of ham, a Bonio or a piece of chicken and he would let the devil himself get up close and personal with his nearest and dearest.

As the memories of the last twenty-four hours start to form in my mind, I realise it's not likely to be a ham-toting serial killer but more likely to be Conal.

Conal, who arrived late last night and had listened as I talked, who had asked to see the photo I'd taken of the ultrasound screen. Who had listened when I said I had to accept I am going to be a granny. Who laughed uproariously when I told him how Laura had mentioned his mother had referred to herself as a GILF.

'God, I miss her,' he'd said when he stopped laughing.

'She was an incredible woman.'

'There are a lot of those about,' he said, his smile shy and soft.

We'd talked until the small hours, cuddled on the sofa, until we were both yawning. So I invited him to stay over.

No. It was not about sex. We did not have sex. We both seemed to understand that we were tired. I was emotionally wrung out. We were not at our best. It was a relief, to be honest, because my legs are hairy, I need a shower and I am most definitely not at my most alluring.

We just held each other and slept. Until now, when I sense his presence in my bed.

'Morning, Becs,' he says, his voice a little croaky and tired. 'Did you sleep?'

'I did. Surprisingly well, in fact. Thank you,' I say, reaching for my phone on the nightstand to check the time. It's still dark outside but given that it's January that could mean anything up until about half eight. It is, in fact, just after half seven and Daniel's paw on the bed and mournful look of 'Please let me out into the garden now before I pee on your deep pile' makes me grateful I didn't sleep beyond that.

'I need to let the dog out,' I say, pulling myself up to sitting.

Both Conal and I are still fully dressed. We did at least take our shoes off though. I think by the time we had climbed the stairs, I was just too exhausted to do anything more than the very, very bare minimum. God only knows how rank my morning breath is, or how awful my face looks. It will be a mess of yesterday's make-up, destroyed by a night's sleep and a few hours' crying before that. My mouth is like a furry boot even though no alcohol whatsoever was consumed and I can feel my pores screaming for hydration.

I don't turn to look at Conal as I get out of bed and head straight for the door to bring Daniel downstairs. I can nip into the bathroom when I come back up, have a quick freshen up and walk back into the room looking less bog witch and more 'this is a woman I want to have a relationship with'.

'Bloody dogs,' I hear Conal tease. 'Always getting in the way of true love.'

My heart starts at the mention of the L word, which is frankly ridiculous. I know this is just an expression and there is no way there is any love to speak of yet. Well… not that kind of love anyway. I suppose I *sort of* love him and always have because he's the brother of one of my best friends and we used to hang out together back in the day. But that's not the same as *love* love. You know, the big 'in *love*'. It's much too early for any declarations as substantial as that and certainly not in relation to a dog and their need for a morning pee and poo.

My head knows all this to be true but my heart is clearly still on emotional high alert and is not behaving. Maybe because while my heart feels it is too early for *love* love, it knows that it's not too early for icebergs. And isn't that exactly what Conal had done by showing up last night? He'd been my very own iceberg.

The bitter cold of last night has turned to a persistent and dirty fall of rain – the kind that will keep the sky extra dark and makes everything look as if it is being viewed through a murky filter. Heavy splats of rain pepper the patio as Daniel sniffs around for a place to wee in much the same fashion a sommelier sniffs a fine vintage.

Why we have to go through this rigmarole is beyond me. Both Daniel and I know he will eventually take his spot by the fence, arse pointed towards next door's garden and their yappy wee shite of a dog.

There's no message from Adam on my phone. I hope he is still sleeping. I hope both he and Jodie had a restful night. I hope Niamh and Paul had a chance to talk through all of their worries.

I hope everyone feels just as content with their lot as I do this morning.

'He's a good sort, isn't he?' I say to Daniel, who is staring at me, unblinkingly, as he squats.

'I'd like to think so,' I hear Conal say from directly behind me. Of course, I immediately startle before remembering my current bog witch appearance. He was not supposed to come down the stairs. He was supposed to wait there in the bed while I threw some water on my face and did a world-record-breaking, dentist-defying tooth-brushing session. He was not supposed to see me big-upping him to the dog. I am mortified.

'Don't look at me,' I squeak, immediately covering my face with my hands.

'What are you on about?' he asks, and I can hear the amusement in his voice.

'Seriously!' I say. 'It won't end well. I'm like Medusa at the minute. One glance at me in my current state and you will turn to stone, or turn to run or something…'

I push past him, leaving Daniel to finish his morning ablutions without me, and straight back upstairs and into the bathroom where I lock the door and assess the damage.

I look… and there is no other way to say this… old. Old and tired. My skin is blotchy, and my eyes bloodshot. My hair has taken on a life of its own. I immediately start picking myself apart with no compassion for the woman who has gone through a traumatic experience. It's so easy to let that little voice in, I realise. I've known her my whole life, after all. She's familiar. A constant. She even sounds like me, so who am I to tell this negative Nelly in my own head to go and – to use a phrase Niamh once delighted us with – 'ride her hand'. It's a colourful one, and not for polite company, but sometimes it is the only way to say it.

I take a deep breath.

'Becs, I'm going to nip out. Get some coffee and croissants from that bakery on Ivy Lane for breakfast,' I hear Conal call. 'I'm taking Daniel with me for the walk. Be back in half an hour.'

Immediately I go to tell him that he doesn't need to take my dog out for a walk, and he absolutely does not need to go and get fancy coffee or lovely, flaky croissants that make my mouth water. I go to tell him he doesn't need to bother doing that for me.

But I stop.

I stop and look again in the mirror at the old, tired face. I take a deep breath, and call, 'Thank you.' And I smile as I hear the front door close behind him. He doesn't need to do all those things for me. But he wants to. Because he's a good man.

I start the shower running, turning the water up as hot as I can tolerate, and before the bathroom mirror steams up I look at myself again.

Instead of picking apart my face, and my body as I undress, I speak the same words of kindness that had been spoken to us at the body positivity session. Our faces, and our bodies, are not only valuable in our youth. Our beauty does not lie only in youth, and positive times and smiling when you feel like crying. Each line, each wrinkle, each tiny red pinprick of my bloodshot eyes is testament to my life, my experience, the people I love and how hard I love them. They are testament to a person who has value whether twenty-four, forty-four or a hundred and four. Who are we to say that beauty is only a smooth face, adorned with make-up, or a perfect, stretch-mark-free body, free of scars?

My body, and my face, is my journey.

And to my surprise, as I step into the shower and let the water pummel me awake, I do not even want to throw up in my mouth at using the phrase 'my journey'.

I use my good shower gel and my favourite scented shampoo. I go all out and put both serum and moisturiser on my face as I dry off. I'd like to say I was a serum and moisturiser every day kind of a woman, but I'd be lying.

I spray myself with perfume – all over and not just on my pulse points – and I dress in one of my favourite long jersey dresses and some coloured tights. I brush my hair through but leave it to dry naturally, and by the time all that is done and I'm walking down the stairs, Conal returns with two cups of coffee and a bag of the freshest-smelling pastries in the world.

'Definitely less Medusa-like,' he says with a smile when he sees me. 'Although if I was less of a gentleman, I'd make some joke about you being even more likely to turn me... or parts of me... to stone now...'

Something flips inside me. I'm not initially sure what it is. It's an odd sensation, but not a bad one. In fact, if anything, it's quite pleasurable. I look at him, and it happens again. A clenching. A turning over. A turning on.

I realise, as my face grows hotter still, my libido is like an old engine. It may have seized up through lack of use but it seems that turning the ignition a few times, and having patience, means it's only a matter of time before it will be purring again.

Dear God, I think, as he steps towards me, setting the coffee and pastries down on the hall table. This is what *longing* feels like. What desire feels like. Real desire and not just the strange attraction I sometimes feel for Ian the paramedic in *Casualty*.

I want to take this man by the hand and lead him back upstairs, leaving Daniel to his own devices locked in the living room, while I have unabashed, passionate, incredible sex.

Conal is closer to me now. His mouth just inches from mine. I can feel the heat of his body, sure that he must feel the heat of mine coming, which is positively pulsing off me in waves. It's my turn to reach up and place my hand against his cheek, revelling in the roughness of his unshaven face. Forget Ian the paramedic.

Not even David Duchovny could have me feeling as feral as I am right now.

'Rebecca,' he half whispers, half moans as his lips close in on mine and... now I finally know what it means to feel utterly undone. My body feels charged with electricity – with the desire to be touched.

My lips tingle as his brush against mine and all I want is to keep kissing this man, long and hard and deep and—

A volley of barks, loud enough to wake the dead, and most certainly loud enough to pull Conal and me apart from each other, makes me jump, which results in an unfortunate and definitely not sexy head-butting incident.

Daniel whizzes past us, his tail whipping our legs as it wags at hyperspeed. Before we know it, he is at the door, jumping up and scrabbling his claws against the woodwork, his barks segueing into pitiful whining.

'Becs!' I hear Laura call. 'Is Conal there? Only I have Lazlo and I—'

I open the door, after giving Conal just enough time to grab the coffees and pastries and dash through to the kitchen, where he will have the chance to regain his composure.

'I'm so sorry,' she says, as Daniel and Lazlo greet each other as if they have been lifelong besties. Laura pulls me into a hug. 'It's just, I have to go to work and I can't leave Lazlo home alone because he will shite somewhere and Aidan will not be happy. But never mind that, how are you? How is Adam? And Jodie?'

'Don't worry about it,' I reply. 'Adam and Jodie are fine, as far as I know. Jodie just has to make sure to take things easy for a bit. Conal's here. He's just getting coffee.' I wonder if she can tell just by looking at me that she has interrupted something that could've been truly earth-shatteringly, body-shockingly amazing.

'I thought he might have stayed the night, but more about that later...' she says with a raised eyebrow, and I almost want to tell her to pull that goddamned eyebrow back down because nothing has happened thanks to some spectacularly timed cock-blocking on her part.

Just then Conal reappears, looking distinctly less flustered than when I had last seen him.

'Sis,' he says. 'Thanks so much for minding Lazlo. You're a star.'

'Sure, I know. I'm the very best. You'd do well to remember that,' Laura says with a smile, and leans across to kiss him on the cheek. 'Hurt her and I *will* break you,' she whispers, not too quietly.

'I really have no plans to,' he says as she turns to leave.

Closing the door behind her, I haven't the chance to gather my thoughts before the two dogs bolt for the pair of us, determined that now is a time to play games of their choosing – and we are absolutely not going back to the one we had come painfully close to playing ourselves.

37

MITTENS ARE A BAD CHOICE FOR ADULTS

You would think writing this article would be easy. I'd had a fabulous time at the weekend. I had spent ages planning exactly what I wanted to say and how I wanted to say it. But I had not accounted for my attention span being completely banjaxed.

I am still, exceptionally, very tired. But also a little blissed out. But also a bit stressed about the article. But also unable to stop thinking about the jellybean and all the changes it will bring. For the first time in ten years, I don't know what my future looks like. I am not only out of my comfort zone, I have moved to the neigh-bouring town and the road back is closed.

It's exactly what Becki (with an i), aged sixteen, would want. She'd be cheering me on. She might be absolutely stunned that I'd snogged Conal O'Hagan last night, but I think in a good way. She thought forty-six was as old as the hills anyway, so maybe she wouldn't be too horrified by my impending granny-dom. Overall, I like to think she'd be telling me I was 'all that, and a bag of chips' à la Ricki Lake's chat show in 1995.

I message Niamh to check in on her, and to my surprise she

calls me back. She sounds as tired as I feel and I'm delighted that she has, at least, taken the day off work.

'I might even take the rest of the week,' she says. 'The head will go mad, but *my head* will go mad if I don't take some time to try and sort it out. This past weekend made me realise how much I need to do something... I had a big chat with Paul last night. About everything. And I can't keep going on just thinking it will all sort itself out.'

'Sweetheart, I'm here for you. Okay. Whatever you need. I agree, you can't keep going the way things are. Something has to give. I don't want it to be you.'

'Oh, I'm going nowhere,' she says. 'I've a grandchild to prepare for. We've some interesting times ahead, Becs. I don't intend on being so strung out from work, or menopause or whatever that I miss it. Last night made me realise that.'

I smile. I'm glad to hear that she has some of her fighting spirit back, and that this time she is fighting against her demons as opposed to with her friends, or her husband.

'How is Paul about it all now?' I ask.

'Well, I think last night was a wake-up call for him too. We don't have the rose-tinted glasses on or anything, but if this baby is determined to hang on in there and get here safely then, let me tell you, I'm going to do whatever it takes to support it, and love it.'

'Me too,' I say, knowing full well there will be bridges to cross and obstacles to overcome but deciding that I will cross them as and when I need to and not any sooner. 'How are Adam and Jodie this morning? Has Jodie had any more bleeding?'

'I heard them up and about at about six. Making tea, I think. But they disappeared back into Jodie's room and there's not a noise coming from there. I'm just going to let them sleep. They've had a fright, and they've heard their baby's heartbeat. That's a lot to process.'

'It definitely is,' I say.

'Right!' Niamh says, and I can hear the creak of a chair as she stands up. 'Look, Becs, I'm going to go because I want to call the doctors and get an appointment for myself about my HRT and my godawful mood. I don't have to keep dealing with that.'

'You're right. You absolutely don't. There will be other options. Other doses. You won't know yourself when the urge to murder your nearest and dearest dies down a bit.'

'And you have to get on with your work! Enough chitter chatter, Ms Burnside. There are articles for glossy magazines to write. Let's show Ms Carrie Bradshaw how it's really done, *Derry Girls* style.'

She's right, of course, I cannot put it off. I need it to be fresh in my mind, and I want to impress the socks clean off Grace. However, Daniel is looking up at me, his head cocked to one side, as if he can read my thoughts and thinks nothing of offering a dog-focused solution.

'Okay,' I say. 'Let me get some shoes on.'

If there is one thing I have learned in all my years on this earth it is that one way to jolt myself back into a creative mindset is to take the dog out for a walk – preferably somewhere with a minimal amount of other people around and a maximum amount of nature in whatever form it chooses to take. Even if that involves the aforementioned persistent, dirty fat fall of rain.

I can hear my mother's voice echoing in my ear. 'You're not made of sugar and you won't melt.' I've always thought that to be quite a nonsense phrase. I have never suggested that I am made of sugar and my fear is not melting. It's getting drenched from the top of my head to the soggy tips of my toes. That the rain battering down on me will not be as relaxing as a nice, hot shower is what makes it even less appealing. But still, my mother's voice, and her ability to be right in almost every situation, has me putting on a pair of thick woolly socks over my tights before forcing my now fatter feet into my welly boots. I tell myself they're cool welly boots because they have a leopard-print design, but there is something about wearing wellies that always makes me feel as if I'm six and about to tramp through the snow to school.

Spotting the boots, Daniel takes a mad dose of the zoomies and darts around the downstairs of the house with more energy than the average ten-year-old dog has. There's no backing out of this now. Not when I've already given Daniel more than enough reasons to huff with me over the past few days.

Soon I am doing my very best not to slip on the carpeting of leaves and mud that covers the woods close to our home, while Daniel is break-necking it through the trees and bushes like an all-terrain vehicle.

Trying not to fall flat on my arse is at least distracting me from replaying that almost epic snog to end all snogs, or remembering how deep Conal's voice had sounded as he moved close to me, or how dark his eyes were.

I feel the key turn in the ignition of what was my libido again. It is definitely, without a doubt, coming back to life.

My phone rings and I delve into my pocket, trying to get a grip of it even though I am wearing my thickest, warmest mittens. It's not an easy task but I manage to see that it is Adam calling before it slips from my hands and lands face down in a puddle of very muddy water.

'Fuck,' I say, all ability to replace the bad F word with fudge instead gone. 'Fuckity fuck!' I say again, immediately reaching for my phone, which of course completely saturates my heavy woollen mittens but ultimately does nothing to actually retrieve the phone because these mittens clearly repel anything with a smooth surface. At least, I think, at least it is still ringing, but no sooner has the thought left my head than it stops and I don't think it's because Adam has hung up.

I pull the mittens off, thrusting my hands into the icy, murky water and retrieving one very wet, very dead iPhone. I think this might just be beyond the help of a bowl of rice and twelve hours in the airing cupboard.

Damn it. I don't want Adam to think I'm ignoring him but obviously I have no way of getting hold of him, here and now, and the rain is still coming down in merciless sheets. 'Daniel!' I yell, hoping that he will sense the urgency in my voice and get his furry arse back so we can get back to the car and I can drive directly to Niamh's – and to Adam.

But this is the first walk I have taken Daniel on in three days and so he sees this as an absolute green light to run as far and as fast as his furry little legs can carry him. That there is added mud, squirrels, rabbits and no doubt assorted hallucinogenic fungi is all just a bonus. I should have known this was a bad idea, today of all days.

'Daniel!' I call again, my call now definitely more high-pitched fishwife-like than before. 'Daniel! Come here now! Come on! Be a good boy!'

I just want to get him back on the lead and get out of here but Mister the Spaniel clearly has other ideas. I will myself to keep my cool. I will not become the mad woman of the woods who wanders around in the rain screaming at animals.

Then again, maybe it would just be another step on my path to becoming a fully feral crone and embracing my witchy powers.

If only, I think, I really could embrace witchy powers. If only I had the power to perform spells that could make a real difference.

That could summon Daniel to my side. Or un-fudge my phone. Or make Niamh feel less all at sea.

I call Daniel again, willing him to just come when called. I don't like that Adam has called me and I haven't been able to answer. The doctor's words from last night are still in my mind. We're not out of the woods yet.

Which is ironic because neither am I and I don't want to walk further into them, but I know that's the direction in which Daniel ran. I chide myself for not keeping him on his lead, but this is one of a handful of places where he can actually run free and not have to be on his very, very best behaviour. This is one of the few places where he can go 'full dog' and do the things dogs are meant to do, and I can hardly blame him for wanting to enjoy every last second of it and then some. I know this is what he does when we come here. I know that he runs off and explores until he gets rid of that initial burst of energy born of total freedom and returns to tramp by my side, absolutely delighted with himself.

I just have to have patience, I think. He will come back. And I will get to Adam as quickly as I possibly can. No amount of anxiety or getting stressed about it is going to make it happen any quicker. I need to realise that I am not always in control of how life plays out but only how I react to it.

I breathe in, remembering Peggy's calming words at the retreat, and I re-centre myself. What good will I be showing up for Adam soaked to the skin, covered in mud and with no voice from screeching my way through the woods? Okay, I tell myself, as I turn and start retracing my steps, calling in a calm voice for Daniel. You know how these things go. Adam is fine. Jodie is fine. The baby is fine. Daniel will show up. Everything will work out because it always does. Maybe not in the way we initially hoped – hasn't my entire life proved that beyond a reasonable doubt – but it still works out and we learn to cope with it.

If, I think, I could write a letter to sixteen-year-old Becki (with an 'i') I'd tell her just that. If only time capsules were really multi-dimensional, time-travelling tools, I'd write all this down and pop it back in the shoebox that's currently in my sideboard, and tell her that no matter our plans, or dreams, life will do its own damn thing.

That, I realise, as I hear four muddy paws splashing and sploshing towards me along with the heavy panting of a deliriously happy dog, is how I need to write this piece for Grace. It's how I can absolutely hook her, because I know – or suspect at least – that I am not the only person to think and feel this way.

The retreat has taught me that. Last night has taught me that. Conal has too. None of us can really expect to reach our forties unscarred by life. That's not how the world works. So instead, we have to try and figure out how to navigate it all – and especially how to navigate the detours and plot twists.

'Let's go and get Adam,' I say, and Daniel trots very nicely alongside me as we head back to the car.

38

THE GOOD, THE BAD AND THE HONEST-TO-GOD
TRUTH

To my immense relief, Adam was only calling to ask if I could pick him up and bring him home. There have been no further crises. Please God there will continue to be no further crises.

I would've used picking him up as an opportunity to see Niamh in person and give her a big, reassuring hug but it seemed that she and Paul had gone out for lunch. That has to be a good thing, doesn't it? That they are spending time, just the two of them, together.

I'm telling myself it absolutely has to mean that and not something sinister as we get home. On arrival, Adam becomes my favourite child simply by being here and taking a very muddy Daniel through to the bathroom to get washed.

While I listen to him tell Daniel to be a good boy and behave himself, and reassure the dog that he's being very brave, I get a tiny little idea of what he might be like as a father. Firm yet gentle. Loving and intuitive. He might be so very young, and it might only seem like five minutes ago that he was a little boy himself, but he has shown me in these last weeks, and especially in the last twenty-four hours, just how mature and responsible he can be.

I let those fuzzy feelings warm my heart as I get ready for my second shower of the day. It is, after all, not only Daniel who has come home from the walk in the woods mucked to the eyeballs and shivering with cold.

I need to warm up, feel refreshed and be comfortable and then I absolutely will start to write. Or so I promise myself.

An hour later and I'm looking like a bag lady, but a comfortable and clean bag lady, dressed in some jogging bottoms and my favourite 'Tired and Needy' oversized hoodie (with thumb holes!). The thick woolly socks and Crocs round the look off nicely.

I come downstairs to find that Adam has lit the fire, and Daniel is now dozing peacefully in front of it. Adam has also made me a cup of tea and a sandwich and announces he is going to have a bath himself.

'When I'm done, I think it's about time I started looking at flights back to Manchester and sort things out there,' he says. 'I'm not really happy about leaving Jodie, but at the same time I have to make sure to get my qualifications, don't I? If I'm going to be a dad. I need to have my shit together.'

He gives me a kiss on the cheek and I watch him as he leaves the room. So much is changing, so fast. I'll miss him when he goes back to college, but I'll also continue to be increasingly proud of him. There are many nineteen-year-old boys who would run for the hills faced with their girlfriend's unexpected pregnancy. God knows there are many fully grown men who struggle to cope with not being the centre of attention any more in a relationship.

Once I can hear the bath running upstairs, I bring my tea and sandwich through to the living room and switch my computer on, only to be bombarded with a whole host of emails – which of course I've not seen because my phone has been enjoying a mud bath.

There are several from the agency that oversees my B2B freelance assignments, listing new opportunities and also updating me on some of my existing clients and their next publication. The requests are in for interviews with a CEO, several listicles. Two are serious: on career progression, and on ways to make business customers trust your brand. The other is light-hearted with a Valentine's Day/office romance theme which is a car crash waiting to happen. No HR manager in any company is going to let that through. I flag that to the client and ask for HR approval – which I know will be denied – and go back to reading my emails.

Then I spot an email from Grace which of course I immediately click into. Please God she won't be getting in touch to tell me that Peggy thought I was awful, or that Peggy has been found out to be an actual cult leader and the whole article is no longer needed. And actually, while she's at it, she made a huge mistake and she doesn't actually need anyone else writing for her magazine and if she's being honest she doesn't really like me anyway – and never did. Not even at school. And she was only pretending to like me so she could wreak her revenge for something awful I did to her when we were teenagers which I can't even remember anyway...

I may, of course, just be spiralling. Still, it's with a degree of trepidation that I read what she has to say.

Hey Rebecca,

I hope you had a super weekend at the retreat. I've heard it was a great success – can't wait to hear your take on it. Are you okay to get me the copy over ASAP – those pesky deadlines are already becoming a headache.

Oh, and we need some photos. Did you take any with your

friends that they'd be happy to share? I've one of our staffers down at the site getting snaps of the accommodation and the setting, and Peggy of course. So it's just for a bit of extra colour.

But we will need an official byline shot from you, so can you let me know your availability for this week and I can send a snapper over to grab a pic, or you can call into the office if that's easier.

This isn't a paid promotion, so don't be afraid to be completely honest and if you can inject some of that great humour of yours into it then even better.

About a thousand words?

Can't wait to read it! We'll have to get a good chat about it all too.

Talk soon,

G

Oh, God, she sounds very enthusiastic. I hope I don't disappoint her. There's nothing quite like being told to be funny to absolutely kick your ability to be funny directly up the hole.

But then I remember my walk in the woods, and my realisation that it doesn't have to be *perfect*. I don't have to be perfect. I don't have to be anyone I'm not already. Grace has put me on this assignment based on material of mine she has already read. Based on my ability to be honest. Isn't that more than enough? Isn't that what all this is about in the first place – us being honest with each other? The good, the bad, the absolutely humiliating and the ugly?

I want sixteen-year-old girls to write letters to their older selves having a proper idea of what life can be like when you're older. Even some of the tough times. I don't want them to worry about ageing or needing to fall in love to be whole. I don't want them thinking their worth should be measured by how skinny they are, or how much money they have in the bank. Life is about so much more. This past weekend, including hearing jellybean's heartbeat, has taught me that in spades.

I think of my boy upstairs, my other son in England and how their lives will change. When Adam changes his course and comes home it will be the first time they've lived independently of each other. I think of my mum in the house she now lives in alone crocheting cardigans for a baby who I think will help heal the very depths of her grief over Dad. I think of Deirdre, who has been so lonely but who has hopefully found new friends. I think of my beautiful Niamh, who is in pain but who is finally, finally, putting herself first. Of Laura, who is finding comfort in the universe and the powers beyond our understanding to cope with her loss.

And I think of Conal. The man who arrived at my house at eleven last night because he sensed I needed a hug and who offered that hug without expectation. The man who made my morning easier by taking Daniel out for his early-morning wee, before going to fetch breakfast. How this man has made me feel physical sensations I have not felt in a very, very long time, and all without so much as laying a finger on me.

When I think of all that – all that mess and hope and love – I know that I've got this. I know that in writing about this weekend I will also be writing about the honest side of being middle-aged, menopausal and ever so slightly mad.

I click into Microsoft Word to open a new document and I start to write.

When I was sixteen years old, I thought I knew it all…

39

ALL GROWN UP

It's dark again by the time I lift my head, having lost myself in my writing for the afternoon. My attention is only shifted back into the here and now by the arrival of Adam back in the living room looking well rested.

'Did you sleep well?' I ask.

He nods in response. 'I did. I don't think I realised how tired I was.'

'You hungry?'

He shakes his head. 'Not especially.'

'I can make you something? Or order you a pizza or the like? Anything you want.' I want desperately to spoil him, knowing that most likely, in a few days, he will be beyond my spoiling for a while.

'Nah, I'm good. Thanks, Mum. Maybe later.' He sits down beside me and glances at my computer screen.

'I'm just finishing up,' I tell him, clicking on the save button.

'Is that your article for the magazine?'

'Sure is. Grace needs it ASAP or I'd put it to the side until after you're gone.'

'You would not!' Adam says, defiantly. 'This is what you've wanted to do forever and you're going to do it. I'd not let you use me as an excuse to sabotage this.'

It stuns me momentarily to realise he recognises that I'm prone to self-sabotage. And there was me thinking I was hiding all my toxic traits from my children all these years. I'm not sure I'm awfully happy about having my 'Perfect Mammy' crown tilted a bit.

'Don't look at me that way,' he says, and I realise I clearly have been unable to hide my emotions from my face. 'I love you to the ends of the earth, Mum, but if you think I haven't noticed how you're not one for taking chances then you're very, very wrong.'

'I... well... I...' I stutter. I want to tell him that it's not always easy to take chances when you are raising children on your own, but I stop myself. Now is not the time to put the fear of God in him about how having children will change his life – whether with Jodie, or alone. And it's not like it's his or Saul's fault that I ended up parenting them on my own. I made my choices. As the boys would say – 'that's a me problem'. I will not become one of those mothers who blames her children for how her life panned out differently than how she hoped, because truth be told, if I had to do it all over again, I can't say I'd do anything different.

'I-I-I nothing!' Adam says, mocking me, but in a kind-hearted way. 'Mum, you've said it yourself. This is your chance now and you have to run with it. No skiving off just because I'm home for a couple of extra days. You do more than enough for me, and besides, I'll probably be spending a lot of time with Jodie.'

'You really like her, don't you?'

'Yeah,' he says shyly as Daniel trots over to him, selflessly offering himself up to be petted. 'I really like her. A lot. She's just the best, Mum. Funny and smart and gorgeous. I am definitely punching.' There's a small, shy smile on his face.

'Oh, love, you're funny, smart and gorgeous too. I don't think either of you are punching. I think you make a great pair. And what I have seen, before the pregnancy test, and since, is a young woman who clearly really, really likes you too. I've seen the way she looks at you, pet. I see the way you are with each other. You just have to do your very best to hang on to that. Even when things are tougher.'

'I know,' he says. 'That's what I plan to do. I want to be the person she needs. I want to be the dad our baby needs. I don't want to ever walk away from my child.'

There is an unspoken 'like my dad walked away from me' that I feel like a stab to the heart. Guilt that I played a part in my marriage breaking down isn't always easy to let go of, even if, ultimately, neither of us were the bad guys.

'Then be the dad your baby needs. Even if, God forbid, you and Jodie break up tomorrow...' He looks horrified, but I keep talking. '...you can still be a good dad – a great dad, in fact – without living in the same house. Look, I know that your dad was... is... problematic and not always there for you two the way you wanted or deserved, but that doesn't mean the same has to be true of you. You can break the mould. You can be a good father no matter what.'

'I'm going to do my very best,' he says.

'That's all anyone can ask for,' I tell him. 'So look, while we're here, let's have a look at flights to get you back to Manchester before Saul wrecks the place.'

'He'll be okay without me, you know, Mum,' Adam says. 'I know he can be a bit of an eejit but he knows what he's doing. He'll manage. We have good friends there. It will probably do him the world of good – he'll have to grow up a bit.'

'I hope you're right.'

'I'm his twin. I know him better than anyone. I know I'm

right,' Adam says as I lift my laptop and we start scrolling through flights.

40

FAMILY MEETING

Niamh – Three Days Later

The four Cassidy children are looking at their parents expectantly. Niamh looks around at each of them, taking in their features and their personalities. She marvels at just how different all four of them are. They all have a certain familiarity in their appearance, of course. The Cassidy high forehead is a curse they all have to carry, but when it comes to their personalities they are all unique to themselves. Jodie has always been fiercely independent and very much boss. That she had almost five years as the star of the Cassidy family show before the first of her siblings came along meant she developed an unshakeable belief in her own brilliance. Niamh hopes it never leaves her.

The boys may share the same poor hygiene standards and obsession with gaming, but Ethan has always been the more boisterous of the two. Verging on feral at times, if Niamh is honest, but hilarious enough to get away with it.

Cal is the more contemplative of the pair. A sensitive soul who thinks deeply about the world and everyone in it. He does his best to hide his occasional bouts of anxiety behind a mask of teenage rebellion but Niamh recognises herself in him only too much. She wants to pour all the love and resilience into his world so he can protect himself from those who would make it tougher – people like her Year 11s.

And Fiadh? Fiadh is the princess. Spoiled by everyone in the house, including her brothers. Every day Niamh thanks her stars that her daughter has turned into a loving and caring, if exceptionally nosy, child and not a carbon copy of Verruca Salt from *Charlie and the Chocolate Factory*. Right now, it is Fiadh who is wriggling in her seat, clearly dying to know what has resulted in them all being called together in such a manner. These days, it's rare that all six Cassidys congregate at the kitchen table at the same time. It's usually a Christmas-dinner-only event these days.

'What's going on?' Ethan asks. 'I want to get back to my game.'

'You spend enough time on that game that it won't kill you to give it up now for a wee bit,' Paul says, and while it is clear Ethan isn't exactly enamoured with that reaction, he knows better than to start kicking off.

'Are we going to Disneyland?' Fiadh asks.

'What?' Cal says. 'That's for babies.'

'No. It's not. It's for everyone,' Fiadh says, defiantly. 'Are we going, Mammy?'

'No, love. Not at the moment, anyway,' Niamh says.

It's clearly now her youngest child's turn to look dejected. 'Can we get a puppy then?'

'We're not getting a puppy,' Paul says. 'But we do have some very important things to talk to you about.'

Niamh is so grateful that Paul is taking control because even though she feels so much better than she did even this morning, she still feels more than a little emotionally fragile.

Paul came with her when she went to see her GP. He offered

to actually come into the consultation with her but she had said there was no need and she was happy just to know he was in the waiting area.

She had written down exactly what she wanted to say to the doctor. Over the course of several drafts, her message had changed from 'I think I am losing my fucking mind' to a list of symptoms and a description of how she felt her mental health was taking a battering. She was so glad to have done that because as soon as she saw the kindly face of her GP she burst into tears and struggled to regain her composure. It was much, much easier to just hand over her neatly folded sheet of paper and let the doctor read it for herself.

When the doctor had looked up, her brow furrowed with sympathy and concern, Niamh had cried some more, but then as they started to pick through each symptom and discuss treatments and medications, as well as the availability of talking therapies, she had felt the weight start to lift from her shoulders. It might have been in tiny, pebble-sized chunks, but it was lifting all the same.

Life was starting to come into focus again. The doctor warned her it would be a long process, with a healthy amount of ups and downs, but it would be worth it.

'There are lots of things we can try,' the doctor said. 'Don't ever be afraid to come back and say that we're not quite there yet. Menopause, and even depression – well, they aren't exact sciences. There isn't a one-size-fits-all approach. So just because this HRT has worked brilliantly for your friend, that doesn't mean there's something wrong with you because you don't feel the same.'

Niamh could've kissed her. Like properly snogged her. She felt validated. Believed. Sane even. Apart from wanting to snog the doctor, that is.

By the time she had left the health centre and got back into the car with Paul she had in her hand a prescription for HRT gel and for some top-grade antidepressants, as well as a referral to a counsellor. She also had a Get Out of Jail Free card, otherwise known as an 'Unfit to Work' certificate that would give her some breathing space before she had to face Jayden, Ella et al. again.

But work and medication are the not the only things that have to change.

'Right, kids,' Paul says, 'the thing is we have all been guilty – me included – of putting too much on your mum's shoulders. You are all getting older now and you need to start acting your age.'

'I'm only seven,' Fiadh says, clearly sensing that extra house-work responsibilities are incoming. 'I'm only a little girl,' she adds, batting her eyelashes.

'That's true, love,' Paul says. 'But even little girls can put their dirty clothes in the laundry basket and their dishes in the dishwasher.'

'Ha! Burn!' Ethan shouts, which Niamh thinks immediately was a very, very foolish move.

'I'd not be mocking anyone if I were you,' Paul says. 'See that cesspit of horrors you two share? It's getting gutted this weekend. Every manky discarded item of clothing, every empty crisp bag, every dirty cup and every alien life form... you guys will be picking it all up and bringing it all downstairs where you will learn how to use the washing machine, the dishwasher and how to put rubbish in the bin and not just sit it on top of it instead.'

'But we've a gaming league at the weekend,' Ethan moans, and Cal, who clearly knows when they are fighting a losing battle, reaches out his arm in front of his brother as if to signal that he should stop before he makes things worse.

'Nope. Not until that place is clean as a whistle and fumigated of all noxious odours. It's bad enough that your room is that messy to begin with, but the smell? Dear God, lads. Have a bit of dignity,' Paul says.

'And what are you going to do, Dad?' Ethan asks, defiantly.

'Whatever it takes to make sure your mum doesn't want to walk out that front door to go and live in a witchy cottage by the sea all on her own,' he says, and Niamh smiles. He's listening too.

'Well, then, what about Jodie? What is Jodie going to do?' Cal asks.

'Well, that's another thing we have to tell you,' Niamh says. 'Or at least it's something Jodie wants to tell you all.'

All eyes in the room move immediately to Jodie, who grasps hold of her daddy's hand.

'Well, I know that you've noticed I've been a bit sick recently. And Adam stayed over too.'

'Are you going to be dead?' Fiadh asks, filled with alarm.

'Oh, God, no! I hope not, anyway. No. I'm not ill. Not properly ill anyway. The truth is, I'm going to have a baby.'

The room erupts with questions, cheers and the occasional quiet moment as Fiadh takes in the news she won't be the baby of the family for much longer. Niamh just sits and watches it and she has to hold on to hope that this is the start of good things happening for her family.

Even as Jodie explains that it's still early, and there's a chance something might go wrong, Niamh just gets this overwhelming feeling that everything will be okay.

'What are you going to call the baby?' Fiadh asks. 'I think Taylor or Sabrina for a girl.'

'No. No. We're thinking of Ella, maybe?' Jodie says, her hand going to her stomach.

'No,' Niamh says, that name striking fear deep into her heart. 'No. I will give you £500 if you call the baby something other than

Ella. And for the record, Jayden is also off the table. Totally.' She's only partially joking, of course.

* * *

The following day, Niamh meets Laura and Becca at the Green Cat Bakery café for a debrief and chocolate cake session. In a quiet corner of the coffee shop with an extra-large slice of chocolate cake in front of her, she feels no guilt at all not being in the classroom and instead enjoying this leisurely afternoon with her girls.

'This tastes so good,' she says, taking the time to enjoy the texture and taste of the cake and not, as she has been doing over the preceding weeks, simply shoving vast quantities of chocolate down her throat in a bid to give herself an energy boost, or to fill the void that seemed to be opening up inside of her. It hadn't been a particularly effective method of either – any energy boost she got was quick-lived and accompanied by a sugar-rush headache and a severe bout of nausea, while any void it was supposed to fill just widened to now include self-loathing into the mix. 'I think I'd forgotten how to just enjoy and appreciate food, you know?'

Becca and Laura both nod. 'I get it,' Laura says. 'Always rushing from place to place. Not sitting down to eat and relax. Then after Mum died, I just lost my appetite altogether.'

'I wish I was the kind of person who lost my appetite when I'm stressed. I go the other way. I could eat everything in sight, then I get annoyed with myself,' Becca says. 'It's only Adam being home and having to cook him a proper dinner that has kept me on track these last few weeks. When he goes back, I'll have to be extra careful not to fall back into my old habits.'

'When is he going?' Laura asks, delicately.

Niamh already knows the answer. Just as she already knows that Jodie is also going back to do her exams in Belfast next week. She'd tried to encourage her to take a little time off to rest. She can always resit her exams in the summer. But Jodie is as stubborn as her dad and, Niamh is coming to realise, as stubborn as her mum too. She wants to do her exams and has been studying for them. She swears she'll do nothing more strenuous than walking for the bus to get to the exam hall or to the library to study.

'Sunday,' Becca says. 'Saul will meet him at the airport and if I know my boys, and Saul in particular, it will be straight to the pub.'

'I suppose they might as well,' Laura says. 'Things will change soon enough when he has a baby to consider.'

'That's what I think,' Niamh says. 'Because he'll not get away with that nonsense when he's a daddy.'

Immediately she looks to Becca, wondering if threatening her son might have been a bad move. Becca just laughs. 'Bloody right! I've him warned. His granny has him warned too,' she laughs. 'Did you know she is now on to crocheting a second baby blanket? If she keeps up at this rate, there will be a new one for every day of the week.'

'That's so lovely of your mum,' Niamh says. 'I remember her crocheting stuff when mine were wee. I'm pretty sure I still have some of it up in the attic.'

'Me too,' says Laura. 'Actually, Robyn still has one of her baby blankets at the bottom of her bed. I think it's like her security blanket or something. It's definitely seen better days, but she'll never part with it.'

All this chat is making Niamh feel fuzzy and warm, but she accepts that might just be down to the new antidepressants swimming around in her system.

'In all seriousness,' Becca says, 'Adam is already talking about how determined he is to be a good dad. He's a good lad.'

'I know,' Niamh says. 'Sure, look at his mammy. How could he be anything but?'

She's about to take another bite of her cake, which she swears might be the nicest cake she has ever had in her entire life, when her phone rings. Glancing at the screen, she smiles as she sees Deirdre's name illuminated.

'Give me two mins,' she says to her friends as she gets up to go outside where she will have a better chance to hear Deirdre on the other end of the phone. 'It's Deirdre. I'd left her a message earlier.'

41

DEATH BY CHOCOLATE (CAKE)

Becca

'Jeez, Becca, you nearly jumped the height of yourself when that phone rang. Are you okay?' Laura says after Niamh has left us to speak with Deirdre.

'I am not,' I tell her. 'I'm like a fecking cat on a hot tin roof. I've not heard a peep from Grace since I submitted the article on Wednesday morning and this is now Friday and she said she needed it ASAP to get it in print. Surely that means she'll have read it by now? Why have I not heard from her?'

There is a mild hysteria in my voice and even though I have not five minutes ago told my friends I have to make sure not to fall headfirst back into my comfort-eating ways I shovel a spoonful of chocolate cake into my mouth. But my mouth is too dry due to my absolute nervous breakdown state of being and I feel it stick in my throat.

Great, I think, this is how it ends. I can just imagine the headlines now.

'Death by Chocolate'
Local woman chokes to death on cake

And the quotes from shocked onlookers...

'She just horsed the biggest piece of cake into her mouth. It's no wonder she choked on it.'

'I suppose if you're going to die, then at least it's good she died doing what she so clearly loved.'

'Becs! Take a drink!' Laura says, pushing a glass of water towards me. I'm not sure if it's going to help or just make it all gloopier and less likely to shift, but short of the Heimlich manoeuvre I don't have much else to try. So I go for it and thankfully dislodge the cake and allow air to rush back into my lungs.

Laura is just staring at me, wide-eyed and half amused, I think, as well as half very, very concerned. 'Oh, love. She is very busy, I suppose. It can't be easy editing a magazine like that.'

She has a point – quite a reasonable one, if the truth be told, but I'm not feeling very reasonable. It has been one hell of a week and I just need to know if I hit the brief or if, as I fear, I sent Grace Adams and my one tangible chance at achieving my goal of writing for a glossy magazine running for the hills.

In less stressful but no less distracting news, I've also been overwhelmed with impure thoughts of Conal, which I'm clearly not going to admit to in any detail with Laura given that he's her brother and *eeewwwww*.

I've not seen him since our big 'almost' moment on Monday, but we have been exchanging increasingly daring messages as the week has progressed. No nudes or anything like that. God forbid. If it floats your boat, then knock yourself out – I'm not one to

yuck anyone else's yum. But I refuse to believe there is any creature on the planet who will dissolve into a lust-filled frenzy at the
sight of my stretch marks in a blurry selfie on a phone screen.

There's no goddamn way I've ever felt confident enough to
send a picture of my boobs to anyone. Except, I suppose, for the
time I sent one to the girls. I had mastitis and needed some
advice, so obviously it was not in a sexy way and definitely more
about desperation than confidence. There is nothing sexy about
mastitis.

So while no photographs have been exchanged between
Conal and me, there have been several messages alluding to
getting each other alone and finishing what we almost started. It
doesn't need to be explicit to distract me to the point of needing
to take Daniel out on yet another walk to burn off the nervous
energy.

It seems my libido has not only returned from the dead, it is
hungry and demands feeding.

But it's not like I can invite Conal over while Adam is still at
home. It would be too weird. Too ick. I'd have to be too quiet and
I really don't think that by the time I get Conal alone and in my
bed, I'm going to be able to stay quiet.

So, with all that to contend with, I am at this stage wound up
into a giant ball of tension, likely to go off at a moment's notice.
I'd almost been tempted to hijack Niamh's doctor's appointment
to beg for 'some of the good stuff' for myself.

Thankfully I'd managed to wise myself up before I'd embarrassed us all. And yet, here I am choking on chocolate cake like
the gulpen I am and embarrassing us here anyway.

And I've *still* not heard from Grace.

'But it's Friday,' I say. 'And Friday afternoon at that. She's
hardly going to get in touch over the weekend, so I kind of *need* to
hear from her now or else I know it will be at least Monday. I'm

not sure I can cope with a whole weekend of this. My brain keeps telling me she hated it. Which of course she probably did.' I rub my temples to try and fight off an incoming headache – no doubt brought on by my near-death experience with the chocolate cake. 'Laura, I coloured outside the lines a little and didn't write it as a straight review. I'd thought that was what she wanted, you know. Something a bit different? With a sense of voice. But gah...' I stare at the chocolate cake on my plate, knowing better than to risk taking another bite.

'Take a breath, Becs. I'm sure it's perfect. You can write! You know this,' Laura reassures me.

'But can I? Can I really? To the standard *Northern People* needs? Maybe the limit of my talents really is listicles and interviews with personality-devoid CEOs who give one-word answers. Do you know how hard it is to make seven hundred words out of that?'

She laughs and shakes her head. 'No. I don't, but the fact that you can do it proves in itself you have talent. And if you can write proficiently with that level of material, then you can absolutely write a damn article about our weekend in Donegal. But do you know what, *even* if this one article is not for her, she still wants you to write a column. There will be other articles. Hang in there. This is your first go.'

Laura is right, of course. But I don't know how to get across that while this is my first go, there is a part of me that just needs it to be a winner. More than anything I have ever needed in my career before. Maybe that's naïve of me, or ridiculously self-obsessed, but it's how I feel nonetheless.

I want it to be good for me, of course. And for Grace. But I want it to also be a winner for Peggy, and Deirdre and all the women who danced around that bonfire on a cold January night a week ago.

'I know,' I say, cursing my phone for not ringing and trying to tell myself that maybe it's because it took a mud bath earlier in the week. Yes, the rice worked. I will never doubt the power of rice again. But what if it only partially worked and for some weird, mud-related reason it now blocks all calls and/or emails from Grace?

'You're overthinking it,' Laura says, interrupting my overthinking with impeccable timing.

'I know,' I say. 'Honestly. I do. It's a curse. One I need to work on.'

The tinkle of the bell above the door draws our attention to Niamh, who is making her way back to us with a smile on her face. 'Deirdre's in,' she says.

'In?' I ask. 'Here?' I look around.

'No. For the club! Or the group. Or the bunch of friends. Whatever you want to call it,' Niamh says.

Nope. I'm still lost – a fact that is clearly written all over my face.

'Remember last week? At the retreat? We said wouldn't it be great if there was somewhere to do things like that together on the regular? That it can be hard to make friends in your forties and beyond?'

Ah, well, that does sound familiar for sure. It had simply been lost in the craziness of the week that has passed.

'Oh, yes, I remember,' Laura says. 'I liked the sound of that.'

'I haven't had a moment to think about it,' I say, opting for an honesty-is-the-best-policy approach. 'Do you have actual plans?'

Niamh Cassidy might be the only woman in the world who could have a nervous breakdown, support her daughter through a threatened miscarriage and form a club for lonely middle-aged women all in the one week.

'Well, not so much, but Deirdre wants to get on board. And I think, you know, we should invite her out with us. It doesn't have to be anything mad. But we like her. Don't we? And she's good craic. It could be something really positive for all of us, and God knows we could use all the positive we can find right now.'

Just as she says those very words, my phone illuminates, with proof that there has been no Grace-blocking, mud-related anomaly. Her name is there, and she is calling. And I know I have to answer it.

42

SH*TE THE TIGHTS

'Shite the tights!' I say, turning the phone towards the girls. Clearly I say it a little too loudly and it attracts the attention of some of the other customers, who don't look too impressed with my uncouth language. I raise my hands and mouth a quick sorry, while my face blazes once again. What must they think of me? This grown woman who almost dies eating cake then shouts about 'shiting the tights' in a lovely café.

But there is no more suitable expression than the one designed specifically to describe the level of nervousness where you feel as if the contents of your bowels could literally fall out of your arse.

I shuffle through the tables, mouthing my apology again as I go, until I am outside in the cool air and I can hear Grace Adams asking if I can hear her down the line.

'Sorry. Sorry, Grace. I was just in the Green Cat there and wanted to come outside to be able to hear you properly,' I stutter.

'Oh, I love that place. Best. Scones. Ever,' she says – so very casually it's hard to imagine she realises just how much of my future happiness she holds in her hands right at this very minute.

And yes, I know that I am being extra dramatic but it feels extra dramatic.

'Yes. The very best. I've been meeting a couple of friends for coffee.'

There's a squeak in the background, as if she is moving in her office chair. Perhaps getting more comfortable before she breaks my heart.

'Is it Laura and Niamh?' she asks. 'Are you meeting your fellow retreat goers? I remember the three of you from school. Joined at the hip, you were. Seems you still are.'

'Yes, yes. It's Laura and Niamh and yes, we're still close.' I stop myself from immediately launching into a prolonged over-sharing of our back story, the big falling-out, the reunion and the drama of the *situation*.

'Clearly. That really came across in your piece. Look, I'm really sorry—'

My heart plummets.

'—I've not been in touch sooner.'

My heart stops plummeting but now is unsure whether it should continue on a downward trajectory or return to its designated spot in my chest. So it just hovers around my lower lungs, making it feel sort of hard to breathe.

'Things have been so busy at the magazine. We had a big advertiser come in with a last-minute campaign and in this economy that's not the kind of thing you can say no to, so we basically had to replan the full edition and move everything about. Cuts had to be made.'

And off my heart goes again, plummeting downwards. But still, at least, this wouldn't be my fault. It wouldn't be because my article was rubbish. It was just that they had to rejig everything and advertising revenue has to come first. I know this. I'm not stupid.

'Rebecca,' Grace says, cutting into my thoughts. 'So what do you think?'

Shit, is what I think, primarily. I wasn't expecting to have to give feedback on being sacrificed to the gods of capitalism.

'Well, I suppose. I understand. I know how tough the landscape is for print media at the minute.' I swallow the lump in my throat, sending it downwards towards my heart, which is now no doubt sliding past my kneecaps.

'Sorry. You've lost me there,' Grace says. 'I asked did you think the girls would be happy to get photos done. Properly. I know you sent the ones from the trip, but I think it would really top the article off nicely to have a good, professional shot of you all.'

Now it's my turn to wonder if I have slipped off into some alternate universe. 'Wait... you want a picture? For the article? You like the article?'

'Are you okay, Becca?' Grace asks, but I can tell by the tone of her voice that she is smiling. 'You heard me when I said I loved it, didn't you?'

As my heart does an emergency stop and starts to soar, I decide honesty is the best policy. 'To be honest, my brain shut down when you said you'd had to make cuts and I just assumed...'

'God, no!' Grace says and laughs. 'You poor thing. You need to have more confidence in your ability, girl! I loved it. It is exactly the kind of thing I wanted to appeal to our slightly older demographic, provide a fresh voice and something different. Honestly, I think I'm convinced on wanting to go on this retreat the next time it rolls around.'

I listen in surprise as she heaps praise on my shoulders, and yes, I might be crying now but they're happy tears. Honestly. I hastily wipe them away because I don't want the customers in the café to peek out the window and see 'the mad woman' making a show of herself for the third time.

'What I didn't want was a straightforward advertorial-style breakdown of the retreat that sounded as if we'd been paid to only say nice things but not in a genuine way. That doesn't sell magazines, or get us online clicks. What works is fresh, funny and, most of all, with heart. This has so much heart.'

'Thank you,' I stutter. 'That means so much.'

'Good! It should. But back to my point – do you think your friends will be up for getting their photo taken?'

I look through the café window to where both Niamh and Laura are staring at me and making thumbs up and thumbs down gestures in a bid to get me to let them know how this conversation is going. I raise my free thumb and grin and watch as they erupt into spontaneous applause. It seems we really are, all of us, dead set on making a huge impression in the café today.

'Yes,' I tell Grace. 'I think they will.'

'Perfect!' Grace trills. 'So look, if you can speak to your people and let me know a day and time that suits for a photo then we'll get that taken. The bad news, because there is always bad news, is that our deadlines are even tighter now, so if we can make it happen on Tuesday or Wednesday of next week, that would be ideal.'

'I'll see what I can do. I'm sure I'll sort it out,' I say, now smiling ridiculously widely. 'I'm sure it won't be a problem.'

'Thanks, Rebecca. And well done!' Grace says, before she hangs up and I am left standing in the front garden of the Green Cat Bakery doing my own little happy dance – much to the amusement of the departing customers.

'I'm sorry,' I call. 'I'm just really, really happy.'

They smile back, but scurry on anyway.

43

LEAVING ON A JET PLANE

I don't think I will ever find it easy to say goodbye to either of the boys as they head back to England. But it's particularly hard to say goodbye to Adam today. It feels as if we've been on this huge mother–son journey these past couple of weeks. We've become even closer. I've become even more protective. I've seen him in a whole new light and, my God, he shines brightly.

It's nice though that Saul will be waiting for him – and has absolutely vowed to be less of a disaster zone this term. It's true that life is often more chaotic with Saul in it, but it can also be much more fun. Adam needs a little fun now. Even though I'm proud of how he is shouldering his responsibility, I do want him to remember that he's only nineteen and there is a whole lot of living still to be done out there and so much fun to be had.

Adam and Jodie are in the back seat of my car, holding hands. They look suitably loved up in the unselfconscious way that the young can get away with. Niamh is in the front with me and I know she is checking them out in the rearview mirror almost as much as I am. The plan is to drop Adam at the airport, then Niamh and I will bring Jodie to her university accommodation in Belfast. I know Niamh is on her nerves about letting her pregnant daughter out of her sight. This will not be easy for her.

I'm going to be there for Niamh more, I vow. God knows she has been there for me more times than I care to mention over the years. With her larger-than-life personality it has been easy to miss the times when she is struggling a little, and while she is getting help now, this is not a quick fix. She has a lot of big questions to ask herself – not least about her career. She has admitted that's probably been at the core of her struggles – that no longer loving the career she had been so focused on had made her feel untethered and lost. With the onset of menopause, she had simply spiralled, worrying so much about what she could lose that she could not enjoy what she has.

That she has even admitted that, and spoken to Paul and her kids about it, is a huge step. But there are so many more steps to go – the first of which will be leaving Jodie in her halls of residence and driving back to Derry without her.

'It's only an hour and a bit in the car these days,' Jodie reassures her from the back seat. 'If I need you, Mum, or if you need me, it'll only take an hour. Sure, that's nothing. Or we can meet halfway. Get a cheeky KFC at the Castledawson roundabout.'

'I'd love a KFC,' Adam says. 'Mum, can we stop on the way up and get a KFC?'

'Tower burger!' Jodie says in a deep voice.

'Chicken gravy,' Adam growls, and they laugh.

I glance to Niamh.

'I could go a chicken fillet burger,' she says. 'And fries.'

'And chicken popcorn,' I add.

'Yes! And the gravy!' Niamh says.

'Chicken gravy!' Adam growls again in the same low voice, and he and Jodie laugh again. Presumably this is some sort of joke between them, but I laugh too even though I don't get it – simply because it is just so lovely to hear them laugh together.

An hour and a half later, stomachs full, we arrive at the airport and I help get Adam's bags out of the boot. This is the bit I really hate. The big hug and the watching him walk away. It reminds me that such a big stage of our relationship is over now. That he is an adult living his life and I'm now an anchor point, instead of the whole ocean. Which, of course, is how it should be. But it still has the ability to make my heart ache.

Today I'm not even the last person to hug him before he goes. That is, of course, Jodie. I have told him I love him, and while I might be a little more than 'just an hour' away, I am always, always on hand if he needs me and he only has to say the words.

'Stop fussing, Mum,' he said as I hugged him more tightly than usual. 'I'm okay. It's all good. And Saul will keep me right. Thanks for everything. You've been brilliant.'

I squeaked a barely audible response, desperately wanting to hold on to him tighter for just a little more but knowing that he needed the time to say goodbye to Jodie more.

Niamh and I are now standing watching them hug. We don't speak. We simply link arms. We don't need to say anything. We both know what the other is thinking and feeling. It's a whole set of emotions we need to keep a lid on for now, and until Jodie is dropped off too. Then we can cry/sing the whole way back down the road. I've even put together a playlist for the occasion. We'll start with 'I Can Do It With a Broken Heart' from Taylor Swift, segue into some Florence and the Machine, Gwen Stefani, Spice Girls and many more until we circle back to Tay-Tay and 'Shake It Off'. If that doesn't sort us out, nothing will.

Jodie is remarkably stoic when she turns to walk back to us. Adam gives one last wave – an equally stoic expression on his face – and walks through the doors into the airport. For once I am at a complete loss for words, so I just get into the car and allow Niamh the chance to hug her little girl before they join me.

I'm grateful for the minute of solitude where I can tell myself in my sternest voice that I will not cry. That I can go and visit Adam and Saul at a moment's notice. That he will be back in a few months and he'll be close to home then and it won't be long until there is a mini version of him to occupy my time.

The car doors open and both Niamh and Jodie climb in. I feel Jodie's hand on my shoulder, giving me a little squeeze. 'He said to say he loves you, and he'll make sure Saul doesn't wreck the place,' she says, and I nod because my determination to stay dry eyed is being sorely tested.

'He's brilliant,' she says – all twenty-years-old of her. 'I love him, Becca. I think you should know that.'

'He loves you too,' I say, losing the battle.

'And I love you all,' Niamh says. 'Let's face it, we're all pretty damn amazing.'

44

TIKTOK FAMOUS

Niamh

Niamh feels remarkably calm. It could be the increased HRT dose, or the anti-anxiety medication, but she is surprised that she does not feel like throwing up as she helps Jodie put some new finishing touches to her digs.

Yes, she may have gone overboard – insisting Becca take them for a quick run to Ikea to stock up on new bedding, lights, cushions and a rug – but she wanted to make Jodie's room as cosy as possible.

By the time everything is unpacked, set up and the rubbish folded and put in the recycling, the room looks great and Jodie looks delighted with it.

Becca has left them to say their goodbyes and gone to wait in the car and Niamh is sitting beside her daughter on her bed, their backs against the wall, holding hands.

'It's nice, isn't it?' she says.

'It really is. You didn't have to do this, Mum. But I'm grateful that you did. I'm grateful for everything you've done, and Dad too, of course.' Niamh gives three little squeezes to her daughter's hand – their secret code for 'I love you' that has survived since childhood.

'Sure, you're our daughter. We'd do anything for you,' she says.

'A new car and a holiday in Ibiza?' Jodie asks hopefully.

'Nice try.' Niamh laughs as her daughter rests her head on her shoulder. 'You know exactly what I mean, young lady! I need you to believe that. We are here for you. In whatever way you need, and there is still time for you to pull out of these exams and arrange to do them in the summer.'

'I know, but I'll be fine, Mum. I've no plans to go on the mad tear up here. I'm too tired and too nauseous, for a start. I'll be taking it easy and any sign of anything untoward and I promise I will phone you.'

'You bloody better!' Niamh says. 'Whether it's three in the morning or the middle of the day. My phone will be on. I will be here for you.'

'You're the best mammy,' Jodie says with a smile.

'Sure, don't I know it?' Niamh laughs. 'But you'll be a great mum too. Not as good as me, of course,' she says, happy to tease her daughter, 'but good enough.'

'That's the goal,' Jodie says and laughs. 'But promise me, Mum, promise me you'll look after yourself too? And keep the boys cleaning their own rooms?'

Niamh nods. 'I fully intend to.' She has a lot of things she wants to do, and top of the list is getting better.

She even considers getting her photo taken with Laura and Becca on Wednesday for *Northern People* part of her mission to get back on her feet properly.

She hadn't been keen on the idea initially, but then she had given herself a good talking-to. If this article could help other women of her age feel less alone then she was happy to get 100 per cent behind it. Just as she was excited to look into more ways to get involved with helping women feel less lonely and more valuable. She'd spent the last two nights reading some of the papers and articles Laura had sent her about different cultures and how they celebrated their older women – as well as looking into some of the physical and chemical changes which take place during menopause.

She isn't sure what it is she wants to do just yet, but she knows she wants to do something. She'll take her time figuring it out. Just as she'll take her time figuring out what she wants to do about teaching.

In the meantime, she has her yoga classes, which admittedly, she has actually enjoyed this week. More than ever before.

She's even taken to practising some of her poses at home. Fiadh has delighted in trying to copy her mum, while Paul has offered to clear out the little-used garden room to make her a space of her own where she could do her yoga, practise her meditation or just escape the incessant shouting of Cal and Ethan. 'Is there a female equivalent of a man-cave?' he asked.

'A witch's lair,' she'd replied dead-pan, aware they'd been cowed by Paul's threat she would move out to her own witchy cottage.

'Mum,' Jodie says, cutting through Niamh's thoughts.

'Yes, love?'

'You know you do *actually* have to leave at some stage? And poor Becca has been waiting for ages now.'

'I know,' Niamh says. 'Just two more minutes and I promise I'll leave.'

'Okay,' Jodie says, snuggling closer into her mother than before. 'But if I have to call security to throw you out, I'm filming it and putting it on TikTok. Be warned!'

45

DON'T WORRY, THE DOG'S NOT DEAD

Becca

My back is aching by the time I get home. I'm so delighted to finally get out of the car and stretch. It has been a long day, at the end of a long week. What I want now more than anything is a soak in the bath, a glass of wine and an hour with a good book before going to sleep.

Letting myself into the house, I sigh with relief. Conal had offered to take Daniel out for a walk earlier and I'd asked him to flick a few lights on and set the heating for my getting back. It makes such a lovely difference to walk into a lit, warm home and I decide as soon as I have my coat off and have checked in on Mr the Spaniel I will text him to let him know just how much I appreciate it.

I can guess what he'll say though. 'You need to stop setting the bar so low, Becs. It's the least I can do.'

I wonder how I can make myself believe him. That I am worthy of acts of kindness and affection. I am worthy of being cared for. What I do know, though, is that I am exceptionally grateful for him and his kindness.

It's strange, I realise, that Daniel has not bounded into the hall already. Normally he takes up sentinel position at the door as soon as he hears my car in the driveway, but not today.

'Daniel!' I call, expecting to hear the scrabble of his paws on the floor as he runs to me. But there is no sign of him. This, I think, can only mean one thing. That I will push back the door to the living room, or climb the stairs to my bedroom, only to find Daniel dead. There is no other logical reason. My heart starts to thud. How will I tell the children? They always ask to see Daniel on FaceTime. And what do I do with a dead dog? Call a vet? I don't want to find him. I don't want to see him still and gone. He's an awful pain in the arse, but he's still my baby.

Panic starts to claw at me. 'Daniel!' I call again, my voice broken and way too squeaky. 'Where's my puppy?' I call in the playful voice I always do. There is no response.

My hand shaking, I take my phone out of my pocket. Should I call Conal? See if Daniel was okay earlier when they went for their walk? Maybe I really should find Daniel first though. So even though I don't want to move, I force myself into the living room where the rug is clear and his favourite spot on the sofa is empty.

He always, always lies on the rug at this time of night. Something has to be wrong. My fear growing, I make my way to the kitchen. Maybe the door to the utility room is closed and he's managed to lock himself in there. He's done it before. Gone in to snarf some more of his food and managed to knock the door closed with an over-enthusiastic tail-wagging episode.

But the door is open. And... And...

The table is set for two. Properly. With candles and wine glasses and my good plates. The rest of the kitchen is absolutely spotless. More so than when we left, with the morning's dishes still on the worktop, along with a collection of mugs and side plates retrieved from Adam's room.

Nothing about this is making sense. I call Daniel again, but he does not come and yet... is that a bark? Did I hear a bark? I try to figure out where it's coming from, hope rising in me that I am not actually going to find a dead dog anywhere on the premises.

That's when I hear the unmistakeable sound of footsteps above. Human footsteps. Someone is here.

'Conal?' I call, trying to think of who on earth might be in my house, and realising that a burglar is unlikely to set the table for an intimate dinner à deux. Not unless he's some completely sociopathic serial killer. But no, I will not allow my brain to go there.

There is no reply and still no sign of Daniel. Great bloody guard dog he'd make, I think, then immediately feel guilty in case he is actually dead.

When I climb the stairs, I see the bathroom door is closed. 'Conal?' I call again, but I can't disguise the shake in my voice.

I reach my hand out to turn the handle just as the door is pulled open and... 'Jesus, Mary, Saint Joseph and the wee donkey!'

In the future, when I tell this story, I will explain that this is the part where Conal O'Hagan screamed like a schoolgirl sucking on a helium balloon.

'I was calling you!' I say, trying not to laugh because he does actually look as if he's seen a ghost. He reaches up and pulls his AirPods out of his ears, his face now transforming from sheet-white to blazing red.

'I didn't hear you!'

'Yeah,' I laugh. 'I get that. Where's Daniel? You haven't made the rookie mistake of trying to bath him, have you?'

I try to look around Conal, wondering if I'm about to get body-slammed by a very soggy dog. Conal, however, steps in my way so I can't see past him.

'Daniel isn't here,' he says, still trying to get his composure. 'He's with Laura. She's keeping him tonight. And clearly this is not going anywhere near as smoothly as I anticipated.'

'Why is he with Laura?' I ask, but one quick glance at Conal's face starts all the pieces slotting into place. 'Oh...' I say.

'No! No! Don't worry. It's not that! This is not some ploy to get you into bed the moment your son has left.' I'm not sure Conal's face could get any redder.

'It isn't?' I ask, not sure whether to feel relieved or disappointed. I didn't anticipate this, not tonight. I'd hoped to at least have the chance to shave my legs and other areas.

'No! Well, not like that anyway. I just... You've had a tough but also brilliant week. I wanted to give you the chance to relax and celebrate. I know you didn't want to celebrate while Adam was here. That's all. So I thought – probably stupidly, now that I see it from your perspective – that I'd get dog-sitters. Run you a nice warm bath and pour you a glass of wine, like so...' he says, stepping backwards and revealing my bath filled with copious bubbles, candles on every surface and a glass of white wine, condensation tricking down the stem, waiting for me on a stool.

I can't speak.

'The plan was then that I'd cook dinner, while you had a soak, but I remembered that I can't really cook so I have a selection of menus from the best takeaways in town and you can choose whatever you like.' He looks so embarrassed that it's actually adorable and I feel the growing need to kiss him.

'Full disclosure,' he says. 'I had hoped, you know, for some kissing. Maybe some light... touching...'

I feel my body tighten in response. If I can feel this way with one word... the mention of touching... I might be in trouble.

He takes one step towards me, bending his head towards mine and taking my face in his hand. I close my eyes as he pulls closer and I let out the smallest of moans when I feel the warmth of his lips on my neck. I want them to stay there forever. Okay, maybe not forever, but for a while. At least that's what I think until I feel his lips brush against my own. Gentle but also so very, very filled with longing. I know the next time his lips meet mine there will be an urgency there that will overtake us both and I am ready for it.

Only, he pulls back, his eyes dark, his hand still on my cheek. 'I swear,' he says, breathless, 'I didn't come here to sleep with you. No matter how much I want to. I want you to feel 100 per cent ready. I can wait. I can wait as long as it takes.'

He says all this without breaking his gaze and while just inches from my face. But his body is like a magnet to me and suddenly I don't care that I'm almost forty-seven with stretch marks. I don't care that I'm wearing my favourite comfy everyday bra and a pair of comfy knickers. I don't care that my legs are on the stubbly side or that I probably smell of KFC right now. I don't care that I'm not as flexible as I once was or that it has been so very long since I had last had sex that I'm not even sure I remember how to any more.

I don't care about any of it, because this is him. And he makes me feel safe. And wanted. And appreciated.

And there's no dog in the house to look at us as if we are depraved animals.

I realise that now is the time for my iceberg moment. He has taken the steps towards me before now. He asked me out. He kissed me for the first time. He has taken the lead, but gently, and allowed for me to follow in my own time. He... well... he is a sexy bastard right in this very moment and I need him to know I feel that way.

I stand up on my tiptoes, closing the gap between us, and I brush my lips against his in the same soft teasing manner he had just kissed me with. But I don't pull back. I am done with pulling back. 'I don't want to wait,' I whisper before I kiss him, properly, deeply, again and lead him back towards the bedroom.

46

EPILOGUE

March

'The front page?'

'The actual front page?'

'Oh my God! Cover girls!'

Niamh, Laura and Deirdre are raising their glasses of champagne and hooting as I hand them each a copy of the April edition of *Northern People*.

No, I did not know that sneaky devil Grace Adams was planning on putting us on the front cover. She'd kept that to herself. Maybe I should've guessed when she had insisted on a professional photoshoot back in January, and we had been treated to hair and make-up when we arrived.

She invited me into her office earlier today to get my hands on the magazine 'hot off the press'. I should've realised, perhaps, that's not normal practice either but look, I'm learning. This is all still very new to me.

'Now, I don't want you to be mad,' she'd said when I arrived and I immediately told myself to take a deep breath and not let my thoughts immediately spiral to some unholy place as is my usual habit. Dead-dog-gate being the perfect example.

'Why would I be mad?' I asked.

'Well, personally, I don't know. I wouldn't be mad if it were me.' Looking very shifty indeed, she'd handed me a copy of the magazine and I had gasped.

Right there, on the cover of the special edition to mark forty years of *Northern People*, were my friends and me, grinning widely, arms all linked together, with the strapline, 'Welcome to your fabulous forties!' across the cover.

I gasped. We looked good. Real. Not airbrushed beyond recognition. I was grateful for that. But good.

'The cover?' I'd asked, eyebrows raised.

'It's such a good piece, Becca. It speaks to all us women, no matter where life has taken us. It's a positive representation of life as you age, without ignoring the challenges that come with it. Peggy is over the moon about it. Truly. She said to tell you that you're welcome any time to go back.'

'That's very lovely of her. She's a real star.'

'She is,' Grace said. 'But so are you. This inspired me to sign up for the next retreat. And talk to my own friends about reclaiming our fun selves again. My friend Daisy and I have already booked for Paris. We've always wanted to go but never did. I read this and thought, "We're not putting this off any longer."'

I smiled. No, I grinned. I felt like I had just been given the biggest, brightest Star of the Week certificate at primary school assembly.

'The girls will die!'

'They seem like so much fun,' Grace said. 'When you manage to get your regular meet-ups going, let me know. I wouldn't mind trying them out myself.'

I'd nodded. 'I will. We will. We've lots of ideas and we're just pulling them all together now.'

'Great! I can't wait to hear the details.'

* * *

I had practically floated out of her office and had FaceTimed Conal as soon as I reached my car.

'I am going to enjoy telling everyone my girlfriend is a cover star,' he'd said with a grin, 'I might tear off the cover and stick it up on my bedroom wall with Blu Tac.'

'You're an eejit!'

'Yeah, but you love me,' he'd replied, and I smiled. Because I do. I do love him and he loves me too. I don't doubt it. I don't question it. And he's helping me start to believe that I do deserve to be treated well.

My mother and Mrs Bishop have said they will buy a copy in every shop they find it in. I've made them promise not to make Uber trips just for that reason.

'I'll do what I want,' my mother said. 'I'm allowed to be proud of my daughter, you know.'

I think we both cried, though we did our best to pretend it was just allergies.

I haven't shown Adam or Saul yet. The boys are coming home this weekend for a break. I'll show them then. If I see them. Adam and Jodie will be joined at the hip. Adam can't wait to get home in time to accompany Jodie to her next hospital appointment, after which they are planning to start shopping for some of their baby essentials. Whereas Saul is bringing a friend back to show him the sights and sounds of Derry. I've not met this friend, who goes solely by the nickname of Wigan, before. I'm told he's 'great craic' and that he and Saul are going to seek out digs together once

Adam moves back. It's very reassuring to see Saul make new friendships, and to know that he will have people to rely on without the safety net of his twin on hand.

For now, though, I'm toasting my girls and it feels so lovely.

'Sixteen-year-old you would be proud,' Laura says. 'That's a big one ticked off the list. Published in a glossy magazine. So what's next? Marrying David Duchovny?' She raises an eyebrow.

'I have my own real-life David Duchovny, don't you know,' I reply, and she makes fake sick noises. But I know she doesn't mean it. She's delighted for Conal, and for me.

'Well, since we're celebrating,' Niamh says, 'I might as well let you in on my news.'

We all look directly at her, knowing that she has been deciding what she wants to do about her no longer fulfilling career.

'I'm going back to teaching,' she says.

'What?' I am confused. Very confused.

'Only until next year. I'm going to look at the early retirement pathway, and while I'm still teaching I'm going to do some learning of my own too. I'm going to train to be a yoga and wellness instructor. Particularly focused on women.'

'Oh, wow!' Laura says. 'That's amazing.'

'It is. I've already been putting some feelers out. I've been speaking to Peggy, actually, about what I want to do. I want to do whatever I can to support us all, particularly through menopause and beyond. Sixteen-year-old me didn't have that plan in her letter because she was daft as a brush, but me now – that's what I want for myself. To feel as if I'm making a difference and not just getting buried under admin or being terrorised by Year II.'

I am so incredibly proud of this woman. 'You're amazing,' I say.

'You really are,' Laura echoes.

'Since we're making announcements,' Laura says, 'would you mind if I added to the list?'

'The more the merrier,' I say.

'Good!' she says. 'Well, I'm taking the money from the sale of Mum's house and I'm going back to school too. Deirdre has been giving me a little guidance behind the scenes. I didn't say anything before now because I didn't know if it would be doable, but it looks like it is.'

'Back to school?' I am incredulous. The Laura I know did not particularly like school the first time. She couldn't wait to be done.

'Women's Studies,' she says. 'I'm going to study my passion for a bit, and because I can for a while. There's enough money to cover my loss of earnings for a few years, so I'm going to prove to myself that I can. I know I don't need to. I've done well enough without it. But I think Mum would approve. And I know I want to.'

'Oh, Laura.' I feel suddenly emotional, thinking of her taking on such a challenge.

Glancing down at the magazine cover again, at our smiling faces, I think I can't wait to see what comes next.

47

EPILOGUE PART TWO

Niamh – August

Niamh is incredibly calm. Much calmer than she thought she would be when the time came. The same cannot be said for Paul, or Cal, or Ethan who are running around like headless chickens. Niamh doesn't think she has ever seen Paul Cassidy this nervous before – not even when his own children were being birthed.

But this is different. This is his baby having her baby. He just wants everything to go well for her. As does Niamh, but she knows that now is not the time for her to let her true emotions bubble to the surface. So she exudes calm, allowing only the faintest traces of her excitement and nervousness occasionally to escape.

Jodie – well, Jodie looks young, and nervous, but Niamh knows that her daughter is absolutely ready to meet her baby. They stand together in their kitchen in the early hours of the morning, Jodie's face devoid of make-up, her hair pulled back in a ponytail, and wearing joggers and a hoodie. She is circling her hips as Niamh rubs the small of her back.

'I think they're getting closer, love,' Niamh says, tenderly. 'I think we should think about going to the hospital now.'

Sitting at the kitchen table behind them is Adam, his face sheet-white, while Becca rubs his hand and a very eager Daniel – absolutely delighted to be out of the house at this insane hour – nuzzles his head into Adam's lap, looking for a cuddle.

'It will be fine,' Becca reassures him, and Niamh can't help but smile. She knows just how excited Adam is to become a father, but how he is absolutely shit-scared of what's about to go down in the delivery room. He made the fatal error of watching one too many YouTube clips of birth – all taken from an up-close-and-personal angle. On one occasion, Jodie had ended up comforting him as he came round from a pretty impressive faint. It's something she hasn't let him live down.

'I know, Mum,' Adam says. 'I'm just scared.'

'*You're* scared?' Jodie laughs as she breathes through another contraction. 'You've got the easy job. Stay up at the business end, hold my hand and allow me to call you bad names and you'll be fine.' She winces as the pain peaks and Adam looks to his mother for some sort of reassurance.

'She's right, pet,' Becca says. 'Just be there for Jodie, and when it's all done with, bring her flowers, chocolates and whatever she wants. And for the love of God, when the midwife brings her tea and toast afterwards, don't be like your dad was and try to steal a slice.'

'You never told me that!' Niamh says, although when she thinks about it she probably shouldn't be surprised that Simon Cooke would prioritise his own desire for toast over the needs of the woman who just birthed his babies.

'Oh, yes. Then he asked the midwife if she could pop another couple of slices in the toaster. You can imagine the response he got,' Becca says, but she's laughing.

'Dad already warned me not to do that,' Adam says. 'He said under no circumstances was I to even attempt it.'

Wow, Niamh thinks. Simon gets it right for a change.

'Do you want to call him to let him know what's happening?' Becca asks, and Niamh thinks for a moment how lucky she is to have Paul under the same roof as her, by her side. Not that Becca would want Simon by her side. Oh, no. She is very happy indeed with Conal. It's almost, but not quite, sickening. The pair aren't long back from a long weekend in Rome and her friend is sun-kissed and glowing with happiness. Between Conal and her magazine work, Niamh isn't sure she has ever seen her best friend this happy.

'I already messaged him,' Adam says. 'He said to let him know as soon as there is news.'

Niamh is watching this exchange while continuing to rub Jodie's back, only for her daughter to let out a little yelp.

'Shit, what is it? Did I hurt you?' she asks as Jodie springs up to standing.

Daniel immediately darts to her side and Niamh doesn't have time to fully process how lovely it is that Daniel is so intuitive before she notices him lapping at the floor.

'Oh, you dirty wee shite!' Becca calls just as Niamh registers the darkening stains on Jodie's joggers and the increasing puddle of fluid on the floor.

'Mammy!' Jodie squeaks. 'I think my waters have just gone!'

'Paul!' Niamh shouts. 'Let's go!'

Within five minutes, and not before Ethan has made a badly timed joke about Jodie wetting herself, only to be handed a mop and told to clean it up before Daniel makes himself sick, two grannies, one grandad and two parents-to-be are all crammed into the one car on their way to hospital.

In the back of the car, Niamh sits on one side of her daughter while Adam is on the other. It's amazing how quickly her daughter's contractions have ramped up since her waters went. It's also amazing, and not in a good way, how they are managing to hit every red light on their journey.

'Mum! What if I have this baby in the car?' Jodie asks.

'You won't. You're a first-time mum. It will be ages yet,' Niamh soothes, but she has also noticed that the contractions are now only two minutes apart and lasting longer and longer. She doesn't want to scream at Paul to drive faster but she really bloody wants him to drive faster. She had fully expected to have to tell him to slow down, but instead he is driving like an eighty-five-year-old with glaucoma and a car that doesn't go above third gear – and is more comfortable in second.

'Paul,' she says, trying to keep her voice calm. 'Any chance we could just, you know, reach the speed limit?'

'It's a limit, not a target,' he retorts. 'And I have very precious cargo in this car. I want to make sure we all get there safely.'

Jodie lets out a wail as another contraction hits, and Paul swerves the car just a little.

'Paul,' Niamh repeats. 'Do you hear that? That's a woman in labour. We need to get there as quickly as possible.' Niamh doesn't want to alarm anyone, but that was only ninety seconds since the last contraction and Jodie is wriggling around in the seat as if she's about to star in the creature-bursting-out-of-her-tummy scene from *Alien*.

Adam is doing his very best to comfort his girlfriend and keep her calm. Becca is clearly rigid with tension.

'We won't be long,' Paul says, not changing his speed at all. 'Better to get there safe rather than sorry.'

How Niamh wishes she was driving instead. They'd already be there. Jodie would be on the ward and sucking on gas and air by now.

When Jodie unbuckles her seatbelt and starts to try and turn around so she can kneel on the car seat, Niamh starts to feel the panic build.

'Jodie, love,' Paul says. 'You need to sit down and put your seatbelt on. Precious cargo.'

'No offence, Dad,' Jodie growls in a voice that sounds positively demonic, 'but this precious cargo is about to force its way out of my vagina, so if you don't mind I'll do what I fecking well want.'

'Okay! Okay!' Paul says, finally picking up speed.

'Muuuuuummmmm!' Jodie growls. 'The baby is coming! I think it's coming.'

'*Pull over!*' Niamh yells as Jodie, her face flushed with sweat, her knuckles white, looks at her and is unable to stop her body from pushing.

Adam seems frozen to the spot, his eyes wide with terror.

Niamh knows she has to take control. 'Becca, phone an ambulance. Tell them we're just outside the hospital but this baby isn't going to wait any longer. Paul, grab Jodie's bag and get the fresh towels out of it. Adam...'

Adam blinks at her.

'Adam, you hold your girlfriend's hand and you be there for her. It's going to be okay.' She then says a quick prayer to herself, before twisting in her seat and gently easing down her daughter's joggers.

The sight of a baby's head is not what she was expecting to find. Not so quickly. 'Holy shit, Jodie. You're doing it!' she says, trying to stop her voice from breaking. Her car door opens and Becca hands her towels.

'Paul's hyperventilating on the roadside,' Becca says. 'Ambulance is on its way.'

'So is the baby,' Niamh says, as she places her hands under Jodie, ready to catch her grandchild.

'Oh my God,' Becca says.

'I know!' Niamh takes a deep breath. She can hear Jodie's shaky breathing and can feel the trembling of her legs. 'Jodie. Listen. I can see a little face. You are so very close now to meeting your baby. Take a deep breath for me and we'll get ready to say hello.'

Jodie nods, while Adam declares his love. And then, well, then Jodie pushes and a beautiful, perfect baby girl slides into the world and into her granny's waiting arms. Clara Niamh Cassidy. The baby they have already named and have been waiting for.

It's a moment that Niamh wants to freeze forever. Her baby's baby. She falls immediately, and totally, in love.

Only the sharp cry of this most precious newborn, followed by tearful elation from both Jodie and Adam, brings her back to the here and now.

She guides the baby up to her mum as Jodie turns to sit down, and as Adam and Jodie stare at their daughter, she slides out of the car. This is their moment now.

Unable to speak, she gives two thumbs up to Paul and watches as he starts to cry. Then, just as the ambulance pulls into the layby, she catches Becca's eye. They grin through their tears. This is it. They are both in their granny era. And they are going to rock it.

* * *

MORE FROM FREYA KENNEDY

Another brilliantly uplifting book from Freya Kennedy, *The Fabulous Forties Club*, is available to order now here:

www.mybook.to/FabulousFortiesBackAd

ACKNOWLEDGEMENTS

Writing this second instalment of The Fecking Fabulous Club brought me such joy – and I want to very sincerely thank all at Boldwood Books who have allowed me to continue telling the story of these three wonderful friends.

First of all to my editor Rachel Faulkner-Willcocks for her vision and patience. It really is a privilege to work with you. Thanks to the marketing, sales and production teams, with special nods to Jenna, Claire and Ben who continue to be so very helpful. Thanks to the copy-editor, designer, and proofreader for making this book zing with as few errors as possible. And of course thanks to Amanda Ridout, a force of nature in the publishing world.

As always I have to offer my thanks to my agent Ger Nichol who continues to be everything an agent should be, and more.

Thanks also to Hannah at The Rights People for overseeing my foreign rights sales and pushing my books out further into the world.

Thanks to the book bloggers, reviewers, librarians and booksellers who make this job possible.

Thanks to all my readers – especially those who have stuck with me through thick and thin and everything in between. You are never, ever, taken for granted.

To my writer friends – especially those who give unfailingly of their time and friendship. A big shout out to all the incredibly supportive members of Team Boldwood.

To those real-life friends and family who keep me sane when deadlines are flying in all directions. Thanks especially to Julie-Anne, Marie-Louise, Fiona, Fionnuala and Erin.

Thanks to my parents, who I love with my entire heart, my sisters Lisa and Emma, my brother Peter – along with their assorted spouses and offspring, both human and furry! Thanks to my husband for a room to write in and listening to my long explanations of how publishing works. Thanks to my amazing kids – Joe and Luka.

Finally, thanks to each and every one of you who picks up this book and gives it a chance. Without readers, a writer is nothing. Thank you.

ABOUT THE AUTHOR

Freya Kennedy is the alter ego for bestselling thriller author Claire Allan. A former journalist from Derry, Northern Ireland Claire has published eleven novels. Now, as Freya, she is writing warm, funny women's fiction for Boldwood.

Sign up to Freya Kennedy's mailing list for news, competitions and updates on future books.

Visit Freya's website: www.claireallan.com/freya-kennedy

Follow Freya on social media here:

f facebook.com/ClaireAllanAuthor

instagram.com/claireallan_author

BB bookbub.com/authors/freya-kennedy

ALSO BY FREYA KENNEDY

Boldwood

Boldwood Books is an award-winning fiction publishing company seeking out the best stories from around the world.

Find out more at www.boldwoodbooks.com

Join our reader community for brilliant books, competitions and offers!

Follow us
@BoldwoodBooks
@TheBoldBookClub

Sign up to our weekly deals newsletter

https://bit.ly/BoldwoodBNewsletter

Printed in Dunstable, United Kingdom